D0445228

GLASS MOUNTAIN

R. M. KOSTER

GLASS MOUNTAIN

W. W. NORTON & COMPANY
New York London

Copyright © 2001 by Richard M. Koster

All rights reserved
Printed in the United States of America
First Edition

For information about permission to reproduce selections from this book,
write to Permissions, W. W. Norton & Company, Inc.,
500 Fifth Avenue, New York, NY 10110

The text of this book is composed in Bembo with
the display set in Trajan and Locarno Italic.
Composition by Molly Heron
Manufacturing by Quebecor Fairfield
Production manager: Julia Druskin

Library of Congress Cataloging-in-Publication Data

Koster, R. M., 1934–
    Glass mountain/R. M. Koster.
        p. cm.
    ISBN 0-393-02007-X
    1. Vietnamese Conflict, 1961–1975—Veterans—Fiction. 2. Ameri-
cans— South America—Fiction. 3. Children of presidents—Fiction.
4. Undercover operations—Fiction. 5. Kidnapping, Parental—Fiction.
6. Hispanic Americans—Fiction. 7. South America—Fiction. I. Title.
PS3561.O84 G58 2001
813'.54—dc21   00-052715

W. W. Norton & Company, Inc., 500 Fifth Avenue,
New York, N.Y. 10110
www.wwnorton.com

W. W. Norton & Company, Inc., Castle House, 75/76 Wells Street,
London W1T 3QT

1 2 3 4 5 6 7 8 9 0

Otilita

There is surely nothing other than the single purpose of the present moment. A man's whole life is the succession of moment after moment. If one fully understands the present moment, there will be nothing else to do and nothing else to pursue. Live being true to the single purpose of the present moment.

Everyone lets the present moment slip by, then looks for it as if he thought it were somewhere else. No one seems to have noticed this fact. But grasping this firmly, one must pile experience on experience. And once one has come to this understanding, he will be a different person from that point on, though he may not always bear it in mind.

When one understands this settling into single-mindedness well, all his affairs will thin out. Loyalty is also contained in this single-mindedness.   —*Hagakure,* THE WAY OF THE SAMURAI

If we take eternity to mean not infinite temporal duration but time-lessness, then eternal life belongs to those who live in the present.

—*Wittgenstein,* "PROPOSITION 6.4311"

GLASS MOUNTAIN

PHANTOMS

 I *W*hat he does is steal children."

"*Translation, please, Vincent.*"

"*Jack and Jill split up, she gets the kids. Or him, it doesn't matter, somebody loses. So maybe they're a sore loser. They get hold of Carlos, Carlos gets them their kids.*"

"*Kidnaps them.*"

"*Well, that depends a lot on your point of view. It was your kids, you might call it repossession. Especially if you got yourself a judgment. In another state, you know, that awarded you custody.*"

"*I see a connection. It's a bit like what he did on his first tour.*"

"*You mean, bringing out pilots.*"

"*Yes. Don't you think so? Recovery. But a bit, let's say, tarnished. Is he proud of himself, do you think, doing what he does now?*"

"*How the hell do I know?*"

"*You served with him nearly a year on a long-range patrol team. Four or five men together for weeks at a time, under stressful conditions. I assume you get to know each other quite well. You should be able to estimate his feelings.*"

"Mr. Knox, about me, I don't mess inside people. This shrink at Bragg
. . . They were drafting civilian doctors, slapping things on their collars. This
one had a leaf. Asked me all kinds of shit, my dreams and so forth, did I
ever dream of making it with a guy. I said no, but there were probably guys
in the stockade who'd let him blow them for a couple of dollars. That's what
I think of messing inside people. What I know about Carlos is, first, he's
from somewhere down there, but you can't tell by how he looks or how he
talks English. Two, he knows the jungle like I used to know Newark. Guy
with us, he gets himself a bad toothache about ninety klicks the wrong side
of the DMZ. We were in Newark, I'd find him a dentist. Carlos finds him
a plant works better than novocaine, and the bum tooth just falls out in a
couple days. Three, he doesn't gab a hell of a lot. Like, he won't come up
and put your hand on his tit and tell you how he doesn't like himself.
You want a profile on him, get someone else. My job was to find him."

"How did you do it? We didn't even know he was in this hemisphere,
or even alive."

"I got lucky. We had this guy on the team got hurt pretty bad. Not on
patrol or anything. Some dipshit ran him over with an APC. Black guy
named Sobers. Cut him in two. I mean, the tread got him right in the joint
and mashed him like a bug from there to the knees. But not anything vital,
so the doctors, they managed to save him. Half anyway. It was me, I'd rather
be dead. He's in a VA hospital in Charleston. I looked him up and went
to see him, asked if he knew how to reach Carlos. He said no, then a couple days later he called me. His mother had found a number for him."

"In San Diego."

"An answering service, ask for Carl Marengo. All I had to do then was
call some guys I know. Once I had a name."

"Marengo."

"That's the name he uses with the lawyers. He's got a Wyoming PI ticket under it. I wouldn't be surprised he had other names. Or if his actual base is over the border. I had more time, I'd have more information."

"You have all we need. You did well, Vincent."

"I got lucky."

"It's beyond luck. That you found him at all is amazing. More, that you found him as soon as you did. And even more so that he does what he's doing. Ape Thomas is psychic. He had that reputation, but I put no stock in it until I served with him. He jumped with the Brits at Arnhem, did you know that? Liaison between them and the Eighty-second. The story was he knew before they took off that they'd be jumping on top of two panzer divisions. Mythology, thought I, but he had hunches like that in Southeast Asia. Now it's 'Get me that kid that Bobby Paley sent us, the one that raided solo north of the Zone!' says the Ape, or bellows, rather, in his charming manner. 'His poppa was president of one of those countries! He's going to be my pathfinder platoon!'

"I said, 'Yes sir!' of course. If you decide to take part in this exercise, Vincent—and I think I can persuade him to take you—don't ever, ever question one of his orders. If he asks you something, by all means answer frankly. But don't question an order. He's perfectly capable of killing you on the spot, or making you wish he had. I said, 'Yes sir!' and after I assigned you to look for Carlos, I took steps to locate others with similar skills. I thought it would more likely take three years than three weeks—that is to say, if Carlos was findable, period. When we PCS'd back to the States, he stayed on over there, doing something or other for the Agency. No one has heard from him since the fall of Saigon. His brother pestered DOD for years. The Ape, on the other hand, knew he'd turn up. He's psychic."

"What if Carlos doesn't want to go?"

"That's the point I've been making. He's in recovery, getting things back. That's what Ape's mission is, though I don't know myself what or who they're supposed to recover. Carlos does it for money. The mission pays well. Why shouldn't he go?"

"It could be a mess, that's why. Ape Thomas, what I hear, is very good, but he's been out to stud for five, six years. And I don't care who's in charge, you take a team down there, it could be messy. You going?"

"I'm staff, Vincent."

"Yeah. Well, I'm not going either."

"I'm sorry to hear that. Judging from your combat record and what you've done for us, you'd be a valuable addition."

"Yeah. But I kind of lost my taste for being shot at. I'm not even sure I still like shooting people. He could feel the same way."

"I thought you didn't 'mess' with inner feelings. Are you suggesting that he's lost his nerve?"

"All I said is, maybe he won't want to."

"What he wants doesn't matter. Stealing children does seem a comedown from three tours of operating in North Vietnam. If his nerve's gone bad, perhaps Ape won't want him. But if Ape wants him . . . Never, ever disappoint the Ape. We have fraud at least. Illegal entry into the U.S. I doubt Carlos files tax returns. Kidnapping here and there wouldn't surprise me. If all else fails, Mr. Keegan has friends in Mexico. He'll go."

"Mr. Knox, there's another thing I know about Carlos. He's not the kind of guy gets pushed around."

"Come on, Vincent, I know him too. He was my platoon sergeant. I wasn't always staff, believe it or not. If he's the man he was, he'll jump at our offer. If his nerve's gone bad, we'll explain, and he'll go crawling."

2 *T*hat's about how the conversation must have gone. Knox would have guessed that my nerves might be a bit shaky. Vince wouldn't have mentioned all he told Digby Sobers. If he guessed Dig knew all along where I could be contacted, he wouldn't have mentioned that either. I'd stayed in touch with Dig. We were both basketcases.

After Vince left, Dig called my service. We ended up speaking that afternoon—afternoon for me, I was in Tijuana. Ape Thomas was mounting an op in Central America and had asked Geoffrey Knox to recruit me for it. I told Dig he did well not giving Vince my number, and asked him not to call till further notice. Knox wasn't above tapping his phone. I would have gone down to Oaxaca or Chiapas and lain low for a while—that's how little I longed for excitement—but I'd pledged to recover assets, or at least try to, for a man I didn't care to disappoint. I'd honor my pledge and lie low later.

I might have left it there, and things would have been different. Instead I changed my mind. Some people believe in blind chance, others in destiny. I'm in the middle. As I see it, at any given moment there may be a number of potential futures loitering in the ante-room of time, like actors in a casting director's lobby. One gets the part and goes on, the rest never happen. The number of possible futures is certainly finite, yet one isn't mindlessly shoved on a set course, like a billiard ball or a steer in the stockyards. Now and then, in a limited way, one can choose. I did.

Had I stuck with my first judgment, Vince wouldn't have found me. I wouldn't have joined Ape Thomas's operation. Instead, two days after Dig called I called him back and asked him to tell Vince Giobbe where to reach me. Exactly what would happen wasn't foreseeable, but things might well get messy. I might be killed.

Did that mean, since I was no longer adventurous, that I harbored a death wish? No. When I chose, I was dead already in matters that count. Everyone gets to be dead sooner or later, so to be dead while you're living is a great waste.

3   *H*iding out from Ape Thomas conjured a series of torments. Or the case I was involved in conjured them. Either way, they came on and around my thirty-fifth birthday, May 16, 1984. The first was succinct, a crisp flick to the scrotum, without any hors d'oeuvres of warning or foreplay of threats. I opened a box, and flames came out of it.

The box might have been a cigar box, if cigar boxes were made of metal and lockable. In it were two rubber-banded, dark blue U.S. passports representing Carl Marengo and C. J. Wagram. Carlton Austerlitz and Charles Borodino were in a bank vault in Denver. Carlo Jena, a naturalized Mexican, was in my pocket. The box was behind the back panel of my TV set. I got it out, took it into the bathroom, set it down on the sink. I lifted the lid of the toilet tank and set it down on the seat. Then I procto'd in the upright, over-flow drain tube, extracting a flat key glued to a small magnet. I unlocked the box. When I opened it, yellow flames jumped out at me, *whoosh!*

No, not so, there was no petroleum *whoosh*. My auditory cortex didn't participate. Maybe it hadn't been asked. Or maybe it simply disdained playing third banana to touch and vision. Whatever the case, the flames brought heat and light only. They were enough.

My flinch upset the box. It clattered on the tiles, spilling out passports. I wasn't surprised to find them uncharred, or to see that my lids weren't singed when I looked in the mirror. Even while I was flinching violently from them, I knew the flames had no physical substance. That made them more dreadful.

No. Strike "more." Whatever happens is worse. When the flames are real, you wish them imaginary; when imaginary, you wish they were real.

I sat down on the floor cross-legged with my face in my hands.

No, I opened the tap and spritzed my face.

No again. I crouched and righted the not-the-least-searing-hot box. I gathered the unscorched passports and dumped them in it. I put the key back in the keyhole. I rose and put the box back on the sink. I had a plane to catch. More to the point, I was familiar with dread.

Dread, I had found out, is fear's elder brother. As with many siblings, there's a resemblance, but they aren't really very much alike. Fear, for instance, can be a good companion. Having him around can whet mind and senses, particularly one's sense of being alive. It depends on accepting his company gracefully—if not actually seeking him out, at least not avoiding him.

Fear doesn't bear snubs, though. If you class him a boor and avoid his hangouts, if you shun his approach and take off at the least sign of him, then when you nonetheless meet him—and fear, you'd best acknowledge, gets around, and can show up in unlikely places—then he turns nasty. He harps on unpleasantnesses that might happen, both likely and farfetched.

Pretending you're glad to see him is useless. Fear has a keen nose for insincerity. And if you pay his nagging too much attention, fear may turn into his grandmother, panic, and panic turns you into a roach—a paralyzed roach, as when kitchen lights go on at two in the morning, or a scuttling roach, as when you try to stomp one with shower clogs on, but a mindless, despicable roach in any case.

Dread, on the other hand, is always a prick. You can't be friends with him as you can with his brother. He has no special haunts, he comes looking for you, sneaks up on you in your bed or even your bathroom. He weighs a thousand pounds but is very light-footed. Wherever he catches you, his M.O. is the same: he sits on your chest and makes you feel like dying.

Like many siblings, fear and dread don't compete. Dread doesn't bother fear's friends. He frequents people who avoid danger. He'd been visiting me for some time, we were acquainted. He'd never dropped by before via hallucination, but dread is dread, his M.O. never varies. Neither does how to cope, you wait till he leaves. Measured activity makes the wait pass a bit quicker.

I took Marengo's passport from the box. I slipped off the rubber band, keeping it on my wrist. Inside were a private investigator's license, a driver's license, a credit card, and a fold of hundreds—fifteen. I put the whole business on the toilet tank lid.

I took Carlo Jena's rubber-banded, green Mexican passport from the left side pocket of my trousers and a wad of Mexican money from the right side pocket. I tucked the wad under the band and dropped that whole business into the box.

I took off my belt and hung it by the buckle on the ceramic towel hook by the shower, holding the free end out in my left hand. Not to strop a straight razor. The inside of the belt was fitted with a zipper. I unzipped and fished out fifties folded twice lengthwise—seven. I spread them and folded them widthwise and put them in my right side trouser pocket.

One by one I took the hundreds from the tank lid, folded them widthwise twice and pressed the folds tight, then fitted them into the belt overlapping each other—ten. I put the rest of the hundreds in my pocket. I zipped the belt, took it down, and put it back on.

Think of a nurse setting up for an operation. She's done it a hundred times, it's mainly routine, but nonetheless she has to do it correctly. She levers up the tray of the sterilizer, selects instruments, arranges them on a green-clothed rolling table—not dawdling but not hurrying either, economical of movement, concentrated. You can't tell by watching her what it's about, ingrown toenail or triple bypass. Nor can you tell that last week she had a biopsy, that this morning she learned the lump in her breast is malignant.

Or imagine a waiter—clean tux and a bow tie that ties, not just clips on—setting up for breakfast in the mirrored solitude of early morning in the dining room of a first-class small hotel. On Central Park South in New York, or in the Retiro quarter of Buenos Aires, or in the city it pleases you most to imagine. Filling sugar bowls, testing salt shakers, setting out slender vases of smokey-gray glass, each with a single, half-opened red rose. He, too, moves unhurriedly and precisely. He, too, concentrates on what he's doing. He believes in that, he's that sort of person, and besides, today it's especially wise. Not because a special guest has checked in. To this waiter of ours every guest is special. But he'd rather not think of the tracks on his daughter's forearms, or maybe of his son who's been arrested, or of whatever it pleases you to imagine as the source of the heart-sickening weight on his chest.

I took Marengo's documents from the tank lid, put the licenses and credit card into the passport, put the band back on and the passport in my left pocket. I took C. J. Wagram's passport out of the box. I slipped off the band, keeping it on my wrist, checked credit cards, business cards, and driver's license. I put them back inside and replaced the band. I put that passport in my right hip pocket.

I closed the box and locked it and rehid the key and put the top back on the tank of the toilet. I took the box into the living room, put it back in the TV set, and replaced the panel. I pushed the TV table against the wall. I took the screwdriver into the bedroom and put it in the top drawer of the bureau. I picked the flight bag up off the bed. I left the room and the apartment.

No. Before leaving the room, I looked at myself in the mirror over the bureau. After a moment the face there smiled back sardonically.

"Happy birthday, *huevón*," said the face in the mirror, though my birthday was still about nine hours off.

 On the plane I read J. F. C. Fuller, *The Decisive Battles of the Western World*, underlining and making notes with a felt-tipped pen.

No. I took the book from my bag but left it unopened when the plastic pen in my shirt pocket reminded me of a gold one, a prep-school graduation gift from my mother with her name, Soledad, engraved beside the clip. I'd lost it years before in Southeast Asia, not in the field, on R&R in Bangkok.

No, in Hong Kong. In Bangkok what I lost was my father's razor, a three-piece, double-edge Gillette, gold-plated but with most of the plate worn off, bent a bit at one flange so that only one edge of it gave a safe shave—the only razor I'd ever used, first borrowing it for more or less needless fuzz-scraping, then inheriting it at fifteen, thanks to the communists.

Or maybe not them, maybe thanks to somebody else, the old-line bunch who opposed his election, or the mafia bunch he threw out of running the casinos, or some politician he fired or refused to appoint or threatened to put in jail if he didn't stop stealing. Or the Guardia Civil or the CIA. Now that the world had grown up there were plenty of candidates.

The CIA would be fitting. Humorous too. Slapping of thighs at Langley when my forms came in. Hey, here's a guy wants to be a contract employee, and we greased his daddy back in the sixties!

There was, for example, the Greek at Long Xuyen, a direct descendant no doubt of Praxiteles, except he worked in C-3 instead of marble. Could mold the stuff to put the blast just where he wanted, stand six feet away and not muss a hair. He might have made the bomb that lasagna'd one's dad. Someone I worked with might have placed it. Someone I worked for might have given the order. The wonder is I didn't make the connection, though a glimmer did come near the end, when I heard of the Delta head-man who'd been terminated—with the idea that Victor Charles would take the rap—because, as they put it, "Sometimes he wouldn't play ball." One's dad didn't always play ball with the gringos either.

Or maybe I'd connected long before, on a more important level than consciousness. Maybe that's why I lost the razor.

I was the one who dropped it, during needless fuzz-scraping the morning of the funeral. If my dad had bent it, he'd have bought another. To him it was something to shave with. To me it was something he'd used for as long as I'd known him.

No. When I was small, he used a straight razor. That he stropped on a regular strop, not on a belt. Not hung on a towel hook either. Tied—with stiff yellow twine, that seemed to be it—to the crank that worked the glass louvres of the window, the window to the left of the sink in the house (not really a house) on Dantón del Valle, a wooden building, painted pale green, with four apartments, two on each floor. First swabbing his face with suds, then turning to strop, then making a horrible face at himself in the mirror, twisting his mouth, stretching the skin of his cheek, then shaving in careful but nonetheless fluid strokes, holding the razor like a violin bow.

Then not wiping the suds from his face there at the sink but wearing them instead into the shower. That, at least, was his M.O. with the Gillette. It must have been his M.O. with the straight razor. Not from economy of movement—one wash does it all—but because, when you live in the tropics, there's no sense in showering first and shaving after, not if you use a straight razor that has to be stropped, since the effort of stropping, no matter how easy you take it, will leave you needing, or wanting, another shower. Which *modus* having become *operandi*, he stayed with it when he switched to a Gillette, from habit more than from economy of movement, and since he slept naked, he shaved naked too, with his spare navel pressed to the porcelain.

Hairless pink puckering two klicks due south of his real one on a scale of ten centimeters to the klick. That I noticed first not in the bathroom at home but at the shower behind the house at Medusa, during post-beach de-sanding. My father pulled his suit down to de-sand inside it, and I said, *"¿Que es eso, papi, ese hueco?"*

"That's no hole," he said laughing, pulling the front of his suit up over his real one, stepping in to let the shower stream play on his chest, where hair-clinging, drop-sized planets reflected the sunlight. "That's my spare navel [*ombligo de repuesta*] that Dr. Schmeisser installed when I was in Italy."

Which quip, when I repeated it at lunchtime, got a roar from my godfather-namesake Carlos Gavilán, my father's law partner, and a frown from my mother, followed by an explanation, and the comment that she thought the quip in poor taste. Which, many years later, I thought about plagiarizing. Which I did in fact plagiarize, for publication to a Berkeley coed, the least receptive of all possible publics, stretching the figure (since mine was a good five klicks west-northwest of my real one) and substituting Dr. Kalashnikov. Which I didn't deliver with anything like his lightheartedness. Which the coed enjoyed even less than my mother. Which led directly to a loused-up evening.

I knew where I left the Gillette: on the tiled rim of the tub, at the end away from the taps next to the wall, in the bathroom of a room in a hotel in Bangkok. I'd shaved in the tub using a hand mirror. I put the razor down and soaked for a while, there being no tubs where I'd be in a few hours. I neglected to put the razor back in my kit. Many hours passed before I missed it.

The pen, on the other hand, could have gone anywhere. Onto the laundry pile in one of my shirts. Into a whore's handbag while I lay snoozing. I was happily zonked that whole week, Saigon to Saigon, on combo punches of speed and heroin—the one gulped, the other snorted, no tracks for Carlos—as prescribed by one of Colonel Ape Thomas's medics, a direct descendant, no doubt, of Hippocrates on the Ethiopian side. All that remained of Hong Kong were a few chunks, floating toward me like asteroids in a sci-fi movie. One of them put me, pen in hand, in a bookstore, copying titles of fairy-tale collections from a catalogue supplied by a muffin-faced Scotswoman. I lost the list too.

When my brother, Camilo, and I were little, our mother read to us during siesta. I was long-range patrolling my past for one of the stories. Our room had curtains the color of drying blood, and most days the sun was strong enough to read by with them drawn, so that she and (by contagion) the scenes of the stories were aura'd in a ruddy glow. Later she read in the evenings in the *sala*, with Camilo and I sprawled pajama'd on the cool tiles and the fiber blinds that by day draped the screened windows drawn up to let in the breeze from the Pacific. Only the lamp beside her chair was lighted, and she sat in a yellow glow that pooled at her feet, diked by the warm gloom.

Sometimes my father would come in while she was reading, and hold his hand up so she wouldn't stop, and stand enthralled, not by what she was reading, but by the scene's tenderness—then, still enthralled, he would peel off his linen jacket, pull his tie down and undo his collar, step back into his hammock, there to lie swaying, pry off his shoes with his toes, and hold out his hand when Cornelia brought him his lemonade.

By that time my mother had moved on from fairy tales to books of chivalry, the very stuff that drove Don Quixote crazy, and stories out of *Las Mil y Una Noches*. She followed the practice of Scheherazade—to save her voice, not her head—breaking off in midstory, or in midchapter when she moved on to Dumas. Then, at the critical point in *The Three Musketeers*, with d'Artagnan racing alone to save the queen's honor, she went to give birth to my sister, Clara.

Camilo cracked first. I found him with the book, his back bent like a paper clip, his forefinger creeping the page like a wounded beetle. The thought of his knowing what happened before I did was unbearable. I begged a copy from my godfather. By the time our mother was ready to read again, he and I were chapters apart and disposed to independent cruising.

The readings stopped. No matter: the damage was done. Camilo and I were warped for life, though in different directions. He was turned inward by the pressure of form, I bent outward by the pull of content. He responded to word patterns, I to adventures, so he went to live in the world of books, and I went to live in the world of hazard.

No, that's too pat. There are hazards in the world of books, and I tended to feel I was living a story.

The story in question, the one I was searching for in Hong Kong, concerned a king's daughter who had to be won by prowess and a changeling prince who ventured successfully for her. The trial was riding to the top of a glass mountain. What lodged in my mind was the moment of trial not of triumph. The prince, who seemed no more than six years old, urged his charger up the glittering slope. The horse, its hooves clicking and sliding, strained for purchase. The maiden watched from above. The whole scene was suffused in a bloody aura.

"The Glass Mountain" was what I thought the story was called. I couldn't find it. I tried to call Camilo from the bookstore. No, from some bar. Camilo would have remembered, or busied himself until he winkled it out. I thought that if I read the story over, I might learn what I was doing in Southeast Asia. I was on my third tour, after all.

—You're not even American, what are you doing here?

—Well, at first, sir, I thought I was saving civilization. Like my father. He served with the French in World War Two. And paying the communists back for his murder. But now I think it may be because of my mother.

—Your what?

—My mother, sir. When I was small she read me fairy stories.

—Don't you know the difference between them and real life?

—Yes, sir! I do now, sir. Fairy tales have a point.

That might have been amusing to try on Ape Thomas, but what I actually said was, "Personal reasons."

"You think this is the fucking French foreign legion?"

"Negative, sir! My information is they got beat by the dinks."

Ape Thomas blew cigar smoke. "Okay, wiseass, you're in."

I was sorry I'd lost the pen my mother gave me. Then I judged I was better off without it. It didn't help me do what I was doing, whatever that was. It was just excess weight. In the story I was living, the prince never even tried to climb the glass mountain. He called Air, and they took it out with high explosive, princess and all. Then he got stoned.

And even if I hadn't lost it, it wouldn't have been in my shirt on that flight to Draco. The razor wouldn't have been in the kit in my bag. I'd have gotten rid of them both, I'd have dumped them somewhere. One thing, another thing, I stopped being their son. I had no right to anything of theirs or from them. Even memories were a mistake.

I wasn't who I was. I wasn't anyone.

That's how I spent the flight from San Diego. Remembering two lost objects, trudging the trails they cut to the places they took me.

Not the whole flight. About forty minutes before Draco I got some relief. I got up to go back to the lavatory and saw that the businessman across the aisle had only one eye. The left side of his face was smooth from nose to ear.

I hadn't noticed the man's face being like that, but, after all, I'd been lost in recollections. The deformity froze me. I caught myself staring. Then I thought, there's nothing so awful about it. Napalm and white phosphorous do worse. The skin wasn't scarred. He must have been born that way, he's gotten used to it. He had his little drop table down and was scribbling away. He didn't seem to mind, so why should I?

But then, when I turned and started tailwards, everyone on the plane was the same way. Men and women. A little girl two rows behind where I was sitting. What looked like a honeymoon couple two rows behind her. They had the armrest up and were snuggling together, one-eyed. Everyone was one-eyed. The left side of every-one's face was perfectly smooth.

Three dudes in Stetsons. Both stews. A guy with a clipped beard who was flirting with them. Me too. That's what the lavatory mirror told me, and I hadn't the courage to put my hand up and check. No left eye, not even a left eyebrow.

I kept my head down on the way back to my seat. I buckled in and took hold of the armrests. Then I sat back and forced my eyes open and looked over at the woman across the aisle one row ahead of the businessman and waited till she had a left eye again. After that I took out the emergency instructions card and studied it until we landed in Draco.

"First of all, I don't try to play God."

Nealy nodded in mock gravity. "Not an easy role, no question there. Even God has lots of trouble with it. Many bungled scenes, few rave reviews lately."

We were in the coffee shop at the airport in Peacock, a well-appointed place two floors above ground. The front of the room projected beyond the facade and had canted plate-glass windows that gave on the field, canted outward toward the top, like a control tower—flashy, perhaps, for an airport with no scheduled flights, but in keeping with the sleek private ships on the apron. On the wall opposite the counter was a mural of an open-cockpit biplane, pilot in goggles, banking above a landscape of neatly plowed fields: "Flying the Mail." The light above the mural was the only one on. Except for Nealy and me the place was empty. No one had even come in yet to start serving. Outside, a thin predawn glimmer seeped across the tarmac but couldn't yet compete with the mural light.

"The question is," Nealy went on, "'How do you avoid it?'" He reached into the thigh pocket of his fatigues, took out a pack of Salems, shook one up and lipped it, lit it from the butt of the one he'd been smoking. "How do you?"

"Self-restraint. You ought to try it sometime with the smoking."

I'd slept a while in the airport hotel at Draco, then drove over to Peacock in a rented car. Faster than I'd planned, so I was early for my meeting with Kendall. I sat down at a table near the plate-glass windows. I must have closed my eyes for a few seconds. When I opened them, there was Tommy Nealy, in the same fatigues and flak vest he'd been killed in, tipped back in a chair, shoulders against the glass, smoking and smirking at me from clever blue eyes.

Horror and fascination, as in a dream you know is a dream but can't wake up from. Or won't, since what horrifies you fascinates you too. And seems appropriate, what you deserve, so that the horror brings a sick delight. And when he questioned me, I had to answer.

Not whining, however, though that's what I felt like doing. I spoke the way I would have had he been real. Old training. A remnant of my old self that I still clung to. Whining didn't happen in my family. One accepted trials and tried to complete them.

I'd been avoiding them, that was my trouble. I knew it but steered shy anyway. So phantoms brought them. Phantom flames, phantom deformities, a phantom buddy. I wasn't up to seeking trials as therapeutic, or as pause from the static buzz of being dead, but when they came old training helped me face them.

What Tommy was trying me on was my approach to the case I was finishing up that morning. I answered him as I would have any real person nosy enough to pry yet close enough to merit a straight answer. I even smirked back at him about smoking.

Nealy flicked the butt through the window. It transitted the glass without bumping and tracered out and down, out of my view. He took a drag on the Salem he'd just lighted. A wisp of smoke spiraled from his right armpit where the round that killed him had gone in.

"Guess what?" he said. "Cancer doesn't scare me. What I should have restrained myself from was saving your ass."

A 105 pilot had ditched near the Red River. The crew I was with went over from Thailand to get him. I rode the hoist down and found him, he had two broken ankles. I was getting him to the hoist when the bird took fire. What they always did was fire at the choppers. The bird came down and exploded, not quite on top of me and the pilot. Something came out of the blast and numbed my shoulder. There we were, in the wrong part of Vietnam, with three arms and two legs between us.

Tommy Nealy's crew came over for us. And some A-1s to suppress ground fire, and F-4s to fly cover for the A-1s, and a tanker to refuel the F-4s, and a C-130 flying command post to keep everything orderly. Half the good guys in Southeast Asia were in on it, but Nealy was point. He came down and got the pilot into a stokes litter. When the pilot was up, he took care of me. Then he came up himself. When he cleared the trees, he got a round in the armpit. He hung on, and we got him in, but he died on the way across to Thailand.

"But I didn't restrain myself, did I? Lucky for you. Lucky for you, my self-restraint was meager. I needed every bit for use in my love life. My method, by the way, was to quote Milton. 'Of man's first disobedience,' and so forth. To myself of course. It worked wonders. Constant rave reviews."

I had to smile. He'd been studying lit at Amherst, I think, or Williams and dropped out in his junior year to join the war. For material. He'd actually started a novel before he got killed.

"I'm sorry you never got your book finished, Tommy."

"Stick to the point. How can you avoid it, you're changing lives."

"I don't try to figure out who they'd be better off with. Or which of the parents has the better claim. I restrain myself from considering those aspects."

"Sounds like not thinking of a white camel." He flicked the Salem away and rocked forward hunching, hands smoothed swami-like over the napkin box. He peered at it, then squinted up at me. "Allah be with you, *effendi*," squeaked holy-man Nealy. "You will have much wealth. But you must not think a white camel. To do so is death!"

He rocked back against the window, smirking. "Then, of course, it's tough not to think about it. Don't the clients bring those aspects up?"

"Usually. Most clients want approval along with the service. The guy today, Oliveira, is an exception. All he wants is his assets back. He approves of himself. Who else does or doesn't makes no difference. But most want to be reassured they're acting correctly. They raise the welfare aspect, stress it in fact. They're better parents, and so on. Which is why ignoring it takes self-restraint. I treat it as an illusion. It doesn't exist."

"Ha! Me, on the other hand, you treat as real! You're fucked up, Carlos."

"Why don't you go somewhere and write a book about it?"

"I wish I could. I like playing God."

"Exactly. That has got to be why people write novels. But it doesn't go with things like I'm doing this morning. Therefore I restrain myself from it. I also restrain my emotions. I guess a novelist indulges his."

"Feelings, too, are illusions, is that it?"

"Some are useful, some aren't. Sometimes I get a 'feeling' about a case. When I'm deciding if I'm going to take it. Usually, I let the feeling guide me. But once I'm on a job I go by rules. Rule One is, Don't try to play God. Rule Two is, No force. No persuasion either, not from me. The kids decide. I explain the rules to the client. The money's up front. No refund if we miss, no bonus for scoring."

"Can little kids decide a thing like that?"

"Two are going to in a couple of hours. Oliveira will make his pitch. He has one minute. Maybe the kids will buy it, maybe they won't. It's up to them."

"Isn't a kid swayed by whichever one's there? Isn't there an obedience factor? Doesn't your client have an advantage? Doesn't the parent who's been absent always seem better? Don't they miss him? Don't they feel guilty for having left him? Aren't they unlikely to grasp what's going on?"

I breathed deeply. Breathing deeply eases the weight a little. "Yes."

Nealy fished up the Salems again. Still smirking. He shook one up and lit it with a Zippo. "So?"

"All that might be true." The terms of engagement were that I had to answer. Answering calmly was my option, if I could manage it. "Oliveira may simply say, 'Let's go for a plane ride.' Without saying where to. He's unlikely to say they might never see Mommy again. But there's no arm-twisting. If the kids are the least bit reluctant, it's no go."

"They always go, though, don't they? You never miss."

"Not often. But it's not a sure thing. I might miss this morning. If he's given them cause to fear him, they'll be reluctant. There are guys who can't miss, guys with no Rule Two, with no rules at all. They guarantee results. I can't and don't. My advantage is a better class of client. I'm recommended by a better class of lawyer: the kind that avoid getting mentioned in kidnap indictments."

"Level with me, Carlos. Do the kids have any real freedom of choice?"

"Fuck you, Tommy! You're dead, you're a fucking figment! You can afford to diddle with moral niceties! The guy has lost his kids, they've been swiped from him! He can't get them back by himself! What's wrong with helping him?"

No, I didn't say that. I exercised restraint and delayed my answer. Besides, I knew what was wrong. Helping Oliveira was too easy. No real risk, so not a valid trial. The worst part was, even so I got satisfaction, pause from the static buzz of being dead. From doing it well. From the few constraints I put in to make it feel chancy.

"Do they?"

"The question you're trying to ask but can't formulate clearly is, Can they choose wisely? Maybe yes, maybe no. Depends on the kid. The point is, they decide. I don't try to play God."

Nealy shook his head in mock admiration. "You're like being back in high school with the Jesuits. Though I remember them saying that God, who you never try playing, is also big on letting people choose. What about the legal side? Is that, too, an illusion?"

"Not at all. I try to stick to cases where the legal side's at least even. Today, for example. The court here has awarded her custody. He has a custody order from Atacalpa."

"Who they'd be better off with doesn't come into it?"

"That's right. Rule One."

"You could just as well be working for her?"

"Right again."

"Ha! If it goes off today, she might hire you next week! Snatch and countersnatch! You could get rich on this one set of kids!"

"I wouldn't try a snatch in Atacalpa. Too much downside."

Nealy had a fit of soundless laughter. It took only a second for me to get the joke. Downside was what was missing. A snatch in Atacalpa might be a true trial. A true cause would be nice, but now that the world had grown up there weren't any. A true trial would do.

"I get it now," said Nealy. "I see how you do it. You're not God with a capital G, you're a god, little g. Like in Euripides, a god from the machine!"

The machine was a green-and-white Kennebec camper on a Bison pickup frame. I'd rented it three months before as C. J. Wagram. I drove it from Los Angeles to Draco, checked the records there, then drove to Peacock.

The problem with that cosy, affluent township was its almost total lack of hustle and bustle. Strangers tended to stand out. I settled in at a tourist camp on the lake, rented a rowboat, and went fishing. I acquainted myself with the region, but stayed prudently far from where Mommy lived.

The custody record said that Ellen Laura Gonders Oliveira had resumed her maiden name and moved in with her father, a widowed internist. It said she'd taken a job with a travel agent. The vehicle record said she drove a white Ibex. When I had been around Peacock for two weeks, I drove to the mall where the travel agent was located, found the car, and while attempting to park in the spot in front of it, carefully backed my tow hitch through its radiator. Then I got Fuller out of the glove compartment and read the account of Hitler's campaign in Russia until the lady showed up.

"Have you seen what you've done to my car?"

C. J. Wagram looked up blinking, then grinned shamefacedly for irate brown eyes. "Yes, uh, yes, of course. I'm terribly sorry."

"You ought to be!"

He bumbled hurriedly down from the camper. "I'll have it fixed, of course. I've been waiting for you."

"I suppose I should thank you profusely for not sneaking off! California drivers!"

Wagram hung his head, but the beating continued. "You bet you'll fix it! Can you possibly be insured, a driver like you?"

"Oh, yes." Boyish nod. "I'm fully covered. I sell insurance, as a matter of fact." He fumbled out a business card: C. J. Wagram Associates. The address was a P.O. box in San Diego.

"Well, Mr. C. J. Wagram?" she said, flicking the card. "What now?"

Mr. Wagram smiled, on firm ground at last. "I suggest your local Ibex dealer. That sometimes runs a bit higher than a body shop, but one's sure of getting good parts and not breaking the warranty. Your husband, of course . . ."

"Poor little me, is that it?" Flash of brown eyes. "A big decision like that! It must be beyond me!"

"I'm sorry, I didn't mean . . . Sometimes a man, I mean a family . . . Particular body shop . . ." Wagram was all flustered again. "Uh, if you think my suggestion . . . The dealer, I mean. We could go now. I'd be happy to take you. Your car isn't drivable, I'm afraid."

"Thanks to guess who? Well, the place I bought the car from isn't far. You might be able to make it there without killing us."

When Antonio Oliveira was referred to me, he and I had a meeting. At his hotel in L.A., over two days. His suite was on the top floor. His suits were made-to-measure, his loafers glove-leather, his Rolex Oyster gold, his left little finger ringed with a square-cut diamond. He was thirty-six but looked a becoming forty due to gray hair at his temples and in his moustache. He was aware that his profile suggested a ladies' man and placed a chair opposite me instead of taking the one beside the sofa. He tried Spanish to start with. When I shook my head, he showed very passable English, strongly accented. His voice was velvet: no rasp of anger, even when he described how his wife took their children from him. His manner was businesslike: nothing odd to the transaction we were discussing. He was almost completely successful in concealing his distaste for gringos, even when, gringolike, I slung my chukka boots up on the coffee table. Once, though, he took a call from Atacalpa there in the sitting room and gave me a glimpse under his sleek surface. The call concerned a third party, who apparently had done something foolish or treacherous—inconvenient to Oliveira, in any case. The caller was disposed to forgive him. Oliveira took a different view, and in doing so showed both crudity and venom:

"Mira, flojito, no vengas con mariconadas. El va terminar con los huevos en la boca."

He didn't raise his voice. He didn't have to. The harshness that came into it was sufficient. Things would go hard for the fellow in question. Given prevailing lifestyles in Central America, the part about his ending up with his balls in his mouth may not have been metaphor. Oliveira was clearly a person of strong wants.

What he wanted from me was his kids back, but in a way that wouldn't foul his good welcome in the States. I explained that there were things I had to know—first of all to decide if I'd take the job, then to do it well. He was quite forthcoming. In an afternoon and a morning I learned a lot about him and his wife. Trying to process it, though, before I met her could breed misconceptions. I let it sleep in my mind like the maiden in the fairy tale. Ellen Gonders's person kissed it to life. By the time I had driven her to the dealer's, then back to the mall with the shop chief and a tow truck; by the time I'd heard an estimate of the cost and had given her the sum in cash plus 10 percent (pointing out that extras always come up); by the time I was driving her home, I had as vivid a sense of her and Oliveira's years together as I might have gained by seeing a movie about them.

Poolside at a hotel by the Pacific, in Albamorada, down the mountain from the capital. Ellen reclines bikini'd on a chaise—lovely, leggy, liberated. Skims a paperback while casting for a suitable layover conquest. Along comes Toni, out trolling himself. Brown eyes glance up from the page and hook him so neatly he'll think till his dying day he made the first move.

The beach that midnight. Starlit, shoes in hand, Ellen strolls beside Toni. Phosphorescent breakers foam beyond them. The breeze tousles her hair, presses the skirt of her A-line against her thighs. A bolero they've been dancing to throbs on the soundtrack. She touches his forearm, turns to him, lifting her chin, and gaffs him smoothly into the fish bin. He clutches her, they kiss, sink to the warm sand. Pan to foaming, phosphorescent breakers.

Macagüita Airport, Chilpanzango. Ellen and Toni pull up in his Fellini. How cool and crisp she looks, how like a poster! Gold and purple Hemispheric uniform, auburn hair bunned trimly beneath chic toque. Toni, flushed and haggard, follows her in, catches up, takes her arm, and turns her to him. She listens to his vows with maternal patience, lets him draw her off behind a pillar. He kisses her thirstily. Her eyes are not quite closed, her face smiles calmly.

The observation deck. Long shot of Toni, apart from groups of wavers. One hand grips the rail, one droops forlornly. Jetliner roars by, lifts above jungled mountains, shrinks into the distance. The handwavers drift away. Toni stands gazing. Faint bolero pulsings on the sountrack. Slow disolve to

Ellen's apartment in Houston. Living room overflows with yellow roses. She enters, somewhat wilted by the long flight. Roommates chirp in mockery-masked envy.

Close-up of Ellen: smile of fatigue and triumph.

Gringa stewardesses! In what had been my country I used to know a man who touched nothing else, the way some men drink only single-malt whisky. He was a man of the world, though. Toni wasn't. Toni was the spoiled son of a coffee planter, spoiled by too much money, by excessive good looks, by birth in the ruling class of a feudal society. Spoiled into a perfect Latin *machito* by his mother and all the women in his family, then spoiled by a lot of success against sham opposition—housemaids, shopgirls, typists, friends' younger sisters. He wasn't ready for a self-sufficient gringa stewardess who picked him up because she liked his profile, fucked his brains out expertly for a weekend, then simply flew off, without leaving him the least sense of having possessed her. The impact was crushing. Ellen rolled over him like Hitler's panzers.

And kept the blitzkrieg going on subsequent layovers. Why not? Toni was handsome, rich, an excellent dancer, tried hard to be masterful yet was easily whipped. She especially loved dropping hints of the men in her life. How he winced and grimaced, how his eyes flashed! She also enjoyed milking the fury from him. How tame he grew then. She snared him in a series of humbling envelopments.

From each he salvaged a remnant of battered machismo and

withdrew behind a barrage of yellow roses. He couldn't give her up: pride and want forbade it. Grimly he hung on and took his beatings. He'd break her yet!

Time was on his side. His cannonade of attentions had little softening effect, but his hinterland of position and money was spacious. The tide began to turn three months after their meeting, when he took Ellen to visit the family *finca*.

Here one notes the value of indirection. At this stage the decisive theater was bed. That was where Toni's *machito* ego was being chewed up. He had to win a battle there to equalize, and his inclination favored that ground, despite the repeated thrashings he took there. But he couldn't bed Ellen under his mother's roof. Taking her to the *finca* thus constituted a maneuver away from the theater of decision and implied reapproaching it by a roundabout route. Observe the effects:

To begin with, the maneuver required discipline since it went against his inclination. As Fuller points out, the first step toward control of the battlefield is control of one's own forces. Then, with bed ruled out, there was nothing to distract Ellen from the charms of feudal existence. The plantation was endless. Someday handsome Toni would own it all. He was doing well already, managing two or three profitable businesses in the capital, but nothing in mere commercial affluence compared with the deference shown by his family's peasants—sombreros doffed and held with both hands at the sternum—when Ellen and he rode among them in the coffee groves. That Toni received it by right raised him in her estimation. That she received it simply by being with him was oddly restful. She began to feel a little weary of flying. She began to think of settling down.

Back in bed in the capital, on the eve of her flight, Ellen lost her customary composure. This had happened before, but never with Toni. For the first time he awed her a little, the way she awed him. He wore the marks on his shoulders very proudly the next day in the country club locker room.

He'd won his battle; her advance was halted. For a time they faced each other in equilibrium. Then Toni proposed marriage, and Ellen accepted, and the initiative swung over to him.

The next phase was too messy and crude to invite study. While Ellen was on the offensive, operations were conducted with sweep and panache. Toni's proposal seemed a capitulation but was, in fact, an envelopment of his own. Once Ellen was caught in it, he ground her down in battles of attrition—plodding, unimaginative, costly on both sides, ultimately effective, but no fun to watch.

She might have refused his proposal and disengaged, winning, but she thought she had him whipped and could collect spoils. Besides, she was in love with him. That is, she enjoyed him in bed and respected him for his claim to social deference. Toni, for his part, was in love with her. That is, he enjoyed her in bed and respected her for her capacity to cause damage—as one will quickly come to respect an ocelot whom one has foolishly taken for a tabby. He wasn't aware of it, but what he intended by marriage was to get title to the beast and domesticate it, exactly what she intended for him. Each could only feel free by caging the other, but neither one had any real self-knowledge. They were locked in mortal struggle and called it love.

Once they were married, Toni had every advantage. The battles were on his terrain. Ellen had no safe base: no job, no uniform, no dawn departures to exotic places, no other men she could drop hints about. Children came instantly, and while she took pains to preserve her figure, and with it the weapon of physical allure, her mobility was painfully restricted. He told her nothing of his business, nor could she glean much about it from others, being doubly unworthy of trust as woman and foreigner. Thus she had little intelligence of a flank vital to him where he might be vulnerable.

She knew more about his monkey business. Having other women, and having Ellen suspect, was tactically effective, besides being personally and culturally indispensable. It reinforced his self-esteem while damaging hers. There were risks to it, however, since the key to sex war is the fraud that no war is in progress. When Ellen caught him, she hit him fiercely. Toni turned the main force of her blows aside with boyish charm and manly contrition and godlike generosity. She counterattacked him in kind, had her flirtations. And made some telling thrusts, but none was decisive, for none could be pressed home to scandalous horning. Toni would divorce her—he'd have little choice—and that would mean she'd lose her children. In Atacalpa and countries like it, adultery is an offense only in women.

Meanwhile, Toni was a good father, to the point where Ellen had trouble seeing him as the enemy. He pampered her. Ease and luxury sapped her will to fight. Meanwhile, Atacalpa was torn by violence. Each day brought a new crop of corpses. This external strife cast Toni as Ellen's protector and distracted her from pursuit of their private war.

At some moment, though, she realized her situation. She was in a war, and she was losing. And when she saw that she could never win it, that every aspect favored the enemy, that his destruction was impossible and hers assured, she brought up reserves of imagination and courage, maneuvered temporarily to favorable ground, and disengaged, seizing priceless booty and withdrawing to what seemed a safe redoubt. She got Toni to take her and the children to Disney

World, waited till he was fed up with the attractions, left him at their hotel, and took the kids—supposedly for a third trip to the Haunted Mansion but in fact to the airport. Seven hours later they were in Peacock.

She'd come through in good order. She hadn't managed to enslave Toni, but had resisted being enslaved herself. She'd salvaged her morale and most of her looks. And she'd captured the children, therefore a margin of triumph. But a pincing in her cheeks, a testiness and snideness in her manner—how cruelly she treated poor Mr. Wagram!—argued that she'd paid a high price. Her buffer of self-assurance was deeply eroded. Wagram would surely do best by remaining insecure—not a sissy exactly, but light-years from a Latin macho.

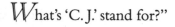

8   What's 'C. J.' stand for?"
Ms. Gonders must have realized early on that abuse wasn't necessary with Wagram, but she continued to bully him—out of habit, or as a surrogate for her husband, or because it was fun. Cutting remarks in front of the repairman. Icy glances, lip curlings of disgust. A bored tone and a refusal to make eye contact. He endured it like a puppy who'd soiled the rug. Now, however, as they turned onto the gravel drive to her home, a large ranch-style set among oaks, it seemed she'd grown glutted. And perhaps ashamed of herself and sorry for him, ready to make amends.

Wagram blushed. "I was afraid you'd ask that. Carol Julius. Terrible, isn't it? In school they were always calling me 'Carrie.' I was always having fights and usually losing."

"I'll call you C. J. My name is Ellen. Won't you please come in for a cup of coffee?"

"I don't want to put you to any trouble. I'm sorry about your car. You've been very nice about it."

"No I haven't. I've been rude. You're the one who's been nice. And a cup of coffee isn't any trouble. Please come in."

But it was hard to put C. J. at ease. He held his coffee as if afraid of a spill and a scolding. Ellen's children came home from school—a boy seven, a girl four. When they chattered to her in Spanish, C. J. was bewildered.

"My husband—we're separated—is from Central America."

"Oh."

It was hard drawing him out. He'd been fishing on the lake. Yes, the fishing was good. No, it wasn't exactly a vacation. Only after much encouragement from Ellen, many signals of gesture and tone that she wasn't a threat, did it develop that the trip was intended as therapy. C. J.'s wife had left him for another man.

"No, we have no children, that's the problem. My wife didn't want them, so I had a vasectomy. Now she does. Kind of funny, huh? I shouldn't talk about it."

"Yes you should. Talking helps."

"Fishing sure doesn't."

"Of course not. All alone out on a lake. Talking's much better. Someday I'll tell you my troubles. What is she like?"

The woman C. J. described reminded Ellen a lot of her husband and a little of herself. C. J.'s sex-war wounds had come as a non-belligerent.

Dr. Gonders came home from his clinic. He and C. J. talked fishing, a manly pursuit, though not brutal like hunting. C. J. was too shy to stay for dinner, but on Ellen's insistence agreed to take a rain check. Ellen saw him to his camper. She waved to him as he drove off into the dusk.

At dinner a week later, C. J. let Ellen's children try to teach him Spanish. He bungled the pronunciation hilariously, setting them wild with glee. They took to him quickly. Without being the least bit patronizing, he made them the center of the conversation. Among the many things they told him was that they met their school bus at seven-thirty, out by the mailbox where the drive met the road.

At the door, as he was leaving, C. J. almost asked Ellen out. He wanted to but couldn't work up the nerve. Ellen went as far as she could to encourage him, even asked him what he did with his evenings. He made another try at getting up nerve, then said he'd brought a lot of books with him.

"How long are you staying?"

"A few more weeks."

"Please call and tell me how you're doing."

C. J. called. He called in person. But not to ask Ellen out or say how he was. Something had come up in his business. He had to get back, and there wasn't time to drive. He'd hired an air-taxi to take him to Draco. Could he leave his camper with her and her father?

"You're the only people I know here. I don't think I can get back for a month or so. I'd like to rent space from you. A hundred seems fair."

Ellen didn't want to take his money. He explained a formal transaction was for his protection. Something to do with the insurance. He'd drawn up a paper for her signature.

C. J. parked the camper near the mailbox, off the drive in among the oaks. He asked for the use of the phone to call a cab, but Ellen said she'd drive him to the airport.

The children went with them. C. J. said that when he returned he'd take them all fishing.

Ellen answered for them: "That would be lovely."

 *A*m I late?"

"—?"

"Am I late, Carl? They're still a ways out. I checked with the tower."

Kendall stood on my left, staring down at me. After a moment he stepped around and sat down on Nealy. Who reappeared at once, a transparency of him, standing in air against the plate-glass window, still smoking and smirking but keeping quiet.

"Carl, are you okay? Has something gone haywire?"

"Yes, I'm okay. No, nothing's gone haywire."

"Good. You look kind of funny. I'm not late, am I?"

I checked my watch. "No. You're right on time."

"Good."

Kendall was the sort of man who instills confidence. Balding, middle-aged, twenty pounds overweight. If he were a dentist, the work wouldn't be too painful; a used-car salesman, the car wouldn't be a lemon; a garbageman, you wouldn't get indicted. Garbageman: cleaner-up of after-job debris.

"Are you straight about this one?"

He sat back in the chair without tipping. "I think so."

Despite the extra weight, Kendall's suit was too big for him. He looked like a public school math teacher, maybe the principal. He had a law degree but practiced exclusively as an investigator. He looked back at me calmly. "Want to go over it?"

"Yes," I said. "How does it work?"

"The client and the driver are on their way in. The three of you will take my car to the target. The new battery is behind the passenger seat. The radios are in the glove compartment. They work. I checked them ten minutes ago."

"You're impeccable, Carlos," said Nealy. "No stone unturned, no avenue unexplored."

I ignored him.

"I stay here," Kendall continued. "I make sure the Lear gets refueled. I make sure the pilot files a flight plan and is cleared for take-off."

"Go on."

"You have a camper on the target's grounds. The driver drops you and the client near it. You take the battery and one of the radios. The driver goes back four-tenths of a mile along Redwood. He parks at the Methodist church. He verifies that he's in radio contact."

"Poke Chop Leadah," mocked Nealy, "this heah Poke Chop Two. Does you read me B'wana?"

I ignored him.

"You and the client go through the woods to the camper. He gets in back. You do an engine check. You install the new battery if needed. If the thing still won't start, or has a flat tire or something, you alert the driver to close up and be ready to bring everyone out. You wait for the assets. When they show up, you call them over. They meet with you and the client in the back of the camper."

"Do Abort first."

"You and the client drive to the church in the camper. You park it there. The driver brings you here. You and the client fly out. The driver and I take your car and my car to Draco and turn them in. I tell the rental place in L.A. where their camper is. I go home."

"What about Go?"

"You drive to the church in the camper. The client and the assets are in back. The four of you transfer to the sedan. The driver brings you here. The five of you take the Lear to Juarez. You and the driver get off there. The client and the assets go where they go."

"Precision planning," said Nealy. "You loved the war, didn't you?"

I ignored him. "What do you do, James?"

Kendall cleared his throat. "As soon as you're airborne, I call the Peacock police. Mr. Antonio Oliveira, a citizen of the Republic of Atacalpa, has just left Peacock with his two children, Tonio and Elena. They have freely and willingly rejoined him. He has a valid order awarding him custody of them, issued by the pertinent tribunal of his country. A copy of the order, along with an authenticated English translation of it, is in the mail to them. The vehicle in which the children left their former residence was authorized to be on the grounds. Copies of the authorizing documents are in the mail to them. No law has been broken."

"Ha!" said Nealy. "And may I add, ho!"

Kendall opened his jacket to show the envelope in the inside pocket. "I mail this downstairs. I turn in your car here in Peacock. I go to Draco and turn in mine. I tell the place in L.A. where the camper is. I go home."

I nodded. Landing lights hung above the reach of the runway. "Is this them?"

Kendall turned to look, then turned back nodding. "Has to be." He stood up. "Got the keys to your car?"

"Under the visor. Space seventeen."

"Mine's in twelve. The driver will meet you there. Good luck."

"He doesn't need luck," said Nealy, "he's got planning. And look at the opposition! Two little kids!"

I ignored him. "Thanks, James. See you next time."

The Lear rolled past the building on the runway. I stood up. I watched through Nealy's belly as it rolled on.

"By the way," said Nealy, "what's she like?"

"Who?"

"Mommy, of course. What's she like, Carlos?"

I looked out through the canted glass. The Lear slowed down and turned onto the taxiway. "Seems like a good woman. She has a bitchy streak, but it's not deep."

"Think she'll miss her kids?"

I turned away toward the mural. Which showed a shell hole full of slimy water. A decomposing dog's head floated in it, then Elena's head, then Tonio's, then my own.

"Well?" said Nealy.

Turning to face him would have been a relief, so I kept looking at the mural. "Yes," I said. "I'm certain she will."

10 We crossed into Mexican airspace around 10:30. Tonio rode the whole way with the pilots, happy as hell. Elena and the stew did coloring books. Oliveira had the armchair opposite them. I sat in the back with Hicks the driver. No one developed deformities, no dead people dropped by. The mission was running—I thought of the thing as a mission. That kept me concentrated, I suppose.

After we landed, though, when Oliveira and his assets were on their way south and Hicks and I were on our way from Juarez Airport to El Paso, the faces on billboards turned to watch me go by. Stopped selling cigarettes and suntan lotion. Acquired sneers or smirks and aimed them at me. At the border, with our cab in a line of cars inching toward the booths, the crow on a Cuervo billboard winked at me and blew kisses. I told Hicks I was staying in Mexico and jumped out.

I walked up and down Avenida Juarez very slowly, up the sunny side and down the shady, counting the people who tried to sell me things. By the time I lost count my breathing had eased. Then I went into a place and drank a beer slowly. Then I had another and some *huevos rancheros*. Perfectly normal by the time I finished, but I didn't feel up to tangling with more billboards. I got a hotel room and went to sleep.

Almost. As I was dozing off a child began to cry in the next room—whimpers, then terrified wails, then outright howling, as if two or three people had hold of a six-year-old kid and were doing something horrible and painful. Then they let go or stopped doing whatever it was, and the screams subsided to sobs and the sobs to silence. Then, as I dozed off, it started again.

The third time I called down.

"What child, señor?"

"The child in the room next to me! He's being tortured! Send somebody up or call the police!"

"What room do you have, please?"

I told him.

"There's no one there, señor."

"What do you mean?"

"Señor. Yours is the only room on that side of the floor that's occupied."

"So someone's got hold of a passkey! They've gone into an empty room and are killing a child there! Send somebody up or call the police!"

No, I didn't say that. I thanked the desk clerk and hung up. I listened to my breathing and my heart, to the air conditioner and faint sounds from the street. After awhile I lay back and looked at the ceiling, yellow in the faint gleam of Mexican sunlight pushing through thick curtains. Then I closed my eyes. As I dozed off it started again, except that now there seemed to be two children.

I got up and took my flight bag into the bathroom. I got out my toilet kit and put it on the glass shelf over the sink. I got out my shaving cream and brush and razor. I lathered my face: right cheek, left cheek, throat, upper lip and chin. Conscientiously, like a barber. I rinsed the brush, then shook it, and then squeezed it, making a ring with my left thumb and forefinger. Then I shaved, very carefully, using short, slow strokes. I rinsed the razor. I put the top back on the tube of shaving cream. I put my shaving things back in the kit. I paid no attention to the screaming children. By the time I was finished, their screams had subsided to sobs.

I went into the shower and turned the water on as hot as it went and then fed in the cold till I could just stand it and got under the scalding stream and stood there a while. Then I unwrapped the soap and washed. Very thoroughly, till the soap was only a sliver. By then, even the sobbing had stopped.

I closed the hot tap and opened the cold all the way. I stood under a while, enjoying hearing nothing but the water. Then I closed the tap and got out and toweled off. I took my bag and kit back into the bedroom, wincing in the refrigerated air.

I would have liked to lie down but couldn't risk it. I took out a clean shirt and clean socks and put them on. I took my trousers from the chair back and put them on. I checked the contents of my trouser pockets. I took notebook and pen from the shirt I'd been wearing and put them in the shirt I had on. I put my soiled shirt and socks in the flight bag. I put the kit on top and zipped the bag. I put on my shoes. I picked up my bag and left the room and the hotel.

No. Before leaving the room I looked in the mirror. The man there looked back at me calmly. His broad forehead and alert eyes suggested a life on the border of theory and praxis: a field geologist, a trial attorney. He was neither tall nor bulky but very fit: a forest ranger, a professional infielder. After a moment he smiled protectively at me. Another beat, the smile became a grin, fraternal concern undercut by sergeanty toughness.

"Take care, jackass," he said. *"Estás en malas condiciones."*

"Lo que falta es música."

II The bartender poked his left forefinger toward the jukebox. *"Allí tiene."*

"¡No hombre! Flesh and bone mariachis, at least a dozen."

The cantina was air-conditioned. Also dark. Not really a cantina, more like a bar. Round cocktail tables on one side, booths on the other. A curved bar with padded vinyl and bamboo stools. Could just as well have been in L.A. or Phoenix, but the sign outside it said "Cantina La Norteña."

The place was empty except for the moonfaced bartender. Fifty or so, with the requisite drooping moustache, skin the color and texture of copper tubing. And Jackass, of course, on the second stool from the right. I watched him in the mirror behind the bar. No question at all, the fellow was in bad shape. Hunched over his glass as if to protect it from predators. Blabbing to a stranger. One drink, and *yak-yak-yak-yak,* as if a selector was jammed and he couldn't get his mouth off automatic.

"Four trumpets. The leader, a guy of sixty, with gray hair cut short, you know, like a toothbrush, and three young guys not worried about their embouchures giving out, who can really blast when the song calls for it. Give me another.

"The three young guys should be tall, so they can stand in the back and toot over the others." To the bartender's back as he turned to the blender: "With their hair slicked down under their sombreros, and each one with a little thin moustache, but the leader is

44

short and clean-shaven, and doesn't wear his sombrero but has it hung at his back by a string around his chest. He should sing besides playing the trumpet. A song here and there, but not slow stuff. Jumpy, despairing tunes like 'La Cama de Piedra.'"

"*Es buena canción.*" The bartender served Jackass another sour. Sugar for energy, lemon for vitamins, tequila for phantom control.

"'The bed is stone, the headboard's stone, / The woman who loves me really has to love me, / Ay, ay!'"

"*Usted canta bien.*"

"*¡No, hombre!* I don't sing well. My pop sang well. One time, when I was a kid . . .'"

Jackass thought better of tempting a visit from his father's phantom and gulped half his sour. "I can't sing much."

"*A mí me suena bien.*"

Nod of thanks, and good-bye to the rest of the sour. "Give me another. Look. Make up three or four. Have one yourself, or whatever you feel like drinking."

"*Está bien.*"

"Five violins." To the bartender's back as he sloshed booze into the blender. "Little guys in their fifties who've been all over and seen it all. That's clear the minute you see them and hear them play. Nothing surprises them, they've seen it already."

"*Mi padre, que en paz descanse . . .*" Serving them each a sour. "*De chico vío a Pancho Villa. Trabajara de botones en el Hotel Ancira de Monterrey, y vió a Pancho Villa entrar en la cantina montado en un caballo blanco.*"

"That's it! They've seen everything that can happen inside a cantina, even Pancho Villa ride in on a white horse. And everything that can happen outside too. It shows on their faces, you hear it in their music. They just saw away. They could be serenading under a twelve-year-old's window or in a whorehouse while a fight's going on. Either way they'd look and sound the same."

"He visto pelea de putas. En Hermosillo, hace muchos años. Era cosa terrible."

"That's it, a pair of whores fighting. Loser gets thrown out into the street. The fiddle players have seen that and everything else. No matter what it is, they've seen it already. That quality is essential to the music. The others shouldn't have it, not the whole band, but it has to be there on the violinists' faces and in how they play. Look, give me what's left in the blender and make up some more."

"Está bien."

"Four guitars. Five with the mandolin the lead singer plays. He's a baritone, this lead singer, and he has a strong voice. He plays the mandolin, but not when he's singing. He steps out in front with his mandolin in his left hand, held by the throat and hanging against his left leg, and the other mariachis curve around him. Not much facial expression, and not a single gesture, but his voice is very powerful and clear. His best songs are unhappy love songs. 'Ella,' 'Noche de Ronda,' 'La que se Fué.'"

"Son buenas canciones," he said, pouring out two sours.

"Yes, good songs, but look, this glass is too small. Why don't you pour the rest into a tumbler? That way you won't be turning around all the time. Give me the rest in a tumbler, and make up some more. I can pay for it, look, here's fifty dollars."

"Está bien, señor."

"The other guitarists sing in the background sometimes, and sometimes they shout, you know, 'Yi! Yi! Yi! Yi!' Except for the bass guitar. He never says anything. He has to be a big guy, as fat as his instrument. Not soft fat, though, not one of your jolly fat guys. A mean son of a bitch, maybe seven-eighths Yaqui, who stares straight ahead without blinking or making a noise. You could hit him on the nose with a two-by-four, and he wouldn't blink his eyes or make a peep. The other guitars, they smile when the music's happy, they look sad when it's sad. His face never changes. Not like the violinists, though. They just aren't concerned. But the guy who plays bass guitar, what he is is angry. He has enough rage for the whole band."

"Está bravo con la vida." He set a tumbler down and poured it full.

"No, not angry with life, angry with God. For not existing. For making the world and then wandering off. He takes it personally, he wants to get even. You can hear his anger in the music. Without his rage the music wouldn't work. And that . . . That's the music I want, the music that's missing. To me . . . If I had that music . . . But look, this stool . . . I'm going . . ."

Jackass climbed down from the stool, gripping the vinyl. Stood for a moment, then lurched with desperate care across the pitching deck of the cantina. He reached the nearest booth and sat down hard with his palms pressed to the cool formica, then slid forearms across the tabletop and crossed them, and let his head drop onto his crossed arms.

For a moment the world stopped spinning, and he heard mariachis, the same mariachis he had been inventing. They were playing "La Golondrina," a common enough song, very old, very sad, but the odd thing was the singer was his father. His father was alive again and singing!

A smile came to Jackass's face. He tried to lift his head to see his father, but in that moment the world began spinning again and dragged him bruskly down into the dark.

12 *A* kid was selling bubblegum in the street. Evil-looking stuff, the size and apparent consistency of golf balls. Colored red and yellow, purple and green. Held up toward me in the lid of a shoe box. Who on earth would buy it?

Late-afternoon glare, sensation of no third dimension. Cardboard facade of curio shops and cantinas. If you peeked behind, there'd be desert, parched rocky hills. Cardboard passersby, cardboard street vendors. I waved the kid off, then thought to give him something, but he'd disappeared.

The bridge. Sensation of walking three or four inches in air. Caused by several wake-me-up drinks, or maybe just another hallucination. I'd fallen in with two couples from El Paso who offered me a lift over the border, but on the bridge I panicked, made them stop, told them to let me out, I'd lost my flight bag. Which was true enough, I'd left it in some cantina, but I wouldn't miss anything in it, not even Fuller, not even the brilliant notes I'd made in the margins.

Steel grates on both sides rose and curved inward. To prevent freedom plunges. Below, the riverbed, dry but for a trickle. Sunset on my right, walking three inches in air back into Mexico.

Flying roaches.

I woke with a raging thirst but not too much headache. After a moment or two I knew where I was, a room in a hotel in Ciudad Juarez.

High ceiling, double-doored wardrobe, large and sturdy bed with a mirror beside it, the kind in a frame you can tip to different angles. I'd wished myself happy birthday in it before crashing, though my birthday had been over for two or three hours. The bathroom door was open, the light on inside. A roach flew out and fluttered toward me.

Very ineptly fashioned aerodynamically. Which is odd when you think of the fine job done on them otherwise. Original design still in use everywhere. No modifications required in millions of years. Biology's Volkswagen, except for flying. They have trouble just staying airborne, and you never see one take off from the ground. Drop from wall or ceiling and flutter like crazy.

I sat up and flailed at the roach but couldn't hit it. It bumped against my cheek and fell in my lap. Lay there upside down wiggling madly, then flipped over and scampered under the sheet. I hunched backward against the bedstead, but other roaches were fluttering toward me. They flew in a swarm from the bathroom, they dropped from the ceiling.

I tried to brush them away, but there were too many. They pelted against my face and body. They fell on me and scurried over my flesh.

I ran naked from the room into the hallway.

No. The floor was ankle-deep in roaches, so I stood on the bed and flailed to keep the filth off me.

No again, I hid my face in my hands and curled into a ball. Not because I chose, sheerly from panic. A quivering mass of roaches covered my body. I felt their wiggly legs and slimy bellies. With eyes clamped shut I could see them—undulating mound, mahogany brown. I knew they weren't there, that made them more horrible. Somewhere nearby a large beast made sobbing noises.

After a time the roaches were gone. Maybe a minute or two, maybe an hour. I lay curled on myself. I'd wet the bed but lacked the will to get up.

Fear and despondency and self-revulsion. Self-pity too, I mustn't leave that out, taking rueful comfort in my isolation. No one knew where I'd sunk. My parents were safely dead. My brother and sister supposed me missing in action. Then I thought, Ellen Gonders knows!—though, of course, how could she? —and I cringed. I lay there waiting for the dirt to be scraped in on top of me.

When the window was showing light, I got up, however. Thought of it as a heroic accomplishment, the wounded knight dragging himself back into battle, though I never had thoughts like that in Southeast Asia. Thought Ellen Gonders would be proud of me. For what? For getting up from a pissed-in bed? I got up and washed and dressed, left the hotel and Juarez.

No winking billboards, no flames from unlikely places. The phantoms, evidently, were worn out. Or maybe they had only come by for my birthday. Or maybe they were on break. When I tried to sleep that night, I'd hear children wailing. Whatever the case, I could kid myself no longer. I was going to pieces. Worse than that, I was dead.

So when I crossed to El Paso, I fed Wagram's credit card number into a pay phone and called Digby Sobers in Charleston, South Carolina—right away, before the act scared me. Then I went home to wait for Vince.

DREAMS

I began to have dreams. Bona fide dreams, while I was sleeping.

Years before I'd stopped dreaming. That was in Thailand, on my first tour. The dreams I was having then were inconvenient. They didn't help me do what I was doing. So I stopped.

Not by getting zonked at bedtime. That only delayed the dreams and made them more savage. What I learned to do was pinch them off.

I'd already learned to snuff inconvenient musings. Riding a cable hoist down into the forest one might wonder if the dinks were down there waiting. Thoughts like that didn't help me rescue pilots, so right away I learned to pinch them off. The logical next step was snuffing dreams.

Nealy transcribed his. In three-by-five-inch black notebooks with graph-paper pages that were good for playing "Battleship" while he and I waited beside the choppers for someone to get shot down over in Nam. Nealy kept a notebook on him at all times to write down things he saw and things he thought of, and his dreams. Dreaming, Nealy said, was mental excretion. I was poisoning myself by inhibiting mine.

"But you, on the other hand, you're healthy! You save your neuroturds in little notebooks!"

"The way to clean your mind, Carlos, is to bring things to consciousness. There's no better way to do that than writing them down. Anyway, I can use them in my book. I'll bet a great book could be done of just the dreams that guys have over here. You know how the fog hangs in wisps above the jungle? Clouds of dreams hang over this war every morning."

"Sure. Well, none are mine. I pinch mine off."

From inside or out-. I learned to know inside a dream that I was dreaming and take myself in hand and pinch the dream off, though at first what I mainly did was squelch recollections. I'd wake with a dream in my mind in the night or the morning, and sing or count or recite or talk to myself till every spark of dream was stifled. Any dream at all, dreams were insidious. I could be dreaming about myself and my brother, that we were at the beach or playing tennis, and the next thing I knew my brother was a dink, and I had my knife out and was sawing his windpipe. So I used a firm hand, I took no prisoners. I broke myself of dreaming once and for all.

Or so I imagined, if and when I even thought about it. After Nealy died I didn't deal a lot with other people at the level where dreams were discussed. If the subject came up, I'd remember I'd quit.

Once a girl asked me if I dreamed about her. I told her no, I'd given up dreaming. Which turned out to be the wrong answer. Which led directly to a loused-up time. Giving up dreams, it turned out, was one of the four thousand seven hundred sixty-eight ways the war could louse you up with normal people, one of the twelve million things they couldn't understand and didn't want to, thus one of the countless enticements to self-pity the generous war kept strewing in my path.

"But you can dream now, Carlos, the war is over."

"Wrong on both counts. A: I broke myself of dreaming. B: The war is alive and well."

I dreamed about a woman. In my dreams I loved her and she loved me. But when I was awake I couldn't place her.

The dreams were vivid enough, more vivid than life. Key aspects of her, though, resisted retrieval. I could recall how it felt to touch and hold her, and how it felt when she touched and held me. I could recall the faint, oniony scent that came on her during lovemaking, that I loved to nuzzle for at the sides of her breasts. I could recall the different ways she said "Carlos," and the throaty laugh she had when animated. But I couldn't picture her face.

I could remember a particular look of hers that she had when she was especially happy, a lovely, womanly way of lowering her eyes and smiling downward, as if she had a wonderful secret that modesty prevented her from disclosing. I could remember that look but couldn't "see" it, couldn't bring her face into focus. The least try made me so nervous I stopped at once.

Her name too. In dreams I spoke it often. Awake, I didn't know it, couldn't recall it, shied from reaching for it with my thoughts, as one might shy from gripping a glass shard. The mere notion of gripping it mentally made me nervous. I never made a real try at bringing it back.

Besides not being able to place the woman, I couldn't recognize myself. I looked the same, was still called Carlos, but it seemed a different man was in my body, an updated version, a reconstructed model. The oddness of it made my head swim. But only when recalling a dream while awake. In my dreams I was perfectly at ease. Not since I was fourteen had I lived so correctly and fully.

In what had been my country, summer and school vacation came in the dry season, mid-December through March. When I was fourteen I spent it in the rainforest, foster son to my father's Indian counterpart. The Indians were smart about adolescence. Since nature doesn't bother girls with it too much, the Indians didn't bother them much either. When a girl stopped being a child, she was a woman. Boys, though, spend years too full of hormones to be children yet too full of crap to be men. The Indians saw this and gave boys what they needed: hardship and practical knowledge dispensed outdoors—canoe-making, blowgun-making, hunting, and so forth. Everything was aimed at enabling a boy to persuade some girl's father that he, the boy, could feed her and her offspring, marriage being the only way an Indian male could lay hands on an Indian female. Education flowed with the current of hormones instead of trying to pole upstream against it.

Morally, I was ready for that summer. In my house one accepted trials and avoided self-pity. My body was fit. Otherwise, I was far behind my Indian coevals—except for hormones and crap, there I may have been leading. Their contempt for my pallid hide and uncalloused feet, their ridicule of my blunders with their language, and their scorn at my ignorance of the forest were marvelously stimulating. They'll see! I told myself and went out and showed them. It never occurred to me that I might fail. In February my father sent to know if I'd like to go home for Carnival. I didn't even think; I didn't have to. I told my foster father to say No thank you. No Carnival could compete with the fun I was having. I wore a breechclout and coating of tree gum. I had scratches and lumps on every part of my body. I was living!

I went back the next year. Going back is always a mistake. It's never the same; you're always disappointed. But my father had just been killed, and I had to be somewhere. Any other place would have been worse.

The Indians were smart about death also. They knew the death of a loved one makes you angry, and that you need a place to put your anger. I spent those months hunting alone. At night I had people around me. I slept in my foster father's house, a wonderful house constructed on stilts and tree branches, with rooms that walked out from the center in three directions, added on for new wives and children. At daybreak, though, on my foster father's orders, I went out alone and stayed out till sunset. Each animal I killed took some of my anger. Still, it wasn't one of my life's good parts. The first summer I spent in the forest was great, however.

So was my first tour in the war, the start of it anyway. I believed a thing called communism existed, a disease that was also a religion. I believed the war was about halting its spread. I believed that taking part was correct, as it was for my father to take part against Hitler. It was extremely correct to rescue pilots. The way they looked at me established that. Very helpless, very glad to see me, stuffed to the ears with gratitude and admiration. Being a savior was wonderfully satisfying.

And also exciting. It was a rare run when we didn't draw fire, and even then things could go wrong. And we flew at night sometimes, and in crazy weather. The whole thing was a high. It was as if I was living in a movie.

Brave people, of course, stay sober and live in real life. They evaluate danger honestly, at retail prices, and don't pretend there's no chance of their having to pay. They accept the fear involved without grudge or welcome. Then they put it off to one side where it won't get in the way of what they're doing.

I knew brave people in Southeast Asia. I admired them and would have have liked to be like them. But being brave wasn't really important, so long as I behaved as if I were. How I managed was my business. I went after danger and fear and got high on them, and whatever might sober me up I pinched off. It was a good time.

After awhile things changed, however. The watershed, I saw later, was when Nealy died, though at the time my response was it didn't matter. Lots of people were dying. One guy more or less didn't mean anything. Made no difference, wasn't a big deal. That's how I took your death, Tommy. I pinched it off. But I also began asking for cracks at firing the machine guns that were mounted in the choppers' doorways. And volunteered to fly gunner on other guys' trips. I still flew my own, but by the end of that tour I was not saving pilots. Not anymore. That wasn't what I thought of myself as doing, or halting the spread of communism either. I was killing dinks, killing dinks pure and simple, and when I reupped I asked for the kind of duty where I wouldn't have to pretend to do anything else.

It was still a full life. No question there, as Tommy used to say. But it lacked a certain measure of correctness.

2 *N*o, not so. That was hindsight. Guilt came later. And was retroactive to include saving the pilots. They handed out all kinds of pain and havoc and might have gone about it less diligently if no one were there to save them when they went down. When I was in long-range patrolling, I found nothing wrong with killing. I was, in fact, quite content: full of anger but with plenty of places to put it.

See us at work. In tiger stripes and face paint, so you won't see us easily, and unless you're on top of us you won't hear us at all. Allard, and five yards ahead of him Digby Sobers, and five yards ahead of him Newton, "Noot the Loot," and five yards ahead of him Vince, humping the radio, and at the point Carlos. Ghosting through a gloom of fronds and lianas; profession predator, older than whoring.

I owned the point from my first patrol. Not that I walked point all the time, no one could do that, but most of the time I was out there, more than all the others together. Half were on their second tours, but even so I knew the forest better, and knew at once when humans had disturbed it. It made sense having me out in front.

Good sense had nothing to do with my wanting to be there. Point is maximum lethality and excitement: no friendly flesh between you and the quarry, no brain but yours between your flesh and harm. Each sound is clear, each glimpse stands out distinctly: the lizard on a vine the same color it is, the pearl of dew on a strand of spiderweb. All the standard senses are sharpened, and others that supposedly don't exist come on line with news you can bet your life on. More than once I "sensed" the tautness of a trip wire two feet in front of me at night, or "felt" the loom of an enemy encampment five hundred yards before we smelled cooking fires.

At point the world moved in slow motion. Birds that screeched and fluttered off ahead waited in air for me to gauge their flight path and judge what may have startled them. Each cell of skin vacuumed up information, yet it all got sorted and filed in plenty of time.

Afterward, of course, I was exhausted. Think of a sarong a peasant woman's been washing, kneading with river sand, flailing on rocks. That's how walking point left me. But while I was out there . . .

Incredible feelings swept through me, yet I had to fight not to credit them fully. That I was naked, for instance—hence the urge to crouch and clasp my groin with both hands. Or the similar feeling that eyes were peering at me, as though I were a germ on a microscope slide. Or that I was invisible, that I didn't exist, or that I existed in a different dimension.

Once we were following a river, moving upstream. The bank was steep, we were right above the water. I looked down to my left and saw some bubbles. Well, bubbles in a river, that's not odd. The river was narrow there and flowing swiftly. We could hear rapids upstream. There was nothing odd about a few bubbles. Still, my hand went up for us to stop. Then I stepped off very carefully to the right, and then, about eighty yards on, circled back left, till we hit the river again above the rapids. It was much broader there, with a strip of smooth stones. A dink platoon was on it taking a breather. North Vietnamese regulars: we were many klicks north of the DMZ. Beyond the strip an eddy had swirled out a pool, and a few of the dinks were washing in it, leaving soap bubbles no doubt.

Watching them from just inside the tree line, I felt I was in a different dimension. I could go out on the stones, and they wouldn't see me. I could shout and they wouldn't hear, I could fire my weapon, set off a dozen grenades and nothing would happen. The feeling was so strong I almost did it.

We let the dinks be. Our business was farther north. Our orders were not to initiate contact. Still, the oddness of that feeling stayed with me.

Or that life was a dream. Walking point fulfilled completely, left no mental space for worry or self-concern, but then I might look up ... Maybe a shard of sunlight touched my hand, and I lifted my eyes to where it pierced down through the trees, and my sense of self would catch up with me for a moment, and I'd wonder, hey, is this real, is it actually happening? But, no, it was so real I couldn't believe it, so much stronger than regular life I'd think, It's a dream.

Or a movie. Seeking the place of maximum exposure reinforced the feeling of invulnerability, the sense that I was living in a movie. Which now and then dissolved, leaving me all but whimpering in terror.

Never when on the move or in action, rarely when on patrol. Sometimes I'd come awake in darkness five or ten minutes before my watch knowing that before dawn I'd be blown to morsels, or paralysed or blinded or mutilated, or taken by predators as angry as I was, and I'd lie soaked in sweat half a heartbeat from soiling myself and twist an ear or bite a fold of cheek or gouge beside my right eye with my thumbnail till pain redeemed me from the lip of roachhood and I could suck deep breaths and get my nerve back and go and pull my watch as if nothing had happened.

Usually, though, dread struck between patrols. I'd be having a beer or lazing or reading something, and all at once the cocoon of illusion would crumble and I'd realize the risks I'd been taking and would take again. Sometimes I indulged myself and wallowed, curled up and bit a knuckle and mewed to myself, there being no need to act bravely there in base camp. Mainly I got zonked for the duration, till the sense that life was a movie returned.

A problem might have come up when I got my spare navel. That was twenty kilometers north of the DMZ, halfway to Dong Hoi. In the forest, when there was no wind (and there usually wasn't), or when what wind there was was wrong, you could be right on top of a thing before your standard senses made you aware of it. One morning my nonstandard senses went AWOL, and I got hit. In less than an hour I was in a litter lashed to a chopper ski with a guy I'd flown with on my first tour passing me plasma. The round just missed my spleen on the way in and just missed my left kidney on the way out, and in less time than you'd think I was fit for duty, but even so there might have been a problem. I might have had some trouble feeling invulnerable, so I took precautions.

First of all, I went back as soon as I could. A brave person would have taken a full convalescence and any R&R that he had coming, but I was hounding the doctors as soon as I came out of anesthesia. When could I go back? How long would I have to leave my teammates shorthanded? Some of this was sincere. Repetition enhanced it. But mainly I knew if I waited and began thinking, I might lose my nerve and my knack for gulping danger. Then I wouldn't get high, I'd be scared all the time, like most of the guys in the line outfits. I couldn't live like that, that would be too awful.

Secondly, I turned my wound around the way I did being point man. Getting hit became positive proof nothing could hurt me. Drilled point-blank, and see, no meaningful damage. Round weaves in and out avoiding organs, and see, in a few weeks as good as new.

I got no arguments from teammates. Lucky guys are good to be on patrol with.

"Some other poor fuck would have croaked, gut-shot like that." This from Vince Giobbe, whose problem was adrenaline addiction. He couldn't feel normally alive unless he was doing something insanely risky. If he hadn't gone to war, he'd have gone to prison. If he hadn't been a lurp, he'd have gone anyway. He'd have gone to Long Binh Jail, which was worse than Leavenworth, and talked back to the guards until they killed him.

Sobers was afraid he was a coward and had to keep proving he wasn't day after day. I should have told him how I went about things. Sobers and I were much alike. I was selfish, though, and kept my mouth shut. I loved having my teammates think I was brave.

We belonged to a priesthood of violence. Our vows were hardship, danger, and aggression. Our selflessness was measured in eighty-pound loads, in two-week missions deep in enemy country. Our piety admitted no safety nets, no softness toward ourselves or toward the enemy.

Or brotherhood, though we were closer than brothers. It wasn't simply that we thought as a unit, which is what a long-range patrol team needs to survive. We tapped a common pool of emotions the way termites share a communal digestive system. Our closeness was wonderful, like nothing I'd known since my family was whole. Then Sobers got run over, and Noot the Loot decided two tours were enough, and Allard, who was going to be team leader, was having a beer in the NCO club when a guy on LSD or speed or something rolled a frag grenade in through the door.

Vince took leave. I could have also, but I was very angry about Allard and Sobers. I didn't want to carry that anger around. I didn't want to join a new team either. I knew people on other teams, guys I'd R&R'd and gotten zonked with, but compared to guys who'd shared my personal danger everyone was a stranger. I couldn't be with strangers the way I was feeling. Nor would strangers want me. So what I did was ask to go out solo. I'd go way in where the dinks felt safe and comfy and pay them back for Allard and Digby Sobers.

My captain let me. He knew I was more or less crazy—as most lurps got to be sooner or later, if they didn't start that way, like Vince. He knew I would cause him less trouble off on my own than on another team or fretting in camp. Besides, the division CO was a body-count junkie who considered lurps his personal death squads. My captain gave me his blessing, but also an admonition in the style of Ape Thomas, under whom he'd served on leaving West Point.

"Sure. Go ahead. But stay in your sector. Stay out of the way of my regular patrols. And try to remember you're in the United States Army. Do all the bad guys you want and keep score for our leader, but make sure they're soldiers. Men of military age, in uniform. No women, no little kids, nobody's great grampa. And no fucking trophies, no ears, no dongs, no scalps. If I hear of you taking body parts as trophies, I will personally blow your head off."

What I mainly took were Claymore mines, for their versatility and high pop per pound. My rifle, of course, but only a few clips of ammo. A single gun can't afford long firefights anyway. Frag and gas and white phosphorous grenades. The latter have a very bracing effect. My knife, my .45, and my machete.

I went way in. I found myself making hand signals to teammates who were no longer there behind me, gaping back in anguish, Where's Vince, where's Newton? And wanting to hum to myself to drive off the solitude—breaking camp at dawn, making camp at twilight—when what I needed was leopard alertness, feral concentration on the forest around me. Each day a bit less, however, as I grasped my new condition and why I'd sought it. All authentic action is pondered unconsciously. We find ourselves engaged, doing this or that, and only then, if ever, pry out reasons. What I was after, going up there alone, was cutting the cord that moored me to civilization. That done, I sailed off into savagery, responsible only to my anger. No past to come to terms with, no future to build, an endless moment crackling with risk and purpose.

I went up to about fifty klicks due south of Vinh, onto the slopes of the Annamite Cordillera, above Uncle Ho's trail. Which wasn't a trail, by the way, but a web of paths through the forest. Most were two or three yards wide with the earth packed solid, but farther east there were paths the dinks drove trucks on.

I made my base on the spur of a ridge. At low elevations the trees go way up, and a triple canopy curtains out the sunlight, so in most spots there's little undergrowth. What I wanted and got high enough up to find was stuff you had to hack through. I picked a spur with flanks too steep to climb. The only way to reach it was down the ridge hacking. I placed a pair of Claymores so that their blasts would angle across my front and snaked the wires off in a long zigzag so someone backtracking along them would be led away from me. Then I made an escape route down the spur with cam- ouflaged hand- and footholds, and a hideout a distance off with a cache of rations where if I had to I could go to ground. Then I began collecting for Allard and Sobers.

My M.O. was to leave my base at midnight and get down to one of the paths before dawn. Part of the way I followed a stream, wad- ing for long stretches in icy water, premiums on safe-base insurance. I'd lie up all day in a thicket noting traffic, then at nightfall move out north or south. Right on the paths usually. All I had to do was stay alert, not do something inane like bump into a sentry. They were very relaxed up there, at least when I started. Groups bound for the war bivouacked beside the paths, shielded from the sky by the tree canopy. When I came on one I'd reconnoiter, and if it posed no problem (which it usually didn't), kill the sentries and go in and cut throats. I brought the war to them, saved them miles of marching.

Amidst sleeping enemies! Absolute immersion in the moment; polar opposite of being dead. One taste and I knew why the ape that went down on the plain and became a killer never went back into the trees.

At first I selected throats on a bivouac's fringes. Obviously, they were the safest targets. Then I thought of the consternation they caused at dawn. From then on I worked the middle. The surprise would be more stunning, no one would feel safe.

That way, too, my act was more exciting, as when the trapezist adds another somersault or subtracts the final scrap of net. Was I asking to be killed, I wonder? Trapezists, I've heard, have a special term, "casting," for the morbid urge to miss a hold and fall. Or was I, in paradox, keeping fear at bay by putting myself ever more deeply in hazard? Was I, in effect, reassuring myself, saying, See, there's no cause for alarm, you can do anything and get away with it? I don't know. There's no question, however, about the excitement, or the exaltation I felt using my knife.

What I took for the general's body count were letters and photos, things I couldn't come by without killing their owners. And maps if I found them. Maps and letters had intelligence value. Searching the sentries' corpses was no problem when I killed them out on a bivouac's edges, but it was another thing entirely when the searchee's buddies were snoozing inches away. That produced a nearly unbearable tension, joyously released in the next man's murder. Then, Should I do three? Should I do four? At least twice I bit off one too many. At least twice someone woke while I was doing his neighbor—in case of which I kept white phosphorus grenades handy, along with a phrase of Vietnamese. The phrase meant "Enemy to the southeast!" I delivered it in a whisper, then tossed the grenade. The flash wrecked night vision and was an attention getter, as were the blast and the howls of those who got splattered. Nothing beats "Willy Pete" for disengaging.

When I had enough clients to warrant the cost—a group of platoon strength, say, or larger—I'd stay a while and rig a proper ambush. My personal best was a two-miner done on a bunch of what had to be raw replacements. I placed one mine on the unit's rear—that is, on the flank farthest from the path—and the other between the path and the bivouac, and ran detonating cords back into the forest. At first light someone found the guys I'd butchered. There followed much surprised jabber, with (I felt sure) many men on their feet. So I blew the first mine. Huge kabloom, screams, wild wails, and so forth. Everyone still mobile bugged for the path. Kabloom again; their war was over.

What I usually did after a raid was make my way east or west while it was still dark and reach another path and lie up beside it, then raid along it the next night. For three or four nights, then slink back to my lair. By my third foray, though, the dinks knew they had a problem and were doubling and tripling sentries. I could still snake into some bivouacs, but my score dropped precipitously. Then they brought in dogs.

Trained not to bay or bark. If their handlers had been as smart, curtains for Carlos. I was in deep undergrowth beside one of the paths, leaning back on my rucksack, half dozing in the heat of late morning, when I heard voices. Very close, and then the doggies' panting—an unnerving sound, no question there. I took a CS/CN grenade from my shirtfront and pulled the pin, keeping the lever clamped while I got my bearings. Then I popped up and lobbed the grenade, dropped at once and scuttled away at right angles. A fusillade drowned out the detonation but was aimed behind me and no doubt high as well. Then, when the firing stopped, I heard the poor doggies. No amount of training could keep them quiet with pepper tear gas in their schnozzles. They wouldn't be tracking anything for a while.

I got a few klicks off and holed up until nightfall, then went back to my base tramping in the streambed, packed my gear and went over into Laos. There I worked north, the direction they wouldn't figure, hunting on the way since my rations were dwindling, cutting heart of palm and digging tubers, forest craft I'd learned when I was fourteen. Then I crossed back and set up a new base camp and went down to Uncle Ho's trail and raided some more.

I made three more forays. The last of my Claymores went during the first. By the end of the third I was out of grenades also, except for two of the three gas grenades I'd brought. And my weight was way down, and I'd been bled out by leeches, and I had bad ringworm on my feet and groin. All of which hit home one night as I was getting ready to go out again.

I was lapsing from a life in the present moment. Awareness of being run down argued care for the future, ditto not having mines to cover my flanks, or white phosphorous grenades to ease disengaging. I made no raid that night. I went back over the ridges into Laos, then south toward home, what I knew as home anyway. Like a civilized soldier. The force under my command was unable to inflict optimum levels of damage on the enemy and liable, should it remain in the field, to jeopardize its future capabilities.

As I moved south, however, I grew restless. With every step I felt less like arriving. Think of a man on his way home from a bender, down from his high, husk-empty in flesh and spirit. He knows that what's best for him now is regular eating, regular sleep, not to mention a bath and a checkup and time to flush the booze and dope from his system. But he misses the booze already, misses the dope, misses the whores and his other piggish pleasures, and burns with shame for having wallowed in them, and craves more booze and dope to salve the burning. What's best for him is one thing, his need's another, which is to get high and stay high till further notice. That's what he'd do at once if he had the resources.

Two days' from home I came on a team bound in ahead of me.

I tracked them and caught up with them the next morning. Touchy making contact without getting zapped, but I managed and was richly rewarded. They'd been recalled three days into a mission and were laden with stuff they no longer needed. I filled my rucksack, exchanged my letters and photos for mines and grenades. Rations too, as much as I could carry, all of which I duly signed for. Then I headed back north. Half an hour was all I spent with them.

"Are you okay?" the patrol leader whispered as I was leaving, an E-8 named Jimmy Burns, a friend of Sobers. "You look a little scrawny. Why not come in with us, rest up a while?"

"Cost me four days' marching, two in, two back here." Even that much talk was an effort. I didn't say I longed to commune with my anger, to slough off the few tatters of civilization I'd put back on, threads that weighed on me like leaden shackles. I turned and went off into the forest.

The next time Burns and I met he was tracking me. That was four months later, up where I was raiding. Four months was Burns's figure. I had lost track. I was fully immersed; time no longer mattered. Or that my mines were finished, and my grenades. My tiger suit, too, was finished for all practical purposes. It had rotted to the point where it tore easily, so I left it at my base and used it for sleeping. Otherwise, I wore a breechclout and tree gum, along with boots and hat and web belt, knife, machete, pistol, and canteen. That was my costume when Burns and I met.

I didn't sense Burns behind me. By then I checked my trail as a point of routine, doubling in a wide arc every so often. I had so many precautions and operating procedures, besides having to catch or find my dinners, that I did a lot less raiding than when I started, but that didn't matter either, that was no sweat. There were too many dinks for me to kill all of them. What mattered was having the chance to kill some. Fear didn't dictate my precautions. I owed it to the dinks to go about killing them in the right spirit, to show them respect. Immersed in the present moment one feels no fear. What in other states might be fear is felt as alertness.

Anyway, I checked my trail and found Jimmy Burns on it with what turned out to be a picked team. Ghosted behind them till they rested, then got up close to where they sat in a circle, five men sitting with backs and packs together, eyes and weapons pointing out.

"Jimmy," I whispered, "don't shoot, it's me, Carlos Fuertes." When Burns saw my getup, his eyes popped.

"All you need is a bone in your nose and a blowgun, and maybe a couple shrunken heads on your belt." That's what Vince said. Oh, yes, Vince was with them. He had insisted. All five, in fact, had volunteered. To find my corpse if they could, or some evidence that I'd been captured. Even when they came on the track of a single marcher in GI boots, they hadn't really expected to find me. "A Montagnard with your boots," Vince said, "that's what we figured."

This came two hours later in a safe spot on high ground. I was surprised they were surprised to see me. "Why count me out?" I asked, once we'd said our hellos and I'd learned their mission. I was really glad to see them, and touched they'd come all that way just for me. But why count me out, I was doing fine?

The others looked around at each other, sheepfaced, and passed the buck to Burns, that's what leading means, and Burns hemmed and hawed a little before speaking. "Carlos, your tour was up three weeks ago."

I blinked and shook my head. What one does when returning to consciousness. I was still 99 percent immersed.

"You've been out five months," Burns went on. "Out of touch almost four. It's been that long since you resupplied."

I looked down, all at once aware of what I was wearing, how I must look, my beard, my hair. Feeling the way you feel when you've done something stupid but still don't see exactly what it was. Lost track of time, but hell that could happen to anyone. Overstayed my tour, but it wasn't as if I'd left early. We were in a war, weren't we? I'd been killing dinks, wasn't that the point?

"Fuck's it matter?" Vince said. "He's okay, okay?" He put his hand on my shoulder. "Fuck it, let's go home."

I pushed his hand off and stepped back. "You guys go, I'm fine, I've got it made here. Leave me a few grenades, a couple of Claymores. I've got my best base ever, they'll never find it. I don't do any raids within a day's march of it, and I'm driving them crazy. You guys go, I'm fine."

Burns's look was enough to hush me. "You think this is a game? Well, you may be having fun, boy, but we're not playing. I got reamed for not bringing you in the last time. I'll bring you in dead this time, if that's what you want."

I was fine for two days, the rest of that day and all the next. We camped at my base. I got back into uniform and collected my rucksack and led them over the ridges and south a few miles, but then, on the third day, I began weeping. For no reason, nothing was wrong, I just wept. Not blubbering, not a sound; tears, that was all. For more than an hour. Then, an hour or so later I started again.

Since my weeping was silent, it wasn't a problem. I couldn't walk point, that was all. After four or five days my weeping stopped. Not a tear for the last three days of our march. Still, I didn't ask to walk point and wasn't asked either.

My status with the army was somewhat ambiguous. I'd been taking the war entirely too personally. I heard the phrase "private vendetta." On the other hand, if my zeal were officially censured,

my escapade would be officially noticed, to the grief of my commanders all up the line. I was allowed to re-up for a third tour. Not
where I'd been, though. I went instead to Colonel Ape Thomas's
outfit with a note of introduction from my captain.

I wanted my high back, my time of savagery and fanaticism. I
resented each day I'd missed, each hour I'd been robbed of. I longed
to be back in action and hoped Ape Thomas lived up to his reputation. A refrain ran in my head, the motto of another unit—not an
illustrious unit, but it had a nice motto: "Killing is our business, and
business is good."

It didn't work out. I'd lost my knack of immersion in the
moment. Later on, when I had some perspective, I realized I had
known from the first, there on the ridge with Vince and Jimmy
Burns. If I went with them I'd never return to full savagery. That's
why I was weeping on the way south.

I didn't disgrace myself. I did a good job for Ape Thomas. If not,
Ape wouldn't have asked Geoffrey Knox to find me. I was very
good at war then, even if I no longer enjoyed it, and my nerve had
only just begun to go. I didn't have much fun, but I did a good job.

I sweated blood before each mission. What we did was raid in
force, fifty-man teams and larger hitting targets that supposedly
were off-limits, that the U.S. claimed it never touched. Before each
strike I sweated. And combed my mind for things to be enraged at.
My father being murdered was what I used most, but Sobers being
mashed was useful also. All sorts of things, girls who'd stood me up,
whatever. Or fantasies of dinks raping my mother and sister. Which
sounds trite—which is trite!—but it works. It's amazing what a person can make himself picture when he's struggling to transmute fear
into anger. My own mother, stripped and pinioned, toyed with by
dinks!

Speed was good also. Eighty mils and you'll take on King Kong, except you have to watch out not to waste buddies. One way or another I did my job. I pulled that tour, then went to work for the Agency—no risk to speak of, no real risk at all, and gobs and gobs of killing, if only by proxy.

Riskless killing, very poor for the nerves. Riskless anything is morally debilitating, but riskless killing is especially noxious. Riskless kid-snatching ditto. By the time I showed up on Keegan's island, my three tours were like something done by another person, an elder brother, say, who was dead now.

4   *T*he island was out in the eastern Caribbean, one of those former Brit colonies that now had independence and belonged to the Commonwealth. It was run by crooks, but they spoke the Queen's English. The police wore shorts and kneesocks and called you "Sah!" Hurricanes aside, the climate was friendly. All told, it came in for less scorn than banana republics. Jim Keegan had bought a large tract on the south coast.

And citizenship. He could not have felt snugger. Then U.S. forces invaded Grenada. What, he thought, if they invaded his island? He might find himself back in the southern district of New York reunited with the charges he'd jumped bail to avoid facing.

Keegan didn't know himself if he was guilty. His mind ranged steppes of finance the law scarcely knew of, coming up with schemes no one else could conceive. He'd have never done anything if he'd had to be certain first that it was legal. Besides, you didn't need to be guilty. Being found guilty was enough. The point had great significance to Keegan, whose indictment materialized shortly after a man he'd annoyed very badly was appointed to an important government post. Jumping bail was the maneuver of prudence. Keegan missed not being able to go to the States, however—more, in fact, than he'd imagined he would. When his island no longer seemed perfectly snug, he began to think about a pardon.

Out loud with a Washington lawyer, who told him one couldn't be had for love or money. To begin with, Keegan wasn't lovable. Even with a bad heart or terminal cancer, he'd be wasting his time appealing to sympathy. As for money, the days were gone when cash dumped into a party war chest could make a federal case go away. Only presidents dispense federal pardons, and the one Keegan's enemy worked for had heard of Watergate.

Still, the lawyer went back and asked how bygones could be bygones. It turned out that Washington would accept a substitute: a high-profile swindler who had taken refuge in Central America. He hadn't jumped bail. He was out of the United States when he learned that he was named in a sealed indictment, and whoever it was in Justice who informed him would get indicted too if his name came out. Keegan's problem would go away when Swindler, whose security arrangements were elaborate enough to rate a newsmagazine article, was snatched and repatriated. That's how it happened that Keegan hired Ape Thomas.

Ape had conditions. He needed help from Washington—satellite photo reconnaissance and use of the diplomatic bag to get gear into the country where Swindler was refuged. Washington, of course, got deniability. Ape wouldn't mount the op from U.S. soil. That's why we rehearsed and staged on the island.

Recruiting snatchers went forward in tandem with staffing. Ape would take only men he had tested in combat, and of those who were not overage or still in the service or unshakably committed to peaceful pursuits, one might be in Africa training mercenaries, another in Asia trying to find MIAs, a third climbing a mountain or chasing a woman or bodyguarding a nervous potentate. Experience said he would surely need at least ten, and might conceivably want as many as twenty, with certain specific attainments martial and otherwise. The sooner they were rounded up the better. So feelers went out to obvious choices. Word was left for X at a roadhouse near Phoenix, for Y at a gun club in St. Paul, and Ape called a friend at the Pentagon to learn who might have mustered out since New Year's and who would be retiring next month. My name came up last. Ape was smoothing details out with Geoffry Knox—Knox was security chief of Keegan's main company—when he recalled a trooper in Knox's platoon along with a fact developed during staffing: a good plan would involve infiltrating the target's establishment.

"Get me that kid that Bobby Paley sent us, that did the solo raids north of the Zone! His poppa was president of one of those countries! He's going to be my pathfinder platoon!"

I flew San Diego–San Juan via Miami. In San Juan I was met by a Dr. Gómez. He drove me to an airfield near Fajardo and delivered me to a man who called himself Spud. Spud flew me to Keegan's island in a Twin Cessna. To a strip on Keegan's tract, not to the airport. Marengo's passport didn't leave my pocket till Ape Thomas collected it.

Except for the Cessna leg I flew first class, but I wasn't comfortable. About when the plane leveled off I grew terribly nervous.

Panic of exposure. Your roach when the kitchen light goes on at midnight. I responded with heroic self-denial, refused a drink whenever one was offered, refused to concoct a false bio for the man sitting next to me, how I was Carl Marengo from wherever, engaged in whatever for legitimate gain. No panic-calming booze for you, little monkey. No camouflage or cover either!

What I did was put the seat back and breathe deeply and think how lucky I was not to have phantoms. In a bit, panic eased to simple terror. That Ape Thomas would see I'd lost it and send me packing. That the others would refuse to pull my dead weight. That no one would catch on, that I'd fool everyone, only to fall apart in midoperation. That I'd be killed—no, worse, that I'd be taken, put in prison, beaten, tortured, raped. That I'd be raped and like it, that . . .

I got up and went back through the curtain to the main cabin and back to the tail along the portside aisle, then up the starboard aisle and on through the curtain and around the front of first class back to my seat. Where I sat back and breathed deeply and counted my blessings, until I had to get up and go walking again.

"Giving up smoking?"

"Huh? No. No. Nothing that useful."

Man in the seat on my left peered over smiling as I settled after my third promenade. Big nose, twinkly blue eyes, early forties. Held his head tipped forward, smiling up sheepishly. Like a kid, I thought, that's why I don't take it as prying. He waited. His smile grew sad and even more kidlike: forlorn Kilroy, nose poked over a wall.

"Nothing that worthwhile, ordinary jitters."

The man nodded, cupped his chin in his left hand. West Point ring very plump against small fingers. "Get them myself."

I leaned back. "Still on active duty."

"Uh-uh, retired." Pause. "I take it you served."

75

I nodded.

"Southeast Asia?"

I nodded again.

"Then you'll understand. I got a reputation for telling the truth. God knows how, but a thing like that can ruin you. COs wouldn't trust me, crummy fitness reports. I got passed over for bird, so when my twenty were in I hung it up."

Lousy as I felt I had to laugh. Laughing, I realized I felt better.

The man beside me offered his army pedigree. He had served three tours in Vietnam also. His truthfulness problem dated from the third, when he was on a division commander's staff. He didn't mind lying to journalists or inflating the body count, but when called on to brief LBJ, he had answered a direct question honestly.

When my turn came, I was surprised to hear myself go on. No gush, thank God, as in the cantina in Juarez. Being nervous was one thing, full-bore phantom-fueled dread something else. Still, I went on. Part was that I felt a lot better talking than stewing in my fears or circling the airplane, but mainly it was the man's talent for listening. I'd say something, then stop. The man would wait. Eyes twinkling, interested but not pressing. I'd say something else, and he would wait. The next thing I knew I was telling stories—Tommy Nealy, raiding alone, stuff I'd never told anyone—while he, his face gone sad, peered over like Kilroy.

He was small, maybe five foot five, maybe one-thirty, with small hands, small fingers, everything small but his nose. He had a bounciness, though, that compensated, energy that showed in his eyes' twinkle. All his life the runt, but he needed no favors. I saw him humping the biggest load in the unit, bouncing along while big guys' butts were dragging.

He looked sly, but disarmingly so, like a kid or a leprechaun, as if he simply loved slyness and would give back anything he swindled. His way of tipping his head and looking up at you may have come from always being the shortest man present, or it may have been to make people feel superior, a ploy he didn't care if people saw through—a runt but always serene, never resentful. I saw him at West Point, in the Beast Barracks, letting the hazing and bullshit glide right by him while other guys fumed and blew their stacks.

He only put me off once. Not when he asked if I had combat flashbacks. That was a reasonable question for one vet to ask another. Maybe he asked because he had them himself. I said no and thought to myself, no phantoms either, not since I'd called Sobers. What put me off came later.

"Was it worth it?"

"I don't know what you mean."

"Are you glad you did it?"

"The war?"

"Yeah. Are you glad you went?"

"I don't know, I never thought about it. I had to go, it was the war they were having. So, yes, since I had to go, I guess I'm glad."

"Why did you have to go? Was it patriotism?"

I laughed. "I'm not even American. And it wasn't anticommunism either, though there was a time when I thought it was. Maybe anticommunism was a small bit of it, why I joined the American army and went to Asia instead of becoming a *guerrillero* somewhere. No, when I was little I made a pact with myself. I was going to have adventures, do brave things."

"And you never grew up."

I looked at him. "When people break pacts like that, or forget them, it's because they *give* up, not because they grow up."

77

As I said it, but not before, I knew it was true.

The man beside me looked back at me. At length he nodded slowly, then looked away.

After that he and I went back into ourselves.

Dusk came, the premature dusk of eastbound jet travel, and with it a clear if bogus sense of accomplishment at having made it through the day. This calmed me to where he could thumb through a magazine, but also made the drinks harder to refuse.

But I've earned one!

Shut up!

Soon making it through the day no longer counted. Now I had to make it through the night. I was less jumpy, though, than before my chat with my neighbor. When Miami was announced, he looked over again. He wished me luck. He was off to Latin America, he said. I felt like saying I was headed there also. What I did say was that maybe we'd meet again somewhere.

"You never know," he said. "You never know."

In San Juan I felt better. Headlight beams halo'd in mist, palms beside the highway. I might have been in what had once been my country. I dozed in Spud's cockpit till sunrise—great red beachball popping free of the ocean fifteen points left of the plane's nose. The Cessna landed five minutes later.

A man with a jeep was there to meet me, part of Keegan's security force not Ape Thomas's caper. In another life I might have postured for him. Now, however, I was starting fresh. It felt like my first day at Bragg, my first day at college, my first day with my father's Indian counterpart.

The airstrip was on a bluff above the sea. The highest part had a big house on it, with a railed mirador out at the cliff's edge, and an umbrella'd table suggesting a swimming pool, and a fenced enclosure, maybe a tennis court, and a dish for picking up satellite TV. A road ran up from the strip, but we followed it only partway. A fork led left around the end of the runway, then downhill into trees and back toward the ocean. There, still above the beach but not so high, were a pair of low buildings. My guide let us into one of them. In a storeroom he issued me boots, two sets of fatigues, four olive green T-shirts, two pairs of fatigue pants cut off above the knee, four pairs of socks, and a nylony baseball cap, Day-Glo, yellow-green, with a local brewery's logo above the bill. Then he led me across to the other building and showed me to a room in it.

"Your people are up on the bluff. Uniform is T-shirt, cap, and cutoffs."

"My people" were working out when I joined them—push-ups, sit-ups, leg lifts, squat jumps, back bends. After that we ran: down to the beach, then along it, then back, seven miles. Men in Day-Glo caps churning in wet sand, soft waves spuming at our ankles. After that we listened.

"This isn't exactly new to me."

Ape Thomas sat hunched forward on the grass, chin thrust at our faces.

"I spent half my career going places I wasn't supposed to. North Vietnam, Laos. Other places I still can't mention, or they'll send some guys around to cut my dick off. You know how it is. All of you were with me one time or another. We're going to go into a place and boogie a little. If asked, we were never there, it never happened. The only thing new is now we're getting real money."

Raspy personality, raspy voice. "You'll like Ape Thomas, Carlos," my captain told me. "He hates people too."

"All of you are on the payroll as of this minute. If someone doesn't make the op, he still gets paid part, but nobody goes home till the whole thing's over. This will be exciting enough without leaks."

Curl of lips, white teeth, don't-fuck-with-me grin.

"These things require meticulous research and planning. We will have both. But what really makes them work is improbability. The whackier a thing is, the surer you can pull it off. What we're going to do is about five-sixths of the way up the whackiness scale, so there's nothing to worry about."

Same thick neck, same thick shoulders, same fitness. PT and a seven-mile run, but his breath was easy. Same Brillo cut, same bright little eyes. The tuft that poked from the neck of his T-shirt was white. Otherwise, the same Ape.

No, he was meaner. Passed over for general, pensioned out. Not much chance to boogie lately.

"We're not ready to start rehearsing, the thing's still being planned. For a while we'll do some squad training, get in shape, get to know each other, build esprit de corps. But first we need names for the operation. It's a kosher op, we're not working for the Russians. But no one's going to give us medals for it, no ceremony on the White House lawn. And there's money involved. All in all, discretion is in order. The name of the exercise is Golden Retriever. I'm Top Dog, or just Top."

"Why not God?" said the man sitting beside me.

"*Code* name, dummy!"

I took the name Carlos. No breach of discretion. Only Top Dog knew it wasn't phony. And I hadn't used it for years. I, too, was taking a name for the mission. Whose point, where I was concerned, was redemptive. I was betting that violence and danger might bring me back to life and to myself. I had to take the trial as Carlos Fuertes.

As always, the struggle was internal—will, flabby at the moment, versus self-indulgence. Running, for instance. We ran seven miles each morning, in rucksacks with sand inside after week 1. I was in better shape than half the men there, but for weeks I was the last to finish. I'd let thoughts of quitting slip into my mind, then have to spend precious energy fighting temptation. Worse were fear and self-pity. It's damaging my heart! It isn't fair! Thoughts like that triple your rucksack's weight.

We drilled in fire and maneuver. With AK-47s, a weapon people associate with rebels, of which Central America had its share—*disidentes, bandidos, guerrilleros.* They got blamed for all sorts of shit, Top Dog observed. Maybe they'd get blamed for Golden Retriever. I was scared I'd tense up and not fire—one of two tip-offs that a man's nerves might be bad. The other is firing the thirty-round clip in one bluster, which I did at the start having revved to keep from tensing. Impotence and *ejaculatio prematuris.* With both the cure is relaxing, but that's like not thinking of a white camel.

Worst, oddly enough, was patrolling. I was certain I'd mess up, couldn't keep concentration even at point, drifted away and then returned in panic—Where have I been? There must have been a program that saw me through, a set of ingrained responses the war had fashioned that enabled me to function although I was zombied. But no, oh no! I was not happy patrolling, and point, where I'd been supreme, was now a torment. I dreaded it worse than any rookie.

Firing was better. We fired the Kalashnikov and the Uzi; the Colt, the Baretta, the Browning, the PPK; bull's-eyes and silhouettes and a mock hostage rescue, where three men burst into a room with six dummies in it, good guys and bad guys according to dress or posture, and have to shoot the second not the first. Our coach, the designated sniper, was Shooter. He had joined the army when he was fourteen. At fifteen he was in battle in Korea.

"I walked all the way from Pusan to the Yalu River, and ran about two-thirds of the way back."

Shooter said "Pew-san," as if it smelled bad.

Shooter wore steel-rimmed glasses for reading and was well-read despite his hillbilly accent. Like any expert craftsman he brought his tools with him, a .50-caliber Barrett M-82, his latest acquisition, and a bolt-action Springfield model 1903 with a pistol-grip walnut stock. The Barrett had more reach and a faster rate of fire, but Shooter chose the Springfield for Golden Retriever.

"I won't have to hit anything a thousand yards out, and I like bolt action. Bolt action makes every round a personal message."

The Springfield was handsome to look at and lovely to hold. Some evenings Shooter and a few of us took recreation with it— blew up little balloons to three inches diameter, and tied them off and tacked them to a post, and shot at them offhand at a hundred meters, calling shots of course, for dimes and quarters.

We swam most days and also did rubber-boat training. The leader here called himself Senior, as in "senior chief petty officer present." He had crooked teeth and a soft, down-east baa. He and his buddy Dude were going to pilot the yacht that would take some of us to where Retriever would happen, but I guessed their background before I learned their assignment. They said "deck" for floor or ground and "head" for latrine, so since Top Dog loathed the

Marines, they had to be Navy. Navy SEALs. He had volunteers from the SEAL teams in his Vietnam outfit.

Men who join elite units and sign on for things like Golden Retriever need or crave or are addicted to the intensity life takes on when life's at risk, along with the rush that comes with discharging violence. Some fret when they're not in action, grow ill-tempered. Dude and Senior relaxed. They knew their turn would come and were ready for it. Faith and ripeness kept them sunny.

We climbed ropes, scaled the bluff and rappeled down it. Gato, the lead climber, could go up a sheer face of rock like a spider, and wedge somehow and hammer in a piton, so that others could come up by rope. He spoke French and German besides English and Spanish. The Alps were as good a bet as the Rockies or Andes for where he learned his mountaineering.

Our medic was Doc, of course, also El Doctor, a Latino though what sort I couldn't figure. He was taller than I but not over six feet, very fit but not heavily muscled, too young to have been in Vietnam but not a kid either. Educated air, impeccable English, not just a medic, a bona fide M.D. with a specialty in emergency medicine. Still, he'd boogied with Top Dog and enjoyed it. When excitement rang, he answered.

Other Latinos called themselves Chivo and Lilo, Toro and Hector. Chivo made the quip about Top Dog and God.

We did mortars and explosives on the beach at low tide where the only ones we bothered were the sand crabs. The lead man called himself Rusty—not for his hair, however, which was black. Maybe his real name was Rustin or Rustici. He was about my age and looked familiar. I must have run into him in service—at Bragg or Takhli or someplace in between, on a hop or an R&R beach or a

landing zone, or in one of a thousand NCO clubs or PXs. I didn't
ask him about it, he didn't ask me.

Rusty lacked the panache of the Greek at Long Xuyen but may
actually have been the sounder practitioner. He had a bouquet of
flash-and-bang effects for Top Dog to fake attacks with, and he
taught me great things to do with C-4 and the low-lethality stuff
police SWAT teams use to stun and disorient without causing casualties. I'd have to place and blow charges in Golden Retriever.

At night we drank beer. There was a rec room off the room we
ate in—couches, chairs, a pool table, a TV, a beer cooler. We drank
local stuff, the brand whose logo was on our caps.

At first I stayed out of there. I didn't feel worthy. I was wary, too,
of drink and talk as compulsions. One sip and I might drink a gal-
lon; one phrase and I might not shut my yap till dawn. The first few
nights I went to bed right after dinner. Then what I did was catch
the last of the sunset and the early stars down on the beach.

One night Hector came out to join me—a young Mexican from
Sonora via L.A., very formal in the Mexican fashion. He hadn't said
a word to me that wasn't business. That night, though, he asked me
to have a beer with him and the others.

I didn't answer. I didn't want to lie and say I didn't drink. I didn't
want to tell the truth either. I didn't want to apologize, so I said
nothing.

Hector went on. "They say you're *famoso*. *Que fué solito a Vietnam
del Norte,* and raided there for months and drove them crazy."

My first thought was, Not me, my older brother. Then I felt like
asking who told the story. Instead I said, "So what?"

"*Nada,*" said Hector shrugging. Then: "*Porque no toma una cerveza*
with us tonight?"

"Okay," I told him. *"Está bién."*

After that I still watched the sunsets and the early stars but had a beer in the rec room before sleeping. One beer, which I sipped slowly. As for talk, I spoke when someone addressed me.

I liked being there. Bonding to a pack is addictive. I began to realize how much I'd missed it. It was what had passed in my life for love and friendship. Pleasant, too, to sit with men whose nerve was sound, to hear their confident talk and be accepted. If it hadn't been for my dreams and wanting to get to them, I'd have had a hard time keeping my one-beer limit.

My exploit cut no ice with Toro. Toro liked to call me "Lone Raider," with just enough comradely gruffness to keep from being openly insulting.

"Hey, Lone Raider, how's it going today?"

I would answer with a comradely nod.

Into camp late, but he made it clear he was one of Top Dog's first choices. Off on an assignment when the word went out, what, where, and for whom he wasn't free to mention. Not that anyone asked. We knew better than to ask a prying question. Even so, Toro said he wasn't free to say anything, while hinting about dirty tricks in Nicaragua on behalf of the CIA.

He was a Miami Cuban, was vulgar and vain, uniting the defects of two distinct cultures. He either lifted weights or did Nautilus. No taller than I but weighed well over two hundred, every ounce muscle. He hoped I would get angry and tangle with him.

Part of this hostile stance was rivalry: there might not be spots for everyone in Retriever. Part was plain ill humor. Toro didn't get on with anybody. And part was envy. Sneering at what I had done clearly meant he wished that he had done it. He hadn't learned that having done something means little, that all it really does is raise tough quesions: Can you do it again? Can you do better?

Why I disliked Toro was simple. He reminded me of myself when I did dirty tricks for the CIA.

Toro's specialty was silent killing. Dogs and humans. Or humans and dogs, if you favor that order of precedence. It was something that might be required in Golden Retriever, part of your rent-a-commando's core repertoire. Toro gave a refresher clinic in it.

Which I took with the others and passed with ease. No flashbacks, no phantoms. The island was doing me good, I was much steadier. Besides, once you've learned how and done it, you never forget. Like riding a bicycle.

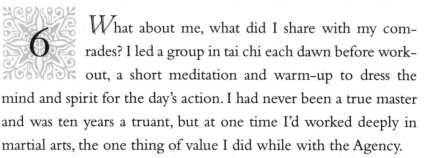 What about me, what did I share with my comrades? I led a group in tai chi each dawn before workout, a short meditation and warm-up to dress the mind and spirit for the day's action. I had never been a true master and was ten years a truant, but at one time I'd worked deeply in martial arts, the one thing of value I did while with the Agency.

One morning before daybreak I was out on the bluff. I'd replayed my dream, then come up there to stand alone and stare at the Atlantic. I found myself moving—rhythmic steps, rhythmic arm and head movements. After about five minutes I sensed someone behind me. I turned around and there were Gato and Hector.

"Will you teach us?" asked Gato.

"Tomorrow."

From then on we met there each morning. In time Senior, Doc, and Shooter joined us.

Top Dog found us there once.

"Carlos, you should have fought krauts with me in the big one. You fought the gooks so long you're turning into one."

Another thing I shared was the art of tracking. To search from three yards out back toward your position, sweeping your head and eyes slowly side to side. To look through vegetation but not at it. To get down at ground level and peer for bent foliage. To avoid looking down at a sign from a standing position, to go to one knee first and then inspect it.

How to tell if a track's author is cautious or careless; lazy, tired, confident, carefree, alert; single or several, leisurely or hurried, able to move at will or convoying prisoners, protecting women and children, carrying wounded, unencumbered or heavily burdened. How to refind a track after you've lost it. How to tell a track's age. How to spot camouflage and deception.

I shared this lore, but not at first. At first I believed I had nothing worth sharing. Then one afternoon . . .

Most afternoons we split in two squads for patrolling. That day Top Dog was to patrol in the scrub past the airstrip but got called to the phone just before he moved out. He left his squad in harness beneath a big fig tree. We double-timed by them on our way to the beach—Senior commanding, Gato, Hector, and Dude, Doc and then me. We followed the beach, then crossed the neck of the headland. There mangrove stretched to the right along the lee shore, mosquito-thick, pasty-mud tangle right down to the water, except where a hump of land a quarter mile on left a meter of beach even at flood tide. That day we followed the coast to where the ground rose, turned inland for a while, then swept round to the left. By the time we regained the coast we'd been out for four hours, conversing by hand signal, resting five minutes each hour, rotating at point every twenty minutes. I'd been jumpy or dazed every step of the way. Now, as we headed home, I was point man again.

Coaching myself: No drifting! Stay in the ball game! Keep alert! Place your feet carefully! Watch out for snags! Then, despite this nagging, my mind wandered. When I returned to myself I was standing stock-still, slouched a little forward, biting my lip. Something was important. I mustn't miss it.

Everyone's felt it. There's something you mustn't miss, an event, an appointment. If you just stand still, it may come to you.

We were near the hump of ground. Off to my right I could see the ocean. Not the ocean itself, the open space over it, letting light in toward us through the tangle. I couldn't hear the ocean, the tide was ebbing, and that coast was sheltered by the headland. What I heard was the hum of mosquitoes, the slosh of Dude's boots, Dude's sigh as he stopped one pace behind. Both my hands were on my rifle. I'd given no signal.

I stood still, but no important thing came to me. I pumped my right fist in the air and started forward. Very slowly, however, completely alert, mind clean of chatter. When I was opposite the strip of beach, I saw what I'd worried about missing. There, and just about nowhere else in the mangrove, the ground was dry enough to leave bootprints. A bootprint was what I saw.

My first thought was of my mother and Camilo, of her reading *Robinson Crusoe* to us, of him squeaking when Crusoe saw Friday's footprint. There were plenty of prints where I was looking, all with their toes pointing toward me, the prints our patrol had made four hours before—or so one might think. Still, the particular print I was looking at stood out as clearly to me as Friday's to Crusoe. The boot that made it was almost brand-new.

My boots weren't new. I'd been tramping in them for a month.

The boots of the men behind me weren't new either. There was only one pair of new boots in use on the island: Toro's. And Toro was with Top Dog that afternoon.

My second look brought more data. Some of the prints had been made by boots with muck on them, others not. There were two sets. The toes of both sets were pointing toward me, but that was irrelevant. On the beach—I knew perfectly well without going out there—there were no prints at all. That cut no ice either.

My fist had gone up at once when I saw the bootprint. It was still up twenty seconds later after I'd gone on one knee to take two looks more. I left it in the air and stood up very slowly. As I did, a breeze brought a faint ammoniac hint of urine.

I slung my rifle and turned around. I held both hands forward toward Dude, then pulled them in toward me. Dude turned and made the same gesture toward Senior. In a minute the six of us were sitting in a circle facing outward—as best we could, anyway, in that muck and tangle. I took out my notebook and wrote, then showed it to Senior.

"Top Dog to our front."

Senior read and passed the notebook to Gato. Then he gave me a grin. He looked like a kid of eleven, his face stained with sweat, muck specks on his cheek, crooked-toothed grin. He had a chance to do something no one had done: counterambush Ape Thomas.

What had happened was this: The call Top Dog took was from Golden Retriever's target country. Preparations there were advancing apace. Things on the island, he judged, ought to liven up. So he brought his patrol around the headland by water, disembarked at the beach, smoothed it of footprints, and walked backward along our earlier line of march to a spot he knew was made-to-order for ambush.

Senior got his notebook out and wrote: "Know where?"

My notebook was going around the circle. I got it from Dude and wrote: "No more than 70 meters. Exactly where I don't know. There's a place that's perfect."

Senior read and nodded forcefully. He wrote in his book, then showed me: "Where the trail goes near the water?"

I nodded.

We had been patrolling the mangrove for weeks. In different teams, of course, different men leading. The first quarter mile had become more or less friendly country. That is, we had come to take the same route in and vary things from the little beach onward. There was a trail therefore—more of one anyway than anywhere else. At the spot Senior and I had in mind, the trail was only a meter or so from the water. Anyone hit there from inland would be unable to disengage to the rear.

Senior grinned, then frowned, then wrote: "Do you think he expects us to think . . . Do you think he figures we'll suspect that spot? That he'll hit somewhere else?"

I thought, then wrote: "No, I think he thinks he's got surprise."

I showed this to Senior, and was going to add that we could take out insurance, but Senior was ahead of me. He flipped to a clean page then drew the position: a verticle line on the right for the coast, a dotted line to the left of it for the trail, and left of the dotted line six Xs for Top Dog. At the bottom of the page he drew a circle: us. Then he drew a line out from the circle to the left, then up the page to a spot left of the Xs. On the facing page he wrote: "Take Dude and Gato and get behind them. Can you be in position in 30 minutes?"

I read and nodded. Senior flipped the page.

"Be prepared," he wrote, "to find them closer to us, this side of the place that's perfect. Don't spook them. I've got a way to let you know when to move in."

I nodded. Senior showed me his watch. I set mine to it.

I poked Dude, then twisted around and motioned to Gato. I stood up and pointed and moved off inland. Very carefully, each movement exact. My hands moved branches aside so they wouldn't snap. My boots touched down toe first and probed for ground gingerly, getting firm resistance before shifting my weight. After sixty steps, say maybe thirty meters, I halted and let Dude and Gato close up on me. I bent, reached down, and got some muck on my fingers, smeared it on my cheeks then on my forehead, smiled at Dude's superior grin—he was brown to begin with. Gato grinned in response and put on his makeup.

Next I fished my compass from a breast pocket, put the needle on N and got my bearing, moved off on a heading parallel to the coast. More carefully than before, ten feet per minute. I found a tree on the right azimuth and worked to it. Then I found another and worked to it, carefully, but in a steady rhythm. Not a shred of bravado, nothing taken for granted, yet it never occurred to me that I might botch things, give my position away or not find Top Dog's.

As it happened, I found them by smell. I couldn't see more than twenty feet through the tangle, but six men who've been exerting themselves in the tropics will give off a pretty potent aroma. A sea breeze gave me wind of them ten trees on, sixty meters past the beach, well before the ideal spot for an ambush. Top Dog had at least given us that much credit, that we'd be super-alert passing that spot.

I held up my hand to Dude, then pointed seaward. Dude smiled and nodded, he smelled them too. He passed the signal on to Gato.

I worked forward a few yards on the same heading so that our skirmish line would overlap Top Dog's. I stopped and faced right, squelching the urge to move in and make visual contact. I knew where Top Dog was just as surely as if I could see him. Senior's orders were clear, and I respected Senior profoundly. "Be prepared to find them closer." Yes siree! I tipped my mind's hat to Senior, and imagined him, off to my right, feeling me do it.

I checked Dude ten yards to my right, standing motionless and facing seaward. I tried to look beyond but couldn't see Gato. I let my arms droop to drain tension from them, moved my head around, spread and clenched my fingers. I took twenty deep breaths and let them out slowly. Then I checked my watch and unslung my rifle, held it at my chest, eight minutes more.

As it happened we waited twelve, maybe fifteen. Mosquito buzz, salt lips. Drag of gear and sticky cling of garments, rivulets of sweat down throat and spine. Stink of fetid muck, of my own body. I was wondering if Top Dog could smell me when I heard a stifled yelp from my right front—close, maybe just a couple meters past Gato. A yelp and Hector's muffled gasp, *"¡La chingada!"*

I raised my hand and poked a finger forward. Dude repeated it for Gato. Dude and I stepped off, Gato too, though I couldn't see him. Stealthily, *ma non troppo*, while Hector gasped. Muffled, scarcely more than normal breathing, but loud enough to carry in the great silence that had suddenly fallen on the mangrove. Surely it was sponging Top Dog's attention. Short staccato gasps, then Senior's stage whisper: "fer-de-lance!"

Later on I put myself in Top Dog's place at that moment and imagined the following data achurn in his processor:

    a. The toxic effects of fer-de-lance venom were bleeding from the bite, the gums, the nose, and the rectum, hemorrhages into the nervous system, and death.

    b. Now that Toro was in camp, Retriever had enough Spanish speakers without Hector.

    c. Doc was in Senior's patrol, so Hector was getting medical attention.

    d. There was pit-viper antiserum in the storeroom.

       1. Should he send someone for it?

       2. Should he get Hector over there?

       3. Both: if Doc says we can move Hector, we send the fastest guy, and get Hector moving, so he and the serum meet at the base of the headland!

    e. Can this be a trick?

These or other data were still churning—Senior's whisper had scarcely faded—when I saw Top Dog's patrol. They lay prone, three yards apart, facing the sea: Lilo, Toro, Top Dog, Shooter, Chivo. Rusty had taken the rubber boat back to the beach, wasn't involved, as he would remind us repeatedly. They had cut the brush at knee level for fields of fire and were ready to go to one knee and open up—pretend to anyway; when we patrolled, our magazines were empty. Top Dog scrambled to his feet. Dude was right behind him.

"Bang-bang, you're dead," said Dude in a normal voice, then added as Top Dog spun around pointing his weapon: "Easy, Top Dog, no one wins them all."

"Whose piss did you smell, Carlos?"

This from Doc. Dinner was over. The cast of Retriever was getting drunk in the rec room. Hooting, howling, wailing. I quit after reaching stage 2. Stage 3 woke me hours later, with Shooter, Senior, and Top Dog outside my window wailing for comrades lost in Southeast Asia, in Korea, in Iran, in Santo Domingo, and in other places I can't mention.

"Whose piss, Carlos?"

"Well, at first I couldn't tell . . ."

"He don't know piss!" broke in Rusty. "That's what I been telling you! Don't know shit either. Thought I was there, and nobody ambushes me!"

"I couldn't tell, they all drink the same brand of beer."

"Drink San Miguel if they was any," said Shooter.

"But when we'd gone fifty meters and still hadn't found them, I knew it was Top Dog's. Only his could smell strong enough to carry that far."

 *A*nother life went on while I was dreaming.

We slept in a low wooden building, a barrack of sorts, with toilets, sinks, and showers at one end, and the rest blocked into rooms off a central hallway—all alike, I was sure, though I saw no one else's: a cot, a chair, a stand, a lamp, a dresser. Glassless screened windows let in the salt breeze. The nights were still but for the sigh of breakers. I lay down in the moral ease of aching muscles, after days that added nothing to my shame, and slept better than I had in years.

But not dreamlessly. On my second morning—my first after sleeping on the island—after our run, we were taking a break on the grass by the airstrip. I lay stretched out, cap pulled down over my face, sun warm on my midsection, feeling my heartbeat slow back toward normal, when suddenly I was thinking of Miami Airport.

What's this about? I wondered. Did I do something wrong or forget something when I changed planes? No, that wasn't it, I'd had a dream! I'd been dreaming when I woke that morning. Now a piece of my dream had popped into consciousness.

Dreaming was news. The dream itself took precedence, however. I held my bit of it gingerly in my mind (just back of my forehead, it seemed, above my closed eyes) and peered at it. The process had me raising my brow, as if to clear mist with it. I was walking through the Miami Airport terminal. Late at night; the place was almost deserted. A few clerks at a few counters, a few weary travelers, a young man sprawled asleep, flight bag for a pillow. Off ahead, a concourse away, a woman was waiting, pacing back and forth, glancing at her watch. My bag brushed my right leg as I strode toward her.

That was it. Except for the honey-sweet triumph that filled me. Never in my life had I felt so favored.

I opened my eyes wide under my cap bill, getting a flood of yellow-green morning brilliance, then scrunched them to retrieve more of the dream, or at least clarify the bit I'd remembered. The woman was waiting for me, that was why I felt favored. But who was she? What did she look like? No way to tell.

No, she was tall. Also very attractive. Another fragment flashed in my memory. I was walking through the terminal with her. Not that same night, the place was full of people, and my mood included pride at being with her, awareness of admiring looks turned her way, and of the qualities she showed to draw them: grace, health, style, energy, spirit. She walked on my right, her arm in mine, looking straight ahead and smiling softly—at something I'd said or just from being with me, a lovely smile that (odd!) I couldn't picture.

I lay there on the grass with a Day-Glo yellow-green cap pulled over my face, holding the dream fragment gingerly. It advised me that the woman's smile was lovely but declined to release an image of it. In the fragment her profile was less than two feet from me, but I couldn't bring it into focus. I tried but got very nervous and stopped at once. Her face was level with mine, though, so she was my height. No, almost. She had heels on—white shoes with sandal straps and two-inch heels. I didn't know how I knew that, but I did.

I lay dazed. The content of the fragments was tame enough, yet they stirred me as much as my birthday hallucinations. Suppose a poor man dreamed of being wealthy. Not fantasized. He has a dream and in it he has money. Not just to feed his kids and clothe his wife, and house them decently and all of that; money to give away, to live in splendor. Recalling a dream like that would stir him, wouldn't it? Well, what if a dead man dreamed that he was living?

The fragments didn't touch the past. I had never walked arm-in-arm with the woman, felt the triumph, been the person she smiled to be beside. Still, the dream was mine and I was in it, alive and living richly also. The shock of it dazed me.

Oh, I came out of my daze when our break ended. The fragments' effect was anything but soporific. I sang through that day's training. For the first time in years I had reason to be on the planet. Pretty soon the day would be over and I would sleep. With luck I'd dream again and live some more!

That was what happened. I set my watch alarm for four A.M., to have time to harvest dreams if I had any. The beep woke me with a dream in progress. The woman and I were in a swank hotel.

Sunlight streamed through tall, gauze-curtained windows onto brocaded chairs and a blue-gray carpet. Through an arch to the left the dining room was filling. She and I weren't staying there, hadn't time for lunch. Could we have a couple Bloody Marys somewhere?

The assistant manager led us to a bar at the back of the lobby and opened it and made us drinks. The woman sat on my left. I stood beside her. We drank our drinks, tasting the freshness of the present moment. We'd made love within the hour. That was part of the moment's flavor. Sunlight on brocade chairs was part of it too. Days and nights together, days and nights apart. We tasted the moment without impatience.

That was it. Except for the wholeness that filled me. It rang in me like a bell, like a bugle at sunset.

I lay still, holding the dream above my closed eyes. Then I let the images play on the back of my forehead. When I was sure I wouldn't lose it, I put on the light and spoke it out to myself so I'd remember it. Then I spent the rest of the hour going back into it.

The assistant manager. He was happy to be with the woman and me, grateful even, as if we were celebrities. Could have said we could have our drinks in the dining room. No, he opened the lobby bar and served us himself. Watched to see if the drinks were to our liking. Beamed when the woman said hers was just right. And was about to say something in conversation, then thought better of it, reluctant to leave yet wary of imposing.

He took the bill I held out and said he'd send the change with a bellman. Was the woman an actress, was she a singer?

The woman. I was sure I'd know her if I saw her face. Back I went into the dream, craning my neck, twisting my head around, trying to see her, only to get nervous and shy off.

Another piece of the dream came to me. It was earlier that same morning. The woman and I were leaving wherever we'd stayed. I couldn't see the room, but I could feel it. I'd been very happy in it, had felt intense joy. I carried my bag and hers out into the hall and turned to let her go by me to the elevator. She smiled at me, a sad smile I knew about but couldn't picture. I smiled back. No, it was more a grin. And said, "Hey, I'll be back," or something like that.

She said, "Yes, you're right, it doesn't matter. An hour together's enough, a hundred years wouldn't be."

The last bit of that dream came to me later, while we were running, slogging along the beach with surf at our ankles, wet sand seizing our boots at every step. Suddenly I felt a familiar prickle that brought back Hong Kong, Taipei, Bangkok, Sydney—all the cities where I'd R&R'd: the queasiness of heading back to danger. That's where I was off to with no time for lunch, back into some sort of war zone.

I dreamed my dreams on location in Miami, undreamlike dreams to have authentic locales. The airport, the hotels around it, the spots on Eighth Street, the Latin city, rear sector of Latin wars, including the thing that I was engaged in—not really a war, more like a resistance movement.

I went to Miami to see the men who ran it, but none of them figured in my dreams. In one the woman and I went out late in the evening to a huge hotel just south of the airport, but the dream didn't follow me upstairs to my meeting. It watched me walk from the woman toward the elevators across a vast refrigerated lobby lit poorly by chandeliers full of dim little bulbs. It left her sitting alone on a bulbous sofa, growing smaller and fainter, fainter and smaller. Then I woke to darkness and the sigh of breakers.

In another she and I were in a restaurant—very late, sitting way in the back, with most tables empty. I'd been to an endless meeting, and then we ate, and now we lingered there like adolescents, though we had a bed to go to a few blocks off. She sat on my right, and as we talked she put her leg over my knee—entirely naturally, taking possession. I felt my heart turn over.

My dreams constituted a special region, the woman's country, planet, universe. Her presence gave the dreams their character even when she didn't figure in them, the way stained-glass windows give a church its atmosphere even if you don't look at them. Her world's center was the hotel we stayed at. As I dreamed the place it was saturated with love, as if love were a perfume someone had doused through it. But not languorous love as perfume suggests. The love I dreamed was appetite for each other, the mutual need to devour and be consumed.

In one I picked the woman up at the airport. We had agreed not to speak till we both were naked. It was her idea and I accepted. What it did was get us violently excited.

Flash of us hurrying along a concourse, I holding her garment bag over my groin.

Flash of me trying to drive while she gropes me wickedly.

Flash of us coupled, still clothed on a still-made-up bed, shoes kicked off, garment bag slung in a corner.

Another dream, no less avid, was the verbal equivalent. Here the room is neat, the bed turned down. She sits, naked, cross-legged, smiling at me. I lie, naked, head pillowed, smiling at her. As she tells me news of her life since our last meeting. Throaty laugh, animated features. Pours herself into me, I take her in thirstily.

In another she bathed me. The dream started with me standing in a bathtub-shower, curtain open, no water running. Then, abruptly, the woman and I were in bed. No picture, no sound at first either, just her warmth and her fragrance, her arm across my hips, her cheek on my chest, like objects strewn on a beach after a gale. Pleasant lethargy and pleasant soreness.

"Carlos, I want to bathe you."

"Umm."

"Can I?"

"Sure. Why not? Not much of a sacrifice."

"Good. Before we leave tomorrow morning."

Then I was back in the bath. Beside me, the woman sank to her left knee, then brought her right beside it to the bath mat, and doing this upgathered her hair and twined it. Her knee bends, her head dips, and her hands rise. Fingertips brush throat, then neck, then shoulders. Gathers her hair on the backs of hands, wrists, forearms; lifts it from where it hangs midway to her waist; twines it in a soft knot and tucks it; the whole movement lovely, deft, and unself-conscious. Next she opens faucets and blends water and (hands respectful, eyes modestly downcast) takes cloth and soap to lave my calves and ankles.

In another dream this handmaiden gave way to a hoyden who smirked impudently and gossiped about male members—"things" or "dongs" as she termed them, their different sizes, shapes, and idiosyncrasies, some nice, some bent, some too thin, some funny-looking—"things" or "dongs" and the men that they were joined to. Gossip offered and taken in good humor, accepted in gratitude even, for how else might I come by the information who had never seen a dong raised in concupiscence, my own aside? What could I know of men, therefore? And if little, what could I know about women?

"What do men want?"

"That's easy, they want to put their things in us."

"And women?"

"The only thing we don't have already: strength."

She spoke mainly well of the men she'd known, usually with

affection, but one man she hated. She spoke of him seldom, but always intensely. Oddly, though, I couldn't remember his name, or anything specific about him. There was a region near the center of her life that she spoke to me frankly about but that I could never recall when a dream was over.

Many of the dreams were erotic. Which was scarcely surprising. No sort of dream is more common to soldiers in training. The odd thing was the content. It often included delights I had never experienced that the woman delighted in providing. How had I learned about them in order to dream them?

This problem had no solution. I put it aside. I accepted the woman as my dreams presented her. She may have been six or seven years younger than I, yet sexually she was more experienced, an attribute that could have put me off, except that in my dreams I was a changed person. One flourish found her spidered above me on palms and tiptoes, her sex mouthing mine softly but no other parts of our bodies touching—a delicate, terrible pleasure, a torment whose torment was that the torment might end, that demanded and received my total surrender.

I looked up at her during it. Her face beamed with pride and power. Her tongue flicked ferally across her teeth.

She knew how to take pleasure as well as give it—and a paradox of love that the dreams taught me is that taking can be a lover's richest gift. So I came to know greedy smiles, lecherous grins, luxuriant feline stretches, pained bitings of her lower lip, and rapacious abandonment to pleasure. And having let pleasure seize her, while recuperating from its throes, a resigned nod, a rueful smile, a mock-outraged "You!"

Then she might look quizzically at me: "You do something that unhooks my spine."

When she lay back and smiled and closed her eyes, there was no one like me on earth, and no one like me before, ever before, and no one like me ever in the future.

The most memorable dream, however, had no sensual element. It was simply a view of her in our room at midday. Sunlight flowed between half-open drapes across a made-up bed on which our bags perched and onto another whose sheets and spread were roiled. She stood between the first bed and the window, across the stream of light from me, the backs of her thighs against a table where earlier I had transcribed some notes from a meeting. She was dressed for travel. We were leaving for the airport in a little. In a moment she would say she loved me, a special vow pronounced haltingly in awareness of the risks that it implied. First, though, she dropped her eyes and smiled downward, past where her hands were clasped lightly below her waist, as at a wonderful secret that modesty forbade her to disclose. That was the dream I most enjoyed recalling.

The person I was in the dreams intrigued me. He was myself but other, a Carlos who'd never existed as an adult. No impatience, no jealousy. Impatience betrays small-spirited worry that you might get edged out of your share. Jealousy shows you doubt you've a share to begin with. I didn't clutch at things or cling to them blindly. The fragility of life caused me no dread.

Because I was loved, because the woman was with me? No, the reverse: she was with me because I was whole and worthy of her. I learned in dreams what I might have learned living. A certain level of health makes you eligible, equips you to give and take love. Then you meet someone in similar condition and make each other healthier and healthier. Everyone around benefits somewhat, which is why people liked to be with the woman and me, bathing in the glow of health we emitted. In that regard we were celebrities.

The struggle I came from and went back to was a key part of my dream persona. My waking self had no clue what it was over. The dream me believed in it, though; that made all the difference. It purged me of pettiness. It gave me the right to love and be loved in return.

Not by being a struggle, by being a thing I believed in, a true cause. I didn't romanticize it, find it a stage for adventure and brave deeds. It was a necessity I might lose my life in. I was conscious of that all the time, in a way I never let myself be in Vietnam. It was as if I'd acquired authentic courage, though having the woman in my life helped a lot. And I helped her. The couple we formed was exceptional.

The structure of my dreams was the same (though their content was different) as the R&R breaks I took in Southeast Asia. What they had up their sleeve, however, so I decided, was to let me be whole a few hours a night. Sex and violence make sense as expressions of feeling. As ends in themselves they're pretty futile, but that was how I approached them in Southeast Asia. I went to bed with women I didn't care for and fought with men I had nothing valid against. At the time it didn't seem a problem. Pointlessness was no bar to performance. I was doing myself grave damage, but for a long while there were no symptoms, except that sex and violence stopped being refreshing. I got disgusted with one and fled to the other, got disgusted again and fled back. Sex and violence, both of which can be cleansing, became two sorts of filth. I used one to wash off the other and just got dirtier.

In my dreams, however, I went from the war to the woman, from the woman to the war, impelled by authentic love and authentic anger. Instead of veering between two sorts of defilement, my life was both balanced and clean.

She found things changed also.

"I love the way you make me nervous, Carlos. On my best behavior. I can be so selfish and ill-tempered—messy, meticulous, passive, violent, moody. But I like the person I am when I'm with you. I admire the courage you have to give me what I really want."

The dreams might have embittered me toward actual life. Returning from them before daybreak might have depressed me. Their effect, however, was exactly the opposite. I didn't mourn to know love only while dreaming, I felt lucky to know it at all. The joy of it was lived emotion. What matter if I lived it while asleep?

Another effect was to make me aware that I was lonely. In my dreams the woman and I were always together, even when she wasn't there. She was in my life, I was in hers. So waking, recalling the dreams, I knew I was lonely. I realized there was no one but me in my life, and I was in no one else's. I was used to being alone, so I hadn't realized, or maybe it was too horrible to dwell on. The dreams, though, woke me up—if one can say that. They made me aware how lonely I was. Not tearfully aware—Poor widdle me! I'd had my choice, I'd closed my life to people. Not just since Allard and Sobers, or since Tommy Nealy. Not just since my mother, since my dad. Twenty years alone, that's what I'd chosen. It didn't make me feel sad, it made me feel stupid. And ashamed: solitude was a risk-avoidance procedure. And amazed in two ways. There I was in my dreams, always with a woman. What an amazing thing for Carlos Fuertes! And, twenty years alone, of my own free will! Of my own dumbness and gutlessness! Amazing!

My dreams showed my life up, no question there, yet rather than make me sad they made me hopeful. In them I was worthy of love, a worthiness that constituted redemption. The dreams I had, the woman who came to me in them, suggested I was aimed in the right direction, as the phantoms had suggested I was lost. They prodded me, made me want to be ready. They were the most important part of my training.

There was one, though, I never got to write down. I was pulled from it by a hand on my shoulder, went from it to Top Dog's growl.

"Chop-chop, Carlos, you're going for a plane ride."

ACTION

I e need a guy inside the other side's setup."

We were in Keegan's limo on the way to the airport, Top Dog and I in back, Dude at the wheel, glass partition zipped between us.

"I don't mean that we'd like it, or that it would be nice. Every doable plan begins with it."

I gazed, still waking up, toward where the headlights stabbed the darkness. Unfamiliar luxe of pliant leather, unfamiliar crimp of collar and tie.

"Our own guy. Turning one of theirs isn't an option."

Whir of radials on asphalt, flare of the trail car's lights in the wing mirror.

"War is a miserable business to begin with. So many unknowns, so few second chances. You better know the people you depend on. You better try to get it right the first time. We won't go for one of theirs, we'll put one of ours in."

"Me, for instance."

"I thought of you the minute the need surfaced. You have the language and background. You have a track record. I mean working alone on enemy ground. In war there are no guarantees or refunds, but a record makes things that much surer."

Eddies of warm wind, salt-pungent sea breath. The sea itself was out of sight.

"Then I found out you're also a devious prick. I don't mean doing stuff for the Agency. They don't cut much ice with me. Can't get out of their own way most of the time. I mean swiping children. I looked into how you do that, I hope you don't mind. If you do, that's tough titty. I don't want my guys getting their balls shot off over loose ends. Leaders are to keep that from happening."

"I don't mind, Colonel."

Top Dog grunted. After a moment he went on. "Devious is good. What we're looking at is a camouflage problem. Our guy's got to be one thing, look like another. Got any thoughts?"

I thought. A bug splatted on the windshield in front of Dude, who worked the washer, then the wiper blades.

"Mainly," I said, "it depends on the situation. Whose confidence you're infiltrating. In general you want to be a flea or a rhino, too small to be a threat or even noticed, or so big they can't believe you're not the real thing. All things being equal, I prefer looking innocuous."

Top Dog grunted assent. "That's what we've been thinking, me and the guy I have setting things up. Less than innocuous, you're not even there. Anyway, that's what this is about, the trip you're taking. Finding the right match, who you should be. Fitting it to you, internalizing the background, the place you're supposed to be from, the landscape, the landmarks. The guy I have, One-One, is ready for you."

Top Dog handed me a U.S. passport and an airline ticket. "You're Eric West, businessman. Your first flight's to Caracas." He handed me a bulky manila envelope. "Open this when you're airborne. It's got orders and another ticket."

I took the stuff and sat back for a moment. Off to the left the sky was graying. Scrub was outlined against it. "Thanks for your confidence, Colonel."

Top Dog looked as if he were going to say something, then thought better of it. He moved forward off the seat into a duck squat and rapped the partition twice with his left fist.

Dude slowed the limo and pulled onto the shoulder. Top Dog was out the door before we stopped. He slapped the roof, and Dude rolled away smartly.

Top Dog's shadow lay stretched on the asphalt in the trail car's lights.

2 *A*erocaribe 690, Depart CCS 1550, Arrive CZN 2105.

I put the ticket back in the manila envelope and put the envelope on the seat to my left. CCS was Caracas. CZN was Chilpanzango, capital of the Republic of Atacalpa.

"Think she'll miss her kids?" asked Tommy Nealy.

No, I heard no phantom, simply remembered. And felt a flush of shame, followed by guilt. Stealing people's kids was a form of self-punishment, but the person I'd damaged most was Ellen Gonders.

Followed by nervousness. Something to do with her was immensely important, but I couldn't face it.

The op, I said to myself, and preparing for it. Nothing else should be on my mind. That was how I pinched off thoughts of Ellen Gonders.

The envelope had maps and a guidebook. I studied them after I'd memorized my orders. I'd been to Atacalpa when I was twenty, playing tennis in the national open. Out of gas in the last set because of the altitude, blew a four-game lead and missed the trophy. I recalled a romantic chasm beside the runway but didn't get to check my recollection. It was after dark when my plane touched down.

Cab to the Camino Real as per instructions. Gringicized the name, overtipped the driver, ditto the doorman but hung onto my bag. Strode across the lobby into the bar, strolled between the tables out onto the side street. A silver Wanderer with mirror glass windows was parked at the curb opposite. As I approached, the driver's window opened.

"*Si, no tenemos guineo.*" I gave the code phrase slowly, wondering for the nth time who the wiseass was who'd picked it.

"*No tenemos guineo hoy,*" replied the driver.

I went around and got in beside him.

Through the city with windows rolled. I spread the street plan out in my mind and zeroed in on the Invictos quarter—Plaza del Unión, Jardines Botánicos, the good hotels, the good shops and restaurants.

"*Carabineros,*" I said, two parts statement one question, pointing at a monument we were approaching.

"*Sí, señor,*" said the driver. Impassive Mayan face, beefy neck and shoulders. Short. He had his seat cranked forward. "*¿Ha estado ya en Chilpanzango?*"

"*Hace quinze años,*" I said, though it was the day's study, not any memory of my first visit, that told me where we were.

Outside a walled house in El Carmen (all the houses were walled) a guard (every house had one) hit a button that made the steel gate trundle aside—pump-action shotgun in hand, revolver on hip, leather windbreaker for the predawn chill. The driver hit a button on the dashboard that made wooden garage doors swing out and slide upward. He parked the Wanderer beside a sedan—the spots for two other cars were empty—and led me through a door into a laundry room, then to a door on the left. He opened it, reached in, and flipped the light switch.

"*Pase, señor.*"

A maid's room. Cot without bedding, straight chair, wardrobe, night table. A manila envelope addressed "Eric West" lay on the springs.

"*Espero afuera,*" said the driver and pulled the door shut.

In the envelope was a plastic wallet with three hundred escudos and an Atacalpan identity card with my picture in the name of one Luis Manuel Blanco Matos. Also instructions. I should undress and leave everything I had brought with me in the room. There were clothes, etc., in the wardrobe. When I'd changed, I should go with the driver. Atacalpan identity was for use in country during the pre-operation stage. I should adhere to it until reembarking. I should consider myself under arms. I should observe operation security. I should report no later than . . . The date specified was nine days later.

I spent less than ten minutes in the house. In the wardrobe I found thin trousers and three faded shirts, cotton socks, work shoes, a cloth warm-up jacket—secondhand, cheap, locally made. Also a plastic bag with toilet articles. Next to the maid's room was a bathroom. I used it, then had a look at the man in the mirror. Who had been eating wisely and sleeping well. Getting lots of fresh air, said his complexion. Avoiding substance abuse, said his steady eye.

"Let's see what you can accomplish," I said to the man. Then I doused the light and went out to where the driver was waiting.

Luis Blanco's business was in La Cañada, a town 350 miles northeast of Chilpanzango. I found myself headed there an hour later. Not in the Wanderer, in a pummeled Lada pickup with bald tires and a whining differential.

"Made in Leningrad by slave labor!" crowed the proud owner, patting the dashboard as if it were a horse's withers. He was called Claudio and was fifty-eight by his own admission. His graying hair and moustache bore it out. He was youthful, though, in gusto.

"The world is my favorite place," he liked declaring. "I'm not leaving it a minute before I have to!"

At first, however, he was dour and sour, silent save for a grunt when I slipped in beside him, stepping across from the Wanderer in the empty parking lot of a shopping center. Then, for a while, he muttered about other motorists—didn't know how to drive, sons of whores, cretins. But when the street became a road and then a highway, as we began to climb toward the cordillera, he broke into a peal of baritone laughter, grinned over at me, and yelped, *"¡Coño, que sabroso!"*

Apropos of what he was doing, shepherding me, helping me prepare for something he knew nothing about except that it would annoy Atacalpa's army. He had been assured in this particular by the man who was planning it, a man he had known for years, who never lied. It was, he said again, full of savor. Some day, months from now, something would happen that would drive the army crazy, and he would know he had helped. Atacalpa would be a perfect country if only the army could be done away with. Strung up by the balls was how he'd do it. That was too much to hope for. One could annoy them, though, and that was *sabroso*.

The army wasn't sweeping the northeast these days. They'd spent the previous year thrashing the region, rubbing out whole Indian villages, murdering select people in the towns, beating and torturing others at random.

"Want to know why? *¡Les gusta!*" He made a plump "goose" of the second word's first syllable. "They like it! The rich want us cowed, the army enjoys hurting people. Outside the capital if possible, where it won't make the foreign businessmen vomit. Strung up, every last one, not a post empty!"

After a long climb the road dipped through a saddle. There was a town at the bottom, a cluster of low buildings left and right.

"We'll sleep a little," said Claudio.

He swung across the oncoming lane onto the apron of a filling station—darkened, no sign of life. Brief crunch of gravel, then we bumped up a dirt street with houses pressed to the edge and pressed to each other. Claudio stopped at the last, got out, waved for me to follow. He rapped on the door and called in a hoarse whisper, *"Doña Estela."*

In a bit a panel in the door opened. An old woman stuck her head out. The room behind her was lit by an oil lamp.

"Agh! It's you! A nerve arriving this late!" She scowled, then beamed at Claudio, then scowled again. "Well? Come in! Or did you just come by to wake me?"

Cement floor, thatch roof on cut-sapling rafters, chairs with leather seats and backs. Claudio and Doña Estela embraced, then stepped apart.

Claudio: *"Doña Estela, el amigo Luis Blanco."*

Carlos: *"A la orden, señora."*

Doña Estela: *"Está en su casa, señor."*

Fringed shawl, calico housecoat, sandals. She sniffed in mock scorn and nodded toward Claudio. "Take care with this one, he's shameless."

And turned, pulling the shawl about her shoulders, shuffled away into the next room, flicked her hand and (without looking back) said, "You know the way," opened a door on her right, went through, and closed it.

The next room was a parlor or dining room, the one after that a gallery where hammocks were slung. It gave on a patio. Beyond that was the kitchen. The toilet was back there too, and a sink to wash at. Claudio showed me to them.

Walking back through the patio, I looked up. We were beyond the high valley Chilpanzango was in, a bowl that held yesterday's smog over till tomorrow. Millions of stars, strewn with immense largesse, tiny, very distant, burning fiercely. I stood and watched them till Claudio called from his hammock.

"On the road in five hours."

I crossed to the gallery and got into a hammock. I was momentarily aware of a curious lightness, light in the sense of unencumbered—no deeds to live up to or shame to live down, no fear or expectation of the future. I was free of all that, I was in action.

I didn't examine, however. I was free of that too. In a moment the thought of lightness was replaced by the thought of what had once been my country. Not the capital, but a countryside composed of cut-sapling rafters, of formal greetings, of woodstoves, of stars.

From where I lay I could see a patch of stars, between the gallery's eaves and the roof of the kitchen. I lay watching them, swaying slightly, then not at all.

In La Cañada, Claudio passed me to Chepi, who was lean and brown and bony, whose arms were taut with veins like telephone cord, who never spoke when he could poke a finger, never poked when he could nod his head. He and I drove the back roads in an antique Peugeot, rode the trails on horses as lean as their owner, hiked footpaths mazed with vines and creepers. Past fields in rice and maize, through pastures with lonely clusters of zebu cattle, to tiny hamlets lost in the bush. Chepi would stop and nod at a feature. I would specify: "The hill?" "The river?" Chepi would nod and force a name through his lips.

At sundown Chepi passed me to Doña Bertilda, who wore the same housecoats and sandals as Doña Estela but was twice as old and three times fatter, who sat all day behind blinds and rusty screening in the oleaginous lowland stifle, rocking, fanning herself, sipping *chicha de tamarindo*, receiving tribute from her numerous cats—a mouse, a bird, a still-struggling cockroach—letting them rub their backs against her shinbones, and (when I arrived) reciting town annals. How Don Fulano cheated Don Sutano. How Don Mengano got his land. How the town burned down one night in the space of an hour, to the heartbreaking moan of boards being chewed to embers, while people stood open-mouthed, enthralled by the spectacle, and red-hot sheets of zinc, which moments before had been the roofs of houses, flew about at great height like magic carpets—a conflagration set (so went the story) by the red-faced Spanish cleric Monseñor Manzaldo, who'd horned every husband of the town aristocracy till he was rebuffed by Doña Inés de Valera and punched in his bulbous jaw by Don Eloy.

Afterward, I transcribed my notes, set down the day's lore in blue copybooks like I'd had in grammar school. Doña Bertilda gave me a new one each evening and collected the one she'd given me the evening before. I would get the books back when my trip was over. They had the raw material of my cover legend and my thoughts on the camouflage problem, how to seem of zero interest, zero threat.

Still later I listened to rain on Chepi's roof, or if the rain had stopped to bullfrogs. Swaying in my hammock, then not at all. I slept deeply and dreamed sweetly, dreams of the same sort I'd dreamed on the island, but now they dissolved and fled when Chepi roused me. I would have liked to keep them but didn't mourn. I was in action now, dreamtime was over. A single dream was enough, a million wouldn't be.

Claudio came to fetch me at week's end. We headed for Chilpanzango and were stopped at the *retén* beyond Cedral.

3

Retén, cognate to retain, a barrier. In this case a poured concrete booth by the side of the road, the right side if you were bound toward Chilpanzango. The door was in back. The front was open from thigh height to the roof, though closable by means of shutters. There was space for three or four men to sit side by side, forearms on a counter, watching. That was it, except for an inscription on both side walls in six-inch letters:

EJERCITO DE ATACALPA
PROTEGEMOS SUS VIDAL

("Army of Atacalpa, We Protect Your Lives.")

In what had been my country a *retén* often came with a counterweighted crossarm painted yellow and black that could be tipped down over the road. At the very least a *retén* had stop signs. Here the citizens were better trained. The cynical lie was enough to make drivers stop and wait for a sign from authority's finger.

This morning the finger was on the left hand of a man who stood outside the booth, right hand on the counter, chatting with the men who sat inside. He was brown-skinned, short and thick. He wore burgandy suede Puma running shoes, dark trousers, a short-sleeved black jersey with the sleeves rolled over thick biceps up onto his shoulders, a tan corduroy cap with little buckles on the sides, and gold-rimmed aviator sunglasses, though the sun was barely clear of the horizon, and the sky was cloudy. When a vehicle stopped beside him, or opposite him in the far lane, he let it sit there. After awhile he turned indolently toward it and studied its occupants, his empty expression expressing contempt and menace. Then, at length, he dismissed the vehicle with his left index finger in a gesture so small the tip moved no more than an inch, but surely of vast relief to those on board. When the vehicle was in the far lane, he brought his hand up to throat level, held it out, and gave the dismissal backhand.

"CIM," said Claudio, pronouncing it "seem." He stopped two cars behind the car that was being let sit at the booth.

"What's that?"

"*Contra-Inteligencia Militar.* Snakes."

"Have we anything to worry about?"

Claudio shrugged. "We're in Atacalpa."

We reached the booth. The man in the cap let us sit. At length he turned to us, looked, and then turned back, said something to the men inside. Still talking, he reached back with his left hand, crooked the index finger, and triggered gently, then brought his arm around in a wide sweep, pointing at the shoulder beyond the booth. He continued to talk while Claudio brought the pickup forward and onto the shoulder, stopped, left the pickup in gear, and turned off the motor.

Claudio and I sat in the pickup, uncomfortably warm without the breeze of driving.

"I was hitchhiking," I said. "You picked me up just this side of La Cañada."

"All right."

I glanced through the back window. "And don't protect me."

"—?"

"We're acquaintances, friends. But even if all I was was a hitch-hiker, if we'd only known each other half an hour, you'd stick up for me because I'm your guest, in your truck. Right?"

"*¡Por supuesto!*" Claudio said. He grinned at me fiercely. "*¡Y por no comer mierda!*"

I grinned back. "You don't eat much shit, do you?"

Claudio held up his thumb and forefinger a millimeter apart: "Not one little piece! Know why?"

I glanced back through the window. "Tell me."

"I might get to like it! So many shiteaters around, I think maybe, if you start, it gets to taste good."

I laughed. "It's worth considering." I glanced through the back window. "But if these people mess with me, don't interfere. All right?"

Claudio looked at me. "If that is what you want."

"It is."

"All right," said Claudio. "*Está bién.*"

"Have you someone you trust around here, like Doña Estela?"

"*¡Claro que sí! En Concepción.*"

"Where's that?"

"Two towns along."

"If they take me, wait for me there till sundown tomorrow. How do I find it?"

"Ask for Doña Josefa, Josefa de Barrios."

"Good." I got my wallet and took out the money. "Hold onto this for me." I left myself forty escudos and handed the rest to Claudio.

"*Está bién.*"

After awhile the man with the cap stopped talking and ambled over. He looked in the window on my side and put his right hand in.

"*Identidad.*"

Claudio and I got out our identity cards. Claudio passed his to me. I passed both through the window. The man in the cap stepped back and examined them. He handed Claudio's back to me. I took it and passed it on.

The man in the cap reached in through the window and tapped my shoulder. He held my ID in his other hand. He pointed his finger at me, crooked it, and triggered. He stepped backward as I opened the door and got out. With the same index finger he pointed toward the bed of the pickup, nodding his head at the same time.

"And my card, *señor*?"

Broad smile. "You remind me of my cousin Nepomuceno, my aunt Eulalia's youngest son. I want to look at your picture a little longer."

"*¿Que pasa?*" Claudio leaned forward, turning his head, looking out through the open door. "*¿Que es lo que quiere?*"

The man in the cap spread his arms and held his hands open. He smiled in false innocence. As he did so, he leaned back, stretching his jersey over the pistol he had in the waistband of his trousers, a thirteen-shot Browning it looked like.

"All I want is a lift to the barrack at Robledo. If that's not too much to ask of you gentlemen." He nodded at me. "This distinguished gentleman can ride in the back."

"Get in, then," said Claudio. "Don't make a dance over it."

"Not so harshly, uncle, you'll scare me."

I sat in the back of the pickup resting my shoulders against the back of the cab. The truckbed transmitted the impacts of bumps and potholes to parts of me sore and chafed from Chepi's saddle, but I felt fine. The slipstream bubbled fresh along my throat. Elder trees bloomed yellow at the roadside, receding like a boat's wake. Beyond, to left and right, lowlands stretched greenly. The hidden sun raised wraiths of vapor from them.

The thing might be to get away right now. Maybe Cap was sincere and just wanted a lift, was only snakish from habit or to stay in practice. Maybe. On the other hand, maybe he didn't like Blanco's ID. Technically, I was in custody already. In about forty-eight hours I had to be at the safe house in Chilpanzango. The book on escape and evasion was to start early. The thing might very well be to get away now, wait till Claudio slowed and go over the side. If I didn't break a leg or twist an ankle, I could make it through the fields into rough country.

As I thought this, a brown sedan came up on the pickup, slowed to its speed, and settled in twenty meters behind it. The driver had been in the booth at Cedral.

I got back into the camouflage I had devised. It wasn't elaborate. For Golden Retriever I would construct a whole person. All I had for now was a mental image that signaled zerohood by expression and posture. I saw myself waiting. In a doorway for a downpour to stop. On a road like this for a bus that never came. On lines for everything. Maybe I had a job—not an uncommon job where Spanish is spoken—running errands for people, standing in line for people who could afford not to. People pushed in front of me. Sometimes people behind me made a fuss. Sometimes they shamed or scared the pusher-in off. I never fussed, however. I just waited.

I pictured myself that way. I sat with my hands dumped casually in my lap looking beyond the brown car at the receding elders.

I gathered myself, and also let go. Think of a swimmer before the start of his heat. The last heat's contestants have clambered out dripping. Those who will swim the next stand about near the starting positions. Some wear terrycloth bathrobes and have towels scarfed at their throats. Some are already stripped to their racing suits. The swimmer we're thinking of doesn't look at the others or really see anything. His eyes are open, but it's as if they were swiveled around staring into his skull. He doesn't smell the chlorine or hear the spectators or feel the moist tiles under his feet. He is drawing himself toward a core inside his chest, and as he does this he twists his head with his chin lifted, dangles his arms, shakes his wrists so that palms and fingers flap loosely. He lets himself drain out onto the tile. He doesn't think of the race, he thinks of nothing. He is going to let the race swim itself through him.

For a moment, though, I had to stifle a grin. I suddenly thought of another reason why Cap might have stopped Claudio's pickup. Maybe he'd been told to. By somebody doing a favor for somebody else, who was doing a favor for One-One, who was working for Top Dog. Maybe getting me busted in Atacalpa was Top Dog's idea of a midterm exam!

3 *T*he barrack was in the center of Robledo facing a park with mango and mamey trees. A high wall surrounded it, painted white, topped with razor wire. The gate was a steel slab that opened sliding. A guard was on duty outside it. The pickup stopped just short of him. The brown sedan stopped behind the pickup.

The man with the cap got out and looked at me. He was holding the plastic bag with my other shirts and toilet articles. The driver of the brown sedan came around the stern of the pickup.

"Any trouble?"

He was bigger than the man with the cap and younger. He wore combat boots and U.S.-issue fatigue pants and a Disney World T-shirt. His expression and stance suggested high blood adrenaline.

"How could there be trouble?" said Cap. "These are gentlemen." He pointed at me and triggered.

"You! Gentleman! Get down!"

I got down from the pickup. *"¿Que pasa, señor?"*

Disney stepped up and shoved my chest with both hands, slammed me against the cab of the pickup.

"You insulted my mother, you son of a whore!"

He put his palm on my ear and banged my cheek against the cab of the pickup.

"Son of a whore!"

The guard came over, unslinging his weapon, a U.S.-model M-2 carbine, World War II vintage, bayonet affixed.

"Any trouble, sir?" he asked Cap.

"For him, I think." He nodded at me.

The guard, who looked seventeen, giggled briefly, then glanced in apprehension from one CIM agent to the other to see if giggling was an approved reaction. It was, and he giggled again.

"*¿Que pasa?*" said Claudio. He stood by the cab with the door open.

"Uncle," said the man with the cap, "you don't want to know. If you think you have to know, we'll take you inside, but what you really want is to be someplace else. Isn't that so?"

I stood leaning against the pickup with my head down, looking at the CIM agent's boots. I heard the pickup's door close and the motor start. As the pickup moved forward, Disney grabbed my shirt and yanked violently.

"Watch out, son of a whore, you'll have an accident."

Cap turned toward the gate. He pointed at it with his left index finger, then flicked finger, hand, and forearm upward. "*La puerta,*" he said to the guard.

The guard jumped and turned, slinging his weapon. The gate had a metal door in it. The guard pulled the bolt back and pushed the door open.

Disney grabbed my shoulders and spun me toward the door, slammed my back with his palms: "*¡Adentro, mierda!*"

I stumbled forward. Cap smiled, held up his finger, and said, "*Un momento,*" as if I were the one rushing things. Where the gate met the wall was an oil drum, painted white, with a phrase stenciled on it:

ESTA PATRIA

ES SUYA

MANTENGUENLA

LIMPIA

("This Homeland Is Yours, Keep It Clean")

Cap held my plastic bag in his right hand. He dipped his left hand in and pulled a shirt out, held it daintily between thumb and fore-finger, flicked it to establish that it concealed nothing, let it drop into the oil drum. He smiled at me and nodded, then pulled out the next item. When the bag was empty, he dropped it in the oil drum.

A slam in my back sent me stumbling toward the door. Cap stepped daintily back and let me pass. As I stepped over the sill and through the door, Disney put a boot on my butt and pushed vio-lently. I rocketed forward, caught my hind shoe on the sill, and went sprawling. Behind me the guard giggled.

Inside the gate was a yard flanked on three sides by stucco build-ings. On the left two soldiers fiddled with an olive-drab six-by-six, one up on the front bumper squinting at the motor, the other in the cab revving. Farther back a group in fatigue pants and olive-green undershirts did calesthenics. As I picked myself up, Disney reached into my collar, seized, and twisted. He dragged me up and along toward the building on the right.

Up the steps and inside the building was a room with a raised desk. The top was at the level of my collarbone. It looked like every military police squad room I'd ever seen. Behind the desk was a ser-geant, heavyset, bronze-skinned, about forty, whose brown uniform shirt was open at the throat showing a triangular patch of olive-green undershirt. Disney thrust me toward the desk and clicked his boot heels.

"¡Mi sargento!"

The sergeant returned the salute with just a hint of condescen-sion, then nodded to Cap, who had come to stand on my left.

"¿Y este?" asked the sergeant, nodding my way.

"This subject," said Cap, "is arrested for having shown disrespect to the Atacalpan Army."

I turned to protest. *"Yo no . . ."*

Disney slammed me forward into the desk. *"¡Quieto!"*

He pulled me back a little and slammed again, repeating the maneuver five or six times, shouting *"¡Quieto!"* each time. I took most of the first impact on my right cheek and the others on my right forearm and shoulder.

"See?" said Cap when Disney was done.

The sergeant nodded gravely. I stood with my head down, rubbing my cheek.

"Keep him for me," said Cap.

"Con gusto," said the sergeant.

The lockup was under the squad room, ten or so meters square, two sides wall, two sides bars. There was a forty-watt bulb in the ceiling outside it, a glassless barred slit near the ceiling inside, a leaky tap in the wall opposite the entrance.

Eight men were inside. Two were Indians, sleeping it off. They lay as if dead, facedown, more or less in the center, naked to the waist and barefoot. Most of the others sat on strips of cardboard. A man tried to sell me one, but the guards had taken my cash along with my belt and shoelaces. Someone had shat in the back corner, but as such places go the smell was mild. I sat down on the floor in the corner between one wall and one row of bars.

After awhile a man swaggered over. He was younger than I and twenty or thirty pounds heavier, with long, straight, dank, black hair. His gut was sleek, his pants stayed up without holding. He lifted one foot to show me a badly worn sneaker.

"No good," he said. "Give me yours."

"Take them," I said.

He bent and reached for my left shoe. I grabbed his hair and dragged his head down. I grabbed his nose with my thumb and forefinger knuckle, grinding it between the two, twisting and squeezing.

He pulled backward, struggling. His shouts came out squeals.

I let go of his nose and grabbed his shirtfront. I let go of his hair, so his head jerked backward. I sworded my hand and thwapped his Adam's apple. Not hard. A hard blow to that spot wasn't required. As I struck, I let go of his shirt.

The man staggered back and sat down. He clasped his throat, gagging. Blood streamed from his nose onto his lips. The other men glanced between him and me.

He put his hands down and crabbed to the far wall. Hurriedly. He stared at me in hate and horror. He nursed his throat and nose, still staring. I stared calmly back till he looked away.

No one approached me after that. Awhile later the man I'd hurt got up and pissed on one of the Indians. Later he sat whispering with two others, shooting glances at me. Planning a night attack, I imagined. Well, if they made it early, they were welcome. Otherwise, I'd hit them. A ruckus would make the guards open the lockup. Then I'd see. By midnight I meant to be loose on my way to the capital. If the CIM agents came back, I had better chances.

I knew the CIM agents. I'd been in the terror business myself. Indeed, during the morning's most troublesome moment, when I was being bounced off the squad room desk, I checked my rage with the reflection that I was getting poetic justice, along with a hint of what my own victims had felt. My camouflage worked at the beginning. I didn't just look meek, I was without anger, even when I was booted onto my face. But when my cheek hit the desk, sudden rage flared in me, and I was grateful for a way to check it. I was grateful, too, for the man with the worn sneakers.

Disney liked hurting people but nonetheless disliked being a bully. He invented slights to his mother to justify cruelty, so he probably longed at some level for balancing pain. Cap had no sign of inner conflicts. On the other hand, he was sotted with power and likely to be overconfident as a result. There were two of them, armed; I would likely be handcuffed. I knew them, they didn't know me. I liked my odds.

I caught myself smiling, then smiled at my smile. There I was, in jail in Atacalpa, more confident than I'd been in years! Well, I still had to get out. I could smile later.

To be businesslike, I took a quick muster. My right cheek was bruised, my left forearm abraded. Neither injury compromised my effectiveness. I'd slept well the night before, I'd had a good break-fast. My body was in prime condition. My nerves were sound, my emotions functioning properly. Appropriate rage stowed where it wouldn't embarrass me, appropriate fear sensed as alertness. My spirits were good, maybe too good for the circumstances. My mind? Time to see.

I arranged my shoulders against the bars and tossed my mind back to when Claudio and I were stopped at the *retén*. I played carefully through all that happened then and thereafter, remem-bering all I could about the CIM agents. That Cap was left-handed, for instance, by how he pointed and how he wore his pistol. That done, I rested a while, then flung my mind forward and played carefully through different takes of the coming evening, visualizing my actions and those of the CIMs. My father had taught me to do that before tennis matches, to watch myself play and beat the boy I'd be facing. The thing was to be ironly honest, so if, in one take or another, a move didn't work, the CIMs made me pay in pain, or with my life. To quote Top Dog, few second chances.

My mind, then, was okay. My will? I'd learn later.

They came after dark, long after dinner. Dinner was rice and lentils spooned into the detainees' paper cups. Which must have been given out with morning coffee. I didn't have one. The Indian with the pots offered to serve me in my cupped hands, but I said I wasn't hungry. Which wasn't true. I could have eaten something and had eaten worse, but I wanted my stomach empty when things started.

The lockup was quiet. Men sat or reclined on their strips of cardboard. The soused Indians had come to and been released. The man I'd hurt had forgotten payback or was waiting until I dozed off. I sat where I'd been all day, legs crossed, back parallel to but not touching the bars, gaze aimed miles away through the wall opposite. My tongue was rolled against the roof of my mouth. My hands lay in my lap, palms up, fingertips touching. Each breath I drew descended past my navel to turn the tai chi ball in my lower abdomen. Each exhalation rose along my spine to the point of my crown and circled past my forehead out through my nostrils. I was nearing *shoong*—total relaxation, yielding, surrender—a stage one isn't in till one's in it completely.

I hadn't been *shoong* for years, had forgotten about it. Which was amazing. How could I? I'd been leading tai chi workouts! How could I forget the spiritual-mental base? Give up and prevail. Fail to surrender fully and be defeated. It came to me after dusk: I ought to be using the time in meditation. Earlier, in the back of Claudio's pickup, I'd slipped in unconsciously. They came before I reached *shoong,* but my Chi awareness was sufficient for me to feel them coming before I or anyone else heard them on the steps.

Both agents were flying. Alcohol, sure, but speed or cocaine also. Cap's eyes shimmered like a woman's in love. Disney sneered and swaggered. He grabbed the guard's club, a three-foot-long mahogany *tolete,* and swept it across the bars, *pong-pong-pong-pong!*

"Who'd like to get fucked with this thing? Line up and bend over!"

The detainees huddled against the wall away from the entrance. I got into my camouflage, hung my head, slumped. The guard twisted a key and swung the door open.

"*¡Tú! ¡Mierda! ¡Aquí!*" Disney stabbed the club at me. "Yes! You! Don't make me go in and get you!"

I slouched out. The guard locked the door behind me. Disney handed the club back to the guard. He took a pair of handcuffs from his belt and opened them with a key from his pocket. I held my hands toward him, wrists together. Cap reached in and took key and cuffs.

"Please," he said to Disney, "allow me." His eyes were glowing. He brushed Disney gently aside and opened the handcuffs, dropping the key into his pocket. He stepped forward and put his left hand under my forearm, pulling gently, separating my wrists. He hooked a cuff over my right wrist. Leaning in, smiling, he placed his hand on my right shoulder. Tenderly. I had a quick thought, Is he going to kiss me?

That wasn't it. He gripped my shoulder, spun me to my left and whipped up on the cuff, wrenching my arm behind my back in a hammerlock. Pain stabbed me. I dropped my head and bent forward. I was just *shoong* enough not to fight the maneuver, just enough toughened by training not to cry out. Cap took my left wrist, drew it up and back, clipped the other cuff to it.

"Pónle la capucha y nos vamos."

Cap lowered my hands, letting me straighten up. Disney took a black hood from the cargo pocket of his fatigue pants, unfolded it and pulled it over my head. Cap let go of my handcuffs. Disney took hold of my elbow and steered me away.

The man I'd hurt was shouting: *"¡Ya verás, hijo de puta! ¡Te van a joder!"*

Stifling in the hood, I couldn't breathe! Untrue, a panic effect, I'd best control it. Fright and despondency—and shame for good measure. I'd made the worst mistake, undervalued the enemy. Cap saw through my camouflage or at least was well trained. My gesture, holding my wrists out meekly . . . He wasn't fooled by it. Cuff a man's hands in front and he's still dangerous.

Rage, half at myself, half at the goons. Who were steering me up the steps, one on each side. Bad temptation to thrash, make trouble for them. Had I ever been cuffed before? Once, in Saigon, when drunk, cuffed by MPs. Had I ever been hooded? Had I ever been steered by the elbows by goons? The jerk whose nose I'd twisted was certainly right. I was going to get screwed. Well, then, get ready.

Hustled through the squad room, down the steps. Jiggity-jog to keep my feet under me. Someone yanked my hands upward, dipping me forward, rammed me forward shouting, *"¡Adentro, mierda!"* Searing blow on my shin, I fell on my face. On the floor of a car, squeezed between front and rear seats. Someone slammed the door on my legs till I pulled them inside.

The car took off at speed, swung one way then the other. Honking, bumping, swaying, accelerating. I was facedown between the seats, weight on my left temple, left cheek, and left collarbone, left hip and thigh. The hump of the driveshaft was under the point of my hipbone. My shins and feet were wedged against the door. My arms were taut behind me, my wrists pinioned.

Panic of helplessness, of suffocation!

No, *incipient* panic, slow your breath.

But the air's stale in this hood, my hands are . . .

It's the air you've got, don't bitch. If your hands can't help, forget them. Slow your breath, you don't need hands for that.

A bump lifted me and dropped me on face and hip point. Sting of pain tensed my arms, they stung in echo, echoed by my wrists as the cuffs bit. Muffled croak.

"How are you, darling?" I could see Cap's eyes glowing. *"¿Estás confortable, amor?* Say something, dearest."

Comfy as shit. And lucky these aren't self-tightening handcuffs. Soon I'm going to be more comfy still.

I hunched forward, levering with my cheek, pushing with my feet against the door. One inch, two inches, till the point of my hip was off the hump of the driveshaft. Next thing was to get *shoong,* relax, surrender. By the time we stopped I'd made some progress, got the tai chi ball started, stopped my mind. We pulled off the road and bumped down a dirt drive. I was loose when Disney dragged me up by the handcuffs, neither angry nor fearful when he snarled, "Out of there, *mierda*!" Steered me a few steps through ankle-high grass—salsa strains, a cantina somewhere nearby. Steered me through a doorway onto cement. Into light, a bit of which seeped through the hood.

"Right there, my sweet," said Cap as Disney stopped me. "Here. We have a necktie for you."

He put something over my head onto my shoulders, then lifted the front and back flaps of the hood. Prickle of rope at my throat. Gentle hands drew the noose against my skin.

"Fit nicely?"

My breath descended past my navel, rose along my spine to the point of my crown.

"*¡Hable cuando te hablan!*" roared Disney.

"No, don't be so harsh, he'll talk, you'll see."

Gentle hands opened my belt buckle. Twitch of arousal, followed at once by terror and outrage as the rational succeeded the conditioned response. Gentle fingers drew my zipper down. Sigh as my trousers sank to my ankles.

"Mmm, what a nice little thing! And neatly trimmed too. We don't see many clipped ones, do we?"

"*Judio de mierda!*" sneered Disney.

Control of breathing gone, but I remained still. Naked to my enemies, where's that quote from? I decided to step out of my trousers, keep my feet free.

"Look what he's doing, we didn't say to do that!"

"That's all right, just saves me the trouble. Now I'll get his little shoes . . . Now his socksies . . . Now his little shirt."

Cap grabbed the neck of my shirt and tore it open, almost toppling me.

"That's it! That's it!"

Cap moved away. I felt his and Disney's eyes on me but had the thought that my nakedness would be unnerving had I been able to see their eyes on me as well. Then something drew the noose upward. It caught under my jawbone, I went up on my toes. Not all the way up, halfway—the noose had stopped rising. It exerted a good, firm tug but didn't cut breathing.

"*Perfecto,*" said Cap.

"Higher," said Disney, "higher."

"No. I'm not a prick. *Soy buena gente.* Don't you agree, Señor Blanco?"

The noose tugged upward twice gently. I closed my eyes. Mustn't be these pricks' accomplice.

"How are we feeling now, a little tired?"

My breath circled past my forehead out through my nostrils. Someone was prowling around me, someone snickered. The sound of my shout surprised me before the pain.

"¡Ayy!" Searing pain in the nuts! Noose biting my throat as I danced to keep my feet under me. Cap hooted wildly. Disney yelled, "Do it again!"

"*¡Ay! ¡Ay! ¡Que bién! ¡Fantástico!*" Cap shouted. "Too bad you couldn't see, you'd have loved it too. But you know, when you're spoken to it's polite to answer. Can we chat now, or shall I shock you again?"

Fucking cattle prod. "What do you want?" The noose had tightened, my words came out croaks.

"Very good! He's speaking to me."

"Do it again!" yelled Disney. "Right in the balls!"

"No. I'm a good person. I'm not a prick. Isn't that so?"

Something poked my chest gently. I said, "What do you want?"

"All right," said Cap. "This morning I got orders to pick you up. Luis Blanco, red Lada, so forth, so on. Detain, convey to Robledo, hold for three days. But they didn't say why. Tell me."

"I'm not sure what you mean." All the way up on my toes to keep from choking.

"Look, are you mocking me? Are you really that stupid? I was told to detain you, but I wasn't told why. I want to know, so I want you to tell me. What have you done? Why was I told to hold you? Don't say you don't know. I'll lose my temper."

"What is your rank? Are you an officer?" Getting a tone of authority into my croaking.

"Son of a whore!"

"Where you're concerned," said Cap, "I'm a general."

"Ven aca, entonces, generalito." Disrespectful familiar address, sarcastic hissed snarl. "Stop trying to be tough, come here and listen."

"Here I am." Cap was right next to me.

Croaked whisper: "Good. I'm an air force lieutenant colonel, Arturo Delmar. Why I am posing as a civilian and why you were ordered to arrest me are military secrets. If you are an officer, I can tell you, but first send the enlisted man away."

 *A*nd he did it?"

"He more or less had to. Curiosity on top of apprehension. He told his bloodthirsty partner to wait outside."

"¡Tremendo! What did you tell him?"

"That my mission was infiltrating a dissident network. Actually, I didn't get that far till later. I began with being assigned to the embassy in Washington. *Agregado aéreo.* After that I got him to take the hood off, and put some slack in the noose around my neck. Then I said I'd been pulled off attaché duty to take part in a countersubversive operation. I'd been outside Atacalpa almost six years, which gave me an edge in working under cover. The main thing, though, was I'd had CIA training. In countries like this the Agency's pretty hot shit."

"I'm aware."

"Then, well, I put it to him directly. 'Had you fooled, didn't I? Never dreamed I was a military officer.' He agreed, and I said I hoped he had no hard feelings. About my tricking him, showing him false ID. Just doing my job the way he was doing his. But, on second thought, weren't his orders clear not to mistreat me? Detain me, okay, lock me up, but not work me over. Not string me up and strip me and electroshock my *huevos*. If they hadn't made that clear, someone would get reamed."

"And if they had, he and his partner would."

"*Correcto*. The shitty part for him was he hadn't mistreated me. Not by his standards. I could still stand, for example. But if he took that line, and I was a prick . . . He was ninety percent convinced I was what I said I was, and if I was a prick . . ."

"You'd do unto him, with interest. They're not so tough when they're on the receiving end."

"Bullying people corrodes your nerve. I know. Anyway, I said I'd tell him the whole story, and tell him where and how to check it out, but meanwhile, could I sit down, could I drink something? Could I put my pants on, did he have a cigarette?"

"He took the cuffs off?"

"Right. I took him out."

"Did you kill him?"

"No. I wouldn't have minded. I'll probably wish I had if I meet him again. But I thought killing him might hurt the operation, that they might go back to you and cause you trouble. As soon as he said he'd had specific orders, I knew for sure you guys had set me up."

One-One laid a forefinger alongside his substantial nose and looked away sheepishly. "Just doing my job."

I couldn't help grinning. "Bastard!"

We were in the walled house in El Carmen, in Chilpanzango. Again it was after dark when I arrived. This time the Mayan, whose name was Nico, led me through the laundry room and kitchen to a room that ran the whole length of the house, high-ceilinged with seigneurial beams and rafters. A single lamp burned dimly at the far end.

There must have been sliding glass doors in the wall on the left, giving on a terrace and swimming pool. The whole wall was probably glass, but blue-gray drapes masked it. The dinner table must have seated sixteen, but there were no heavy, carved chairs to match it and the sideboard. Four metal folding chairs were here and there, and the table was littered with folders, with books and loose papers, with eight-by-ten photographs, with maps. Most of the maps were rolled, but some were spread out, held flat by books placed on their edges. The wall above the sideboard had hooks for pictures, but there were none, just months from a wall calendar stuck on with masking tape. The Mayan led me across the room to an oak door diagonally opposite the swing door from the kitchen, knocked, drew the door open, stepped aside.

"*Pase, señor.*"

The only light was from a TV console opposite the door. Two armchairs were in front of it. A man in the chair on the left waved me into the room without rising or turning. There was a desk to his left, and books on the walls. I stepped in, and the door closed behind me.

"*Tome asiento,*" said the man in the chair. On the screen an attractive woman, very well dressed, came out of a shop and got into a town car. No sound, and the camera jiggled a little. I sat down.

"No popcorn, I'm afraid," said the man beside me, "but we do have beer. Are you still on the wagon?"

Where? San Diego–Miami! Who? Willy Troy!

As soon as it came to me, I was deeply pleased. It was partly the man himself, you couldn't dislike him. Mainly, though, it was a sudden awareness—half rush, half chill—that Top Dog and One-One were considerable devils. They had interviewed me without my knowing. They had manipulated the Atacalpan Army to test me under field conditions. They and Golden Retriever were serious business, and I was part of it.

I breathed deeply. "I'll have a beer if you will, Colonel." Then I let out a sigh of mock disappointment. "I should have known it was you, the parole should have tipped me. What a wiseass choice, 'Yes, we have no bananas!' You're lucky it didn't blow the whole operation."

He had a right to the joke, as things turned out. He and his mother were from a banana republic. His father was American, however, and he was Latino or gringo at his pleasure—authentically, unmistakably one or the other in aspect, accent, gesture, and expression, insight, outlook, worldview, cast of mind. Either way he appeared unremarkable: a small man who said little, of no threat or interest, easily forgotten or lost in a group. He loved this camouflage the way some love a spotlight. When he chose, he could be engaging, but

mainly he listened. And cared about people, so that people felt good
when he listened to them.

His mission name, One-One, came from the war, designated a
raiding team's assistant leader. He'd served with the embassy mil
group in Atacalpa. His contacts in the country's armed forces supposed him still in U.S. government service, and he did nothing to
make them think otherwise. He could ask and get little favors, the
detention of Luis Blanco, for example. His network of local agents
dated from his mil group tour—Claudio, Chepi, Nico the Mayan,
others. They were his own people, though, not part of the network
the U.S. Army knew of and passed along to his successor. Encoun-
tered in barrio cafes and rural cantinas. Sounded out on long drives
through the countryside and late-night beer sessions. Recruited,
tested, trusted, bound to him for life. Why shouldn't they be? He
was bound to them. The whole point of One-One was that he
wasn't professional. Competent, yes, you could believe it, but
amateur in the root sense of the word. He did things for the joy of
them, for love.

Now that I was past the dicey part, however, One-One fell into
something like a professional debriefing mode.

"What about the man outside? I see you've got his shirt on."

"I called him in, *'Ya puede entrar, sargento.'* He was no trouble, I
had the first one's pistol. I'd have kneecapped him on the spot if
he'd turned nasty. I left them cuffed with their hands behind their
backs, and the cuffs interlaced so they'd stay together, each with a
sock in his mouth tied in with a shoelace. And I let the noose down
and looped it around their ankles and hoisted their feet a yard or so
in the air."

"Fun, huh?"

"I was pumped up, if that's what you mean. I felt like kicking the one who bounced me around. Two or three kicks in the teeth. I had put my shoes back on. But hurting helpless people is a form of self-punishment. Besides, it seemed counterproductive. I talked to them all through it. I was infiltrating a seditious cell. I had to make it look like I was a bad guy. I was sorry I had to do it, but not too sorry, not after the shit they'd given me."

One-One nodded. "And none of this attracted any attention?"

"That place is a CIM safe house and torture chamber. Ceiling, floors, and walls all painted black, table covered with stuff for hurting people. If a herd of camels came out of there in broad daylight, nobody would see or hear a thing. I took their brown car to Concepción. The first person I asked knew Josefa de Barrios. I couldn't have missed her house anyway. The Wanderer and Claudio's pickup were parked outside. Apropos, the CIM has its plate number."

"The person it's registered to has been dead for years. We're getting it a new plate and a new paint job."

"Good. Well, I cleaned up and put on my suit and came here with Nico. Soldiers were checking IDs at all the *reténes*, but gringo businessmen must be out of season."

One-One nodded slowly. "You did very well, Carlos."

"What would you have done if I hadn't?"

"Get you out and fly you back to the island and let you hang around there till the op's over. No ripping off epaulets or breaking your sword."

"I mean, who'd have replaced me?"

"That's moot now unless you get hurt in training."

"It was Toro, wasn't it?"

One-One laid his index finger alongside his nose and looked away bashfully.

After a moment he looked back. "Get some sleep. I'm flying out tomorrow, and you've got lots to learn and lots to invent. Here . . ." He got up and went to the desk and came back with the copybooks I'd gotten from Doña Bertilda. "You'll need these for your story. You start work on an infiltration plan tomorrow. This show is about ready to go on the road."

6 *"T*arget is a fifty-one-year-old American . . ."

On screen a color portrait, perhaps from a magazine. Birdish face built around a prominent nose, fleshy lips, weak chin, receding hairline.

". . . who got away with about five hundred million in a real estate swindle."

Click-click, click-click, click-click, more shots of Target. Mounting the granite steps of a public building. Dismounting from a corporate jet. Courtside in tennis rig, poolside in shades. What all have in common is Target's composure, his discreet smirk.

A portable screen has been set up in the rec room. Retrievers sit around in shorts and T-shirts. Senior and Shooter sip beer, ditto Top Dog and Rusty. Doc has his notebook out, Hector has on glasses. A new man sits beside Gato. I'm not in the room, I'm in Atacalpa, but I'll hear about this briefing and other events. One-One stands in back at the projector.

"When it hit the fan he bugged to Atacalpa, where he bought citizenship. He lives with his wife, Diana, in Chilpanzango."

On screen an attractive woman, very well dressed. Comes out of a shop, *click-click,* gets into a town car.

"We're bringing him home."

Pause for effect, *click-click,* air view of a city, misty mountains beyond.

"Like the capitals of many former Spanish colonies, Chilpanzango is in a mountain valley. Here we're looking northeast from southwest, the cockpit view on approach into Macagüita. Left and right, out of the picture, are pretty big peaks.

"The old city and business district, center and right foreground, are at an elevation of twelve hundred meters. To the west, left foreground, is the Invictos quarter—the good hotels, the good shops and restaurants. Behind it is El Carmen, upperclass residential. Further west are the university and the sports complex.

"The rest of the city spreads up onto neighboring hills. West and north these are gentle. To the east and south are steep heights traversed by ravines. Here are some."

Another air view. Four ridges, in echelon, riven by chasms. The crests had streets and dwellings. The flanks were nearly vertical and barren. An archipelago with the water drained.

"The hilltop developments are called '*colonias.*' The second from the top is Linda Vista."

Click-click, a map replaces the air view.

"Here is the southeast quadrant of Chilpanzango, Colonia Linda Vista just about in the center. Contour lines don't appear. Declivity is so steep lines would bunch together. Pink is crest, yellow ravine.

"The hill or ridge Linda Vista is on runs northwest to southeast. The approach from the northwest is fairly gentle. Check the road that runs due east from the business district. We are calling it Road One."

One-One takes a pointer from the table and steps around to the front of the room. He reaches in and traces the road's course.

"Crosses the Rio Tinto, bends southeast; climbs in a long 'S' curve to Colonia Maestro, dips and climbs to Linda Vista. And runs straight through it, climbing all the way, a central thoroughfare with streets branching from it."

One-One traces some streets. They branch at an angle, like fishbones.

"The peak of the ridge is at the extreme southeast. Past it Road One descends in hairpin switchbacks, then heads south and branches. This branch heads south-southeast toward the Pacific. This one, which we're calling Road Two, bends right and heads back toward the center of town, northwest through Colonia San Lucas along a ridge parallel to Linda Vista quite a bit lower."

The new man raises his hand. One-One nods. "Only one road in and out of Linda Vista?"

"Affirmative."

One-One raises his pointer and sights along it. "At the summit is the army commandant's residence. A reinforced infantry platoon is stationed there permanently."

"Reinforced with what?" This from Top Dog.

"Two armored cars, Brit Saladins, wheeled not tracked; seventy-six-millimeter gun and light machine guns."

One-One waits, then continues. "Target lives six hundred meters northwest, on a spur that projects toward the main city. Here."

He taps a place and stares at it for a moment, then walks back to the projector.

"Linda Vista is residential."

On screen a color view of an empty street, high walls on both sides and trees behind them—blue-green cypresses, very tall and plumb-line straight, pinovetas draped with weeping-willowish streamers.

"Walled estates, no parked cars, no pedestrians."

View of a dark wall flamed with bougainvillea. View of a field-stone wall topped with hedge. Snaking through the hedge were strands of barbed wire.

"What's abroad on foot are private guards or soldiers. What's on wheels belongs to residents or guests, or merchants delivering things or police patrolling."

Shooter puts his beer on the floor between his feet. "Sounds like they don't feature getting snuck up on."

"Target does not leave his compound," One-One continues. "Eight or nine months ago he had a bad toothache. The dentist had to take X-rays, couldn't see him at home. It turned out to be a big job, but except for that first visit, the dentist did it all in Linda Vista. Brought his nurse, brought his instruments. Since then he comes to Target's every two months, for control and cleaning. Since then Target hasn't gone out."

Top Dog half turns and raises his hand. "We're going to go in and get him," he says. "We've thought about luring him out but can't figure a way. We've thought about provoking a medical emergency—give him something that makes it look like he's dying, then intercept him on the way to the hospital, but the problem is they might medivac him by chopper, cut down some bushes and bring one onto his property or drive him to the pad at the army commandant's. Going in leaves the initiative with us, and puts him where his defense force feels relaxed. Besides, we've got a whacky way to do it."

One-One clears his throat, but Top Dog has more to say. "And, Mac, don't worry about an extraction from a walled compound with Target's whole defense force blazing away. We have a whacky way to get Target off the ridge too."

"I didn't say a word!" says the man beside Gato.

One-One raps with his pointer, then goes on. "Atacalpa is run by the rich and the military. A nominal government performs administrative and ceremonial functions, but effective power is exercised by a group of men of affairs and general staff officers.

"These men want to keep themselves and their castes in power. They want to preserve the current structure of privilege. They want to increase their personal wealth. They are not squeamish. Atacalpa is run by repression and state terror."

"Preventive counterinsurgency," says Toro.

"If you like euphemisms. They usually signal weakness and obscure reality." One-One took a breath and continued. "Target has the protection of this group and deals directly with at least two of its members."

On screen two portraits of men in their late forties, one in a business suit, the other in uniform.

"Dr. Aristides Yañez handles Target's legal affairs—his asylum in Atacalpa, for example. Colonel Enzo Tovar, who is chief of intelligence, handles Target's security. Target pays for these services, directly and by cutting Yañez, Tovar, and others in on lucrative deals. During his residence in Atacalpa—not quite two years—Target has generated at least twenty million dollars for members of the ruling group. He is useful to them politically also. Like everyone else in Central America they have to take a lot of Washington's shit, but it's not in their interest to look like total flunkies. Harboring a conspicuous fugitive from U.S. justice is a way to demonstrate some independence.

"In short, Target is a valuable asset to the people in charge in Atacalpa. Earnest resistance to Golden Retriever must be expected the moment its existence and purpose are known."

Retrievers draw around the pool table. On it is a model showing broken terrain, two yards square on a sheet of plywood. One-One reaches over it with his pointer.

"This is a sector southeast of downtown Chilpanzango. It was made with data from satellite photos. The important features are, one, Target's estate on the southeastern tip of Linda Vista; two, the junction of Roads One and Two; three, this bit of Colonia San Lucas; and four, the ravine between it and Linda Vista. We're calling that particular ravine the Barranca."

"What's the scale?" asks Rusty.

"One to four hundred. One inch is ten meters, eleven yards."

One-One glances around the group, then looks back to the model. "I'm on its east side. Here's the spur with Target's compound. This street on the northeast we're calling 'T' Street. Here, on the northwest, is another estate. From southwest around to south-southeast, the Barranca.

"The wall is four meters high, one-half meter thick, with coiled razor wire on top of it. We have to assume sensing devices also. At night all inside sectors are lit by halogen lamps placed so as to silhouette intruders without highlighting defenders' positions.

"The gate is sliding plate steel. The guard tower, here, just southeast of it, provides surveillance of 'T' Street from the bend north of the limit of Target's property to where the street dead ends at the Barranca. Immediately inside the gate, in a concrete well, is a plate steel baffle that can be raised when the gate is opened so that a vehicle can't drive straight through. All vehicles are routinely stopped here and checked for bombs.

"This structure, here, to the right of the gate as one enters, was once a four-car garage and machine shop. After Target acquired the estate it was enlarged and converted into a barrack for his defense force. I'll have information about that force in the near future. Target's vehicles are kept next to the barracks, here, in a lean-to with a tin roof—a town car and a four-wheel-drive Trekker wagon. The structure beside it is a tool shed.

"West of the barrack, past some eucalyptus trees, is a tennis court, here, against the wall between Target and his northwest neighbor. The house is to the left of the gate as one enters. I'll have more to say about it and the grounds in awhile, but all approaches to the house are broad enough to provide defensive surveillance and fields of fire."

One-One takes the point end of the pointer in his left hand, lifts his arms, and stretches them above his head, then brings his arms down till the pointer rests against his thighs. "Okay, one last bit before we go through it in detail. The Chilpanzango region is subject to very heavy rainfall during the months of April through November. Where drainage isn't good, there is serious flooding. When Linda Vista was developed, culverts were put in running from Road One to the Barranca."

He reaches out with his pointer to Road One, then draws a line straight south, across Target's property, to the Barranca. "One-meter piping conducts these culverts under people's properties at a depth of maybe a meter. At each street they're open to take the runoff. A few meters southeast of Target's gate, T Street bridges one that we're calling *the* Culvert. It runs beneath the southeast corner of Target's compound and emerges at the lip of the Barranca just outside his wall, here."

"You think he deserves it?"

"Who deserves what?"

"Target. Getting kidnapped."

"He's a crook, he stole half a billion dollars!"

"Everyone deserves everything."

"What does that mean? *Che será, será?*"

"It means we don't have to worry whether he deserves it."

"Maybe what Hector's asking is, have we the right?"

"Being able to do it gives us the right."

"We don't know yet if we can do it."

"We can do it, don't you worry about that."

"Hey, hey, why complicate something simple? All it is, he's further down on the food chain. He's our Target. What we have to do is not be someone else's."

A hill above the beach, fleecy sky, bright sunlight. A six-by-six truck with Hector a few feet in front of it, Doc by the winch on the bumper, other Retrievers behind to the left. All watch a helicopter thudding toward them, forty feet over the hill, thirty yards from it, tilted seaward into the onshore breeze. A length of cable snakes behind it anchored to the bluff two hundred yards off.

The machine passes above, then holds in the air. A loose cable end sways above Hector and settles toward him. Hector reaches for it with gloved hands.

The man flying is Mac—as in Mac the FAC, Forward Air Controller. He flew two tours over the Mekong Delta, calling in artillery and air strikes.

Poking along in a Cessna 0-1 Bird Dog, seventy knots, fifteen hundred feet. Sitting on his flak jacket because Charles loved putting a round up a FAC's bung.

What else was on a FAC's menu? The fun of showing the jets where to dump napalm to save a unit from being overrun, the unfun of seeing civilians murdered. As by destroyers or frigates out in the gulf, plowing a zigzag course, pitching and rolling, their gunnery no more refined than spitting at the ceiling. What did Mac in, though, was a job for the ARVN. He was ordered to help their artillery hit a village where three VC had been reported. He flew over it and all he saw were villagers. He radioed back. Did the province chief really want to hit the village? The ARVN commander said yes, and send the coordinates, but Mac had done that too many times already. He gave the coordinates of the province chief's headquarters and wished them good shooting. They didn't actually fire, but Mac got canned.

He was rated for rotary as well as fixed wing. Top Dog offered him a job with the raiding unit. He probably chauffeured me on at least one mission, but we didn't meet face-to-face till Golden Retriever.

The hanger by the airstrip. Top Dog, One-One, and Shooter sit on folding chairs. Sunlight streams through the open door almost to their feet.

"You want him you've got him," says One-One.

Top Dog nods. "The guy is hyperaggressive, some people don't care for him. But in war, if you err, err on the side of violence. Some people don't care for me either, and I sleep okay."

"What I don't care for," says One-One, "is he's close to the Agency."

"Are they going to be a problem? My number one condition for doing this thing was that the word would go out that we are kosher, not to get in our way or tip off the bad guys."

"The word is out, Top. The diplomats and the mil group will respect it. The Agency, I'm not so sure. They don't always respect the chain of command, particularly in Latin America. They may have their own agenda for Target. Then there are rogue agents. More of them are cropping up, and Target has enough money to give one ideas."

"You in touch with the station chief? Good. Then give him a message. If any of his people fuck with this op, I will personally break his neck with my bare hands."

The island beach by starlight and a half moon. A length of steel tubing a yard or so in diameter, perhaps eighty feet of it, lies well above the waterline on the dry sand. Retrievers stand looking at it.

"Okay," says Top Dog, "first group take your places." He clasps a stopwatch that hangs from his neck by a lanyard.

Gato, Doc, and Toro trot to the far end of the tubing. The thing over Doc's arm is a body bag. Toro carries a coil of half-inch line. He ties one end of it to a loop at the head of the bag. Doc takes a cord with two clips on it from his pocket, clips one end to a loop at the foot of the bag and the other to a belt loop at his back. Mac, meanwhile, has walked away from the group and stands ten or so yards from the near end of the tubing.

"Ready," calls Doc.

"Okay," shouts Top Dog, thumbing the watch. "Go!"

Gato dives into the tube. Doc follows immediately, pulling the body bag behind him. Toro pays out line.

Scrub inland from the airstrip. Retrievers, in fatigues, stand opposite Top Dog.

"Now you get to use your imaginations. You know I like realism. Full-scale mock-ups so you'll know where things are, so you'll feel more at home on the enemy's ground than he does. But the problem is there's two satellites up there, one commie, one ours, and whatever we build will show up on the pictures they're taking. The photo-interp nerds will report new construction. The cameras will zero in tighter and tighter. Next thing you know my sixty-three-year-old ass will be spread across a movie screen in Moscow. Or in Langley, it doesn't matter. People will know something funny is going on here. People will nose around. Our op will be blown. If a mock-up were necessary, I'd build one regardless, set it up at night, take it down before morning. But we don't really need one, we'll use our imaginations."

He steps back and spreads his arms to take in the surroundings. "This is Colonia Linda Vista."

"Zis is ze staircase of ze palace," says Gato.

Top Dog squints. "What was that?"

"Erich von Stroheim in *Sunset Boulevard.*"

Top Dog bares teeth at Gato. "Give me fifty, wiseass!"

Gato drops to the ground and does pushups.

Top Dog looks down at him, shakes his head, then continues. "We're in a walled compound, A for Assault Team's staging area. We've arrived by vehicle after dark, from a safe house over there"—he raises his left arm and points up and away from his left shoulder—"in Colonia San Lucas. The army commandant's compound is six hundred meters southeast. Target's place is eight hundred and twenty meters due south. We're not going to leave it all to imagination. We're going to mark the compounds with yellow tape. Perimeters for the present. We'll add features of Target's compound as data comes in. We'll mark the roads too, everything to scale.

"Marking will take us today and part of tomorrow, but we'll

learn a lot doing it. Then we'll practice A Team's assignments. Everyone will practice every assignment. When everyone's perfect, we'll start rehearsing at night."

Gato gets to his feet. "Fifty more, fuckhead!"

Gato drops to the ground and exercises.

"Don't bother getting up at fifty, clown. Just keep humping till I tell you different." Top Dog looks up at the others and grins. "Fuck doesn't even know what movie this is. I'm not some kraut in some soap opera. I'm Brian Donlevy in *Beau Geste*."

"Thirty effectives of the Atacalpan Army . . ."

One-One and the Retrievers stand around the model. Rain drums on the roof above them.

". . . are stationed at Target's as his defense force—a lieutenant, two sergeants, three corporals, and twenty-four privates. They are organized in three sections that pull four-hour shifts. Exact shift changes we'll have later.

"Four men are deployed outside as sentries around the clock: three on T Street and one on the southeast perimeter, here"—One-One sweeps with his pointer—"patrolling the wall along the lip of the Barranca. They are armed with M-16s and equipped with hand radios.

"After dark the grounds are also patrolled from within. A man is always on duty in the tower. An M-60 machine gun is mounted up there. A guardroom below the tower contains a telephone and the base station of the radio net. A corporal of the guard is always in there. The lieutenant or one of the sergeants is usually nearby."

One-One turns away and sweeps with his pointer, shepherding the others back toward seats and screen. In a minute he has resumed the briefing.

"Target is usually up and about by oh eight hundred, has coffee and fruit on the sundeck off his bedroom, and reads the papers. He has the *New York Times* and *Wall Street Journal* flown in daily. They arrive at his place around twenty-one hundred, and he reads them the next morning, along with articles people send him by fax.

"Target's main activity is managing business interests. Andrés Zamora, a member of Yañez's law firm . . ."

A Latin in his late thirties succeeds Target on screen.

". . . comes every weekday morning at ten hundred with a secretary. They and Target use a two-room office suite on the ground floor. Other local business associates come by irregularly.

"Target is usually in his office until thirteen hundred. Sometimes business associates come by for lunch. Sometimes Target lunches alone, sometimes with his wife. He is usually back in his office by fourteen thirty and stays there until eighteen hundred, though Zamora and the secretary rarely stay that late.

"Target swims . . ."

His smirk returns to the screen.

". . . half a mile every evening in his heated pool. Usually, he and his wife eat dinner alone. On rare occasions they have people over. After dinner they read or watch television.

"On clear weekend mornings men come to play tennis. All are English-speaking, three are Americans. There is brunch afterward, and after brunch drinks. Sometimes the group, or part of it, hangs on till evening. On Sundays others join them for NFL football. The football fans are the same mix as the tennis players: upper-class Atacalpans and American ex-pats. Officials of big U.S. firms have evidently been told not to socialize with Target. Americans in business for themselves seem to value access to him, perhaps as a way of hobnobbing with important Atacalpans, or because he's well-known and access to him is exclusive. The tennis/TV crowd numbers fifteen or twenty.

"A member of military counterintelligence . . ."

On screen a thug in a cheap suit.

". . . is assigned to Target as a bodyguard. Since Target never goes out, the bodyguard's duties comprise protecting Mrs. Target. He normally sleeps away from Target's, driving to and from it each morning and night. He carries a .380 Walther PPK double-action pistol in a shoulder holster under his left arm. When he accompanies Mrs. Target outside the compound, he takes an Uzi with him.

"Mrs. Target, Diana, née Ramos Brin . . ."

On screen she comes out of a shop, gets into a town car, then stares out of a newspaper shot with paintings behind her and people all around.

". . . is a native of Venezuela who attended college in the U.S. and was living in New York when she met Target there five years ago. She is twenty-nine. She and Target have been married four years and have no children. She appears to be loyal to him, no evidence of adultery or other compromising behavior.

"Running her home occupies her almost full-time."

Click-click, click-click—views of Target's house. Facing T Street, a porte cochere and a formal entrance. Facing Chilpanzango, terraces in three levels and a pool.

"Mrs. Target goes shopping most mornings for food or household items. A favorite stop is a plant nursery called El Caballero Verde. In the afternoons she sometimes shops for clothing. She has several female friends of various nationalities, all married, whom she visits in the afternoons and is visited by. She sometimes goes out in the early evenings to movies or art exhibits. Whenever she leaves the compound she is driven by the chauffeur and accompanied by the bodyguard.

"Besides the chauffeur, Target's household includes a cook, a butler, and two housemaids." Portraits from ID-card mug shots flash on the screen. "All have been vetted and cleared by Tovar's people, but that means merely that they have no criminal records, nor any obvious sympathies for the leftist groups with whom the state is perennially engaged in warfare of varying intensity.

"Oh, yes, Target has a new gardener."

A mug shot of me, abundantly moustached, appears on screen. Silence for a moment, intake of breath, then shouts: "Holy shit!" "¡Carajo!" "Way to go, Carlos!"

"I wouldn't buy a used lawn mower from him," says Shooter.

7 There were three slots in Target's household an infiltrator might fill: butler, chauffeur, or gardener. All three were fair platforms for snooping, but if you went on the basis of who looked least threatening, gardener nosed in front. None of your butler's social sophistication, none of your chauffeur's friendship with machines. Sweat on the brow, topsoil under the fingernails—a hick, a boob, a dolt, a dunce, a dummy. Besides, unquestioned, unlimited access to Target's grounds turned out to be very useful in the scheme One-One had come up with for breaching the compound. And consulate records said that Mrs. Target's gardener was on the waiting list for an immigrant visa to the United States.

One-One interviewed the fellow—without his knowing, One-One's favorite game—and found out he was desperate for a way out of Atacalpa and bright enough to help in his own cause. There followed a second interview, this one at the consulate, where a miraculously gringified One-One popped the question: Would he, in exchange for a green card, help One-One pick his successor at Target's? *"¡Ay, cielo santo, que sí!"* was the response.

Next stop was El Caballero Verde. It was owner-managed and successful, but the owner-manager had a gambling problem. One-One bought up his debts and then approached him through an intermediary who all but had "CIM" tattooed on his forehead. For the modest inconvenience of hiring two temporary employees, a delivery man with his own pickup truck and a helper, the fellow could forget his debts forever. Claudio and I went to work there the next day.

My name was Juan Reyes. The name, an identity card, and a sad story had come from a classmate of One-One's now with Immigration, One-One having advised him he was in the market for dead Atacalpans born in the mid 1940s to '50s. The first Juan Reyes had died of suffocation with forty-seven other illegal immigrants locked in a truck abandoned by its driver on a dirt road west of Bisbee, Arizona. One-One liked him because he had done Atacalpan military service and been honorably discharged, a guarantee he'd be cleared to work for Target. He came from a bush pueblo near La Cañada, which was why I had studied with Doña Bertilda and Chepi.

The character model for Reyes's second coming was Doroteo Jiménez, who worked for my father and godfather at their law office. Messenger was his spot on the payroll, but he did everything. He drove my father to work, then took the car around town dropping off and picking up documents, but he always arrived at our house a half hour early and hung around after bringing my father back. If a gate needed paint, if a hinge needed oiling, if a window screen was torn, if a phone cord was twisted, if the chain was off Camilo's bike or the grip coming undone on my tennis racket, Doroteo noticed and saw to it. Naturally and unbidden, as if nothing could please him more. No, not as if: doing things for others truly pleased him.

Doroteo soon passed into my mother's service and became her indispensable factotum. This was why I drew on him. Reyes's way into Target's led through Mrs. Target. Most men don't like to serve women and make sure the women don't like it either. Doroteo liked everything life put on his plate. I gave Reyes this virtue, along with the cheerfulness it conferred.

Besides good cheer, Reyes had beautiful manners. Not the exquisite manners of Latin gentry, the grave, unobtrusive manners of Latin poor: care taken not to offend the pride of others by people whose pride is their only possession. Many people had modeled this trait for me, most recently Hector.

Reyes, besides, was a very quiet person. He watched what went on around him with interest and might ask a question, but such questions were rare and always asked very softly, as if he feared he was making an imposition. Otherwise, he spoke when someone spoke to him. He didn't chatter or make unsolicited comments. Because he was often with Claudio, who talked all the time, Reyes seemed even quieter than he was. Many people think quiet people are mentally slow, and in fact no one thought much of Reyes's intellect. No one thought much of Reyes himself. No one minded him, certainly. Juan Reyes? Wouldn't hurt a fly.

Well, then, I went to live in Barriada Costanza, a casbah of cinder-block shacks on a treeless hillside at the western edge of

Chilpanzango. I went to work at El Caballero Verde. I settled into Reyes's skin. I waited. Meanwhile I found myself a bit uneasy. Not over my nerve. Thanks to Top Dog and One-One and Cap and Disney I had my nerve back. But being about to infiltrate a woman's confidence brought to mind a shell hole full of slimy water with a pair of children's heads floating in it. That is, it brought to mind Ellen Gonders. I hadn't thought of her since the plane to Caracas, yet something about her was still immensely important, and I still couldn't face it. Luckily my uneasiness faded when Mrs. Target showed.

See her get down from the Trekker in jeans and T-shirt, taller and less pampered in life than in One-One's video. Her gardener got down with her. Her chauffeur and bodyguard sat tight. The owner-manager rushed up fawning with Claudio behind him. There followed a slow pavane through the nursery, the owner-manager leading, pointing out bargains, she turning from time to time to consult her gardener, the gardener and Claudio attending gravely. At a certain point she nodded, the gardener said, *"Buena idea, señora,"* and Claudio called, *"¡Juancito, ven aca!"* Up trotted Juan Reyes, tugging a figurative forelock. He lugged the bush in question to Claudio's pickup, then jogged back in search of other errands and so became part of the entourage.

The Trekker climbs the switchbacks below Linda Vista. A blue Lada pickup climbs behind it. In front a tinny radio blares a Mexican ranch song. Claudio wails happy despair along with it. In back are Juan Reyes and a bush.

Diana and her gardener walk past the graveled car park toward the porte cochere. Claudio follows, admiring her mobile, shrink-wrapped rump. Juan Reyes follows Claudio lugging the bush.

Reyes finds himself in Mrs. Target's garden, at the newly acquired bush's destined site. "Can you plant it?" the gardener asks him, then looks to Diana. "He's a nice fellow, let's see if he can learn. I'll show him where to get a spade and trowel."

Three days later the gardener was laid up with a back ailment. On his suggestion Juan Reyes came to Linda Vista to fill in. I rose before dawn to be up there at 0700. I had bread and coffee in the kitchen. I received directions from the gardener, laid up in his room. I mowed the lawn beside the lower terrace and trimmed with a machete where it met the flagstones. I was clipping hedges when *La Señora* appeared.

"*¿Juan?*"

"*Mand' Usted, señora.*" Tipping the shears up to deliver the phrase with a figurative sombrero clasped at my sternum. Smiling.

"*Hoy pondremos califas en la teraza.*"

"*Bien, señora.*"

She laughed richly. "How do you know if it's good? You don't know what they look like?"

Shy smile. I shook my head. *"Es cierto, señora."*

"Come, I'll show you."

The shrub in question had thickly veined dark leaves and drooping red blossoms. *La Señora* had four, all very young. She thought two would go well on the upper terrace. With her regular gardener she would have asked if her idea was a good one. Here she simply proposed.

"*¡Son hermosas!*" said Juan Reyes when he saw them. Minutes later I was digging one up under her direction.

And thinking about her, a woman who was attracted to money.

Or to nerve and imagination. Target had to have them to steal as much as he did. So say she liked all three, she liked a winner, what evolution had programmed her to go after. Having captured a winner, she was fulfilled. No puffy cheeks, hence no tears or insomnia. No sallow skin, no circles under the eyes. Good humor, health, and just a touch of makeup, a kerchief at her neck, a straw sombrero, and lots of light brown hair across her shoulders.

"¿Juan?"

"Mand' Usted, señora."

"Where are you from?"

"The north, señora. A village near La Cañada."

"Have you children?"

Scraped with my trowel. "No, señora. Not even a wife."

No sign of claustrophobia. She wasn't the prisoner. Could go where she liked and seemed to like her home. Not bored or restless, healthy, nothing to prove. The healthy ones hunt for business not for pleasure. First to get proficient with their weapons, then to capture a winner. Bagged a prime specimen, therefore was fulfilled. Bored in a few years if she had no kids, but not now. Which didn't mean she couldn't take mild amusement in broadening a polite peasant's horizons.

"¿Señora?"

"Sí, Juan."

"These plants, are they from here?"

"No. The nursery brought them for me from the Caribbean. A book I have says they're originally from the East Indies."

"¿Las Indias?"

"Sí. The Spanish or English must have brought them to America."

"The book, does it cost a lot?"

Soft smile. "I'm afraid so. It's in English anyway."

I looked down and troweled. "And they're for the terrace?"

"Yes. Till after Christmas. Then we'll bring them back and put something else there."

I smiled up at her shyly. "They'll look very nice on the terrace, I think."

She smiled back. *"Gracias, Juan."*

The shrubs, in pots, went up to the terrace by wheelbarrow. I was setting the second by the steps to the lower levels, when Target came out of the house.

"Darling, what a lovely surprise!"

"You like them!"

He had seen his share of Cary Grant pictures. Peck pictures too, maybe a little James Mason. Blazer, tan twill trousers, blue shirt, rep tie. Would he have noticed the plants had he come out later, with the things sitting there as if they'd been there for years? Probably. In any case, she loved him and he enjoyed that. Went to her, gave her a kiss, paid no more attention to me than he did to the wheelbarrow. She dismissed me when the kiss was over. Craved her husband's company every minute she got. Might be nice to have a woman like that.

Sudden, unfocused pang of regret and longing. Which then focused on the woman in my dreams. Whom I hadn't thought of—God!—for over a month. Or dreamed of. Interesting, and no doubt important also, but it wasn't helping me infiltrate Target's household.

I ate with Target's defense force, made mental notes. Clipped hedges, tidied the garden and the orchard. Huddled in the shed beside the barrack while rain poured, then removed the cover from the pool. I'd arranged with Claudio not to be picked up till after dark and spent the empty time helping out. I gave people cause to like Reyes then and later.

I helped Raimundo the chauffeur polish the town car, helped the maids hang up laundered sheets and towels. Julia the cook was from a town on the Caribbean, blue-black, wide of girth, gap-toothed, and jolly. All she asked was that a man eat *con gusto*, heap his plate with rice, plump milky kernels, ladle on black beans, strips of boiled beef, tomato, onion, celery, pimento, splash the lot with flaming *salsa piquante* and set to. But Reyes saw the pantry bulb was out and got the ladder and climbed up and changed it, so that Julia needn't ask Marco Tulio the butler. She was too fat for climbing ladders herself. The smile she gave me displayed the slim, shy schoolgirl Julia had been four decades before.

Marco Tulio was always grumbling. No one appreciated him, no one thanked him, no one thought of him, no one cared. The house would fall apart in an hour without him, but no one noticed, no one gave him his due. I caught him one afternoon polishing silver and took the stool beside him and polished too—the nutcracker, the grape scissors, the cake knife—without a word to mar his keen of self-pity. It dwindled and died out in a few minutes. Marco Tulio grew grudgingly grateful, allowed himself a grunt in my direction. Then, abruptly, he turned glum again, sat with a grumpy frown, polishing, polishing, distraught at being unable to feel slighted. Which deprivation constituted an injury. A bitter smile crossed Marco Tulio's face. Soon he was grumbling again as if nothing had happened.

Justo the bodyguard had a reptilian stare that he used as an instrument of intimidation. The sight of him brewed a visceral loathing in me such as some people have for large scuttling insects. Reyes, however, took pity on him, one day finding him on the gravel behind the house aiming his stare at a number of bags of groceries. *La Señora* had returned with them in the town car, and when Raimundo had unloaded them, she sent him off on another errand.

"Justo, please take the bags up to the kitchen."

I heard her as I went to the toolshed. When I came out, she and the town car were gone. Justo and the bags were alone on the gravel.

I went over. Justo held his Uzi in his left hand and stared at the bags. He wouldn't put his hands on them, that was pat. He'd no more carry them in than put on rouge and lipstick. On the other hand, they wouldn't go in by themselves, and if he went in to tell one of the maids to get them, *La Señora* might be there and repeat her order. He swung his stare to me as I approached.

"It's all right, your honor, I'll take them."

"What do you mean it's all right? You making fun of me?"

"Not at all, your honor." Juan Reyes met his stare with wide-eyed sincerity. "You're in your suit and all, carrying a weapon . . ."

I bent and took four of the bags—easily, willingly—hooked my fingers through the loops. I stood up with a smile and walked off toward the house.

"*¡Cretino!*" Justo muttered behind me, abuse that merely heightened my enjoyment.

Being Reyes was fun and emotionally restful. I thought I might try to be like him in actual life.

The gardener's back healed miraculously when Juan Reyes was cleared by security. Less than a week after that the gardener got his long-awaited visa to the U.S. He told *La Señora* at once. She said she would miss him. On the other hand, she could scarcely ask him to stay. He said he thought Juan Reyes could fill the position. *La Señora* agreed; Juan Reyes would do very nicely.

I moved into the gardener's room above the barrack. One-One had a long list of things for me to snoop at, but he didn't give it to me the day I moved in. My sole mission at first was to be accepted as harmless, so that what I heard, saw, and did would flag no one's interest. Those first days were the best part of being Juan Reyes. In a sense *La Señora* was glad her gardener had gone. The garden had really been his. Now she was taking possession. One way she did this was introduce me to it.

Some names were familiar: orchid and frangipani, jacaranda and jasmine. The jasmine had leathery leaves and trumpet-shaped flowers. Of evenings the air was swollen with their fragrance. The jacaranda's cool violet stood out among more warmly colored flowers—bright red anthuriums whose waxen bracts looked lacquered, *mendietas* that bloomed yellow-gold, then turned apricot orange.

There were alocasia whose leaves were five feet long and enclosed foot-long flowers that gave off a rotting odor, and three kinds of heliconia, three variations on a gaudy sheath theme. In one, which had paddle-shaped leaves, the sheaths were lobster red and climbed ambitiously. In another they were orange and drooped. In the third they were pink and edged with green and yellow.

A poinciana spread its fiery blossoms beside the porte-cochere where the drive circled. Dwarf poincianas grew against the house, with lacy foliage and prickly branches, and butterfly-shaped flowers sacred (so said *La Señora*, reading from her book) to the Hindu god Siva. Lignum vitae stood among the shrubs, small evergreens with heart-shaped fruit and felty blue flowers. *La Señora* had a tiger's claw tree also. In what had been my country the Indians made soup from the flowers of the tiger's claw, and arrow poison from its seeds and bark.

La Señora had two young poui trees, one pink, one yellow. The yellow tree was called *araguaney* in her country and bore the Venezuelan national flower. She had a datura tree whose blossoms hung bell-like below its branches and exhaled a mysterious, musky perfume. She had mango trees and lime trees, avocado and guava, all of which gave fruit for her table, and two great cashew trees, each forty feet tall, with cacao bushes sheltering beneath them.

Where it fronted the Barranca, and clockwise to the tennis court and beyond, the compound wall was covered with flowering vines. Much was coral vine with flowers like tiny pink hearts. Bees loved them and hung murmurously near them. Beaumontia clung to the wall by the tennis court, white blossoms six inches across, delicately scented. Beaumontia grew on the tennis court fences also.

Clearing the court for play was the gardener's duty. I had just finished this task on my fourth Sunday . . .

By then my comings and goings were of no more interest to Target's protectors than those of *La Señora*'s cat. By then I'd received a snooping assignment. The defense force's armament, its changes of guard. Its postings, its command structure, its combat readiness. The names, ranks, ages, and hometowns of its members, the level of their loyalty and discretion, the place and time their food was fixed and served in case it might be possible and useful to bop them with the runs or botulism. One-One meant to debrief me that morning of what I'd gleaned so far, so I stayed in my room longer than usual, debriefing myself on paper so as to etch the data on my cortex, then burning the sheets. Target and three guests were already on the court when I finished sweeping the leaves and pods into a pile. They were hitting before I had spaded them into a wheelbarrow. I trundled the barrow out and around toward the toolshed and was scared half out of my pose as Juan Reyes. Antonio Oliveira came striding toward me through the eucalyptus grove.

The polo shirt he had on was swankily logo'd. The racket case he was swinging looked like ostrich leather. Serengeti Drivers, Rolex, ring. Tommy Nealy had a fit of soundless laughter.

I grabbed myself and stuffed myself back into Reyes. Modest downcast gaze, deferential slight stoop, no slavish shuffle though, that would be excessive. Deferential nod as we neared each other. Oliveira strode by without taking the slightest notice.

I walked through the fragrant grove among shafts of sunlight. From behind me the twang of rackets, a cry of "Good shot!" Then, "Here comes the merry widower, or whatever he is. Why don't you go back to bed, we have four already." Then, "Pay him no mind, Antonio, he envies your love life. Come and take my place, I'll play the next one."

Tommy Nealy said, "You're impeccable, Carlos."

On Sundays Claudio picked me up at Target's and drove past spots from which Nico checked us for tails. When Nico was sure we were clean, he pulled in behind, and we drove to where I could transfer to the Wanderer. Then we went to El Carmen, mirror windows zipped up. The whole procedure took a couple of hours. That Sunday I spent them wondering if I should tell One-One about Oliveira. I found him on the scrambler phone with Top Dog, holding the receiver at arm's length from his ear as Top Dog howled through it.

"I heard you, Top," he said when things calmed a little. "I'd have heard you without the phone, but I still can't help it. Central America, as you know well, is a war zone, the only war we happen to have at the moment. Between active duty guys and mercenaries, you couldn't walk through Macagüita Airport without bumping into ten men you've led in battle. Everyone knows that Appley Thomas means trouble. You have to stay under wraps, so you go by water. Your friend Toro too, no phone booths out on the ocean. We'll fly you out from Tiltenango."

That provoked more abuse. One-One grinned at me as he bore it. At length he got a chance to be mollifying. "Good news, Top, our Agency worries are over." Pause, then One-One laughed. "Yeah, he got your message. Said you have an iron hand in an iron glove. But the main thing is, they don't like Target either. We're welcome to him, and you're going to love why. The Agency got him to set up a weapons airlift to the Contra bunch in Nicaragua, arrange it and pay for it, they'd furnish the guns. Promised a pardon, maybe his face on Mount Rushmore. Reagan wants the Contras in, but Congress passed a law against helping them."

One-One listened, nodding, then spoke again. "The weapons are from the Israelis, captured PLO stocks. They come down from Texas to strips in Central America. Target set it up through a partner called Oliveira. The Agency loved it. They didn't know Oliveira's in with the cartels. What he and Target have been doing is load cocaine on the planes for the trip north. The flights, of course, are Agency-protected, not to be fucked with by Customs or anyone else. It puts Uncle Sam in the drug war on both sides."

There was another pause, then One-One continued. "They'd kill him if they could get at him. They can't close the airlift down, the White House loves it. They can't stop the drugs, the pilots are hooked on the money. Their hands tremble when they open the morning papers. I think it's why the idea of snatching Target was put in Keegan's head."

Pause and more nods. "I know it came from Justice. They all talk to each other. The people who'll be in the shit if this comes out are second-level political appointees. Four years ago they were congressional aides. Four years from now they'll be lobbyists. They have buddies just like themselves in every department, and all they do is deal favors back and forth. It seemed odd that Justice okayed snatching a conman, even if he swindled half a billion. Cocaine smuggling is a different story, not to mention making the Agency step on its dick."

The last topic was timing. "Yes, they work on Christmas Eve," said One-One. "They work on Christmas Day if there's an emergency." Then, after listening: "Christmas Day oh four hundred, I like it, Top. It'll be a nice present for Target, and if something screws that date up, we go on New Year's."

After One-One hung up he debriefed me. After that we went over communications. Claudio and I had a speech code built around items a gardener might need from a plant nursery—that was if I had an urgent message to send. Meanwhile, One-One had a deal with a pair of disc jockeys. One was on early in the morning, the other at night. He paid them some money, they played special requests. When he needed to send me a message he requested a song for one lady or another. The title and the name encoded the message.

One-One's debriefings left me drained emotionally as well as of information. The communications drills were exhausting too. I rested then while One-One composed a new laundry list, information for me to collect about Target's defenses. Then he fed it into my long-term memory. By the time we finished it was more or less evening, and I still hadn't told him I knew Oliveira—or, rather, that an Atacalpan I'd met in my previous life turned out to be an intimate of Target's. It looked like I wasn't going to tell him either.

Oliveira hadn't spotted me, I wasn't blown. Why jeopardize my part in Golden Retriever? Chords of shame were still vibrating in me. Why jeopardize my shot at redemption.

By nightfall I was back inside Juan Reyes, and Reyes was back in Target's compound. D-day for Golden Retriever was four weeks away.

RETRIEVER

*D*ude and Senior left first. Air taxi to Antigua, where they went on board *Princess Nan*—twin diesel, ninety-six feet, top speed forty knots—for two days of getting to know her at sea and dockside. They and the others had drafted bios from which a friend of One-One's had prepared "legends"—stories complete with documentation to justify their visiting Atacalpa. Some had chosen personal things to take with them—for Senior a pair of opera glasses strong enough to be useful in the field yet small enough to drop in a shirt pocket; for Shooter his Springfield. At first he chose not to take it for fear he might lose it, the stock made by a comrade now long dead, but in the end he put it, cased in leather, in the bag that was going over to Miami and then to wherever they packed diplomatic pouches. Clinging to possessions was no way to live. Everything, life itself, was lost sooner or later.

Dude and Senior provisioned for several weeks' cruising and ran up to the island taking their time, rounding the headland by starlight so as not to show up on screens in Moscow or Langley. Rusty brought their passengers out to them: Top Dog, Shooter, Gato, and Doc in the first load, Toro and the baggage in the second—a surly, sullen, hugely pissed-off Toro, who'd been told just twenty minutes before embarking that he was going by sea not via Miami. By then Top Dog had broken the news that no one would be left out, that everyone would have a part in Golden Retriever.

Senior and Doc had the first watch, Dude and Gato the mid, Shooter and a still-steaming Toro the morning. PT on the afterdeck at 0530 while the sun shrugged from the ocean dead astern: push-ups, sit-ups, leg lifts, leg kicks, squat jumps; yacht on autopilot, Senior leading. Flapjacks by Top Dog for breakfast, then one-on-one sessions. He examined his shipmates on their mission assignments, their own first, then everybody else's, doing Dude and Shooter that first day. Those waiting their turn studied maps of Atacalpa. In the afternoon a round-robin arm wrestling tournament, won by Toro, which eased his fury somewhat.

The next morning at the end of his session with Top Dog he asked if he could bring up a personal matter. They were on the flying bridge in folding deck chairs—honey-colored wood, canvas seats and backs—Top Dog in bathing trunks and garish sport shirt, purple, rose, and turquoise splashes, the kind of cloth once used for barter with savages. He sat facing the stern, Toro to his right front. Shooter had the con one deck below, minding the empty sea and radar scope as *Princess Nan* cruised west at twenty-six knots.

"Go ahead," said Top Dog.

"Why did you change my travel at the last minute?"

"I didn't."

Toro's shoulders jerked, his face showed puzzlement.

"I changed it last month. What I did at the last minute was tell you."

"Why?" asked Toro. "Why the change?"

"I felt like it. How do you greasers say it? *Mi di la gana.*"

Toro glared. *"'Me,'"* he said very softly, pronouncing it 'may.' *"'Me'* not *'mi'* is the reflexive pronoun."

Top Dog shrugged. "Whatever."

He looked out over *Princess Nan's* wake at the eastern horizon. The sun hung midway between it and the zenith. A cloud the size of his hand hung to the southeast. "I'm concerned you may compromise operation security." He looked back at Toro pleasantly.

Toro opened his mouth. As he did, Top Dog raised his left forefinger. "Think before you say anything. If you give me hurt pride and bluster, things will get worse."

Toro bit his lip and thought, then said, "Why me?"

"Let's turn that around. Why might I doubt your trustworthiness?"

"I don't know. I took part in a raid you led in Pinar del Rio. I did well, you said so yourself. *You* called *me* for this mission."

"All true. So what's come up since?"

"I don't know. Maybe someone said something against me."

"Suppose someone did, what they said would still have to hold water. What's happened lately?"

"I don't know. I did some work for the Agency."

Top Dog grinned, showing his teeth. "See how easy it is?"

Toro sulked. "I did some work for the Agency, so what?"

Top Dog sighed. "Those guys, there's no north to their compass. They make up what's important as they go along. So of course you can't trust them. People who work for them tend to become like them. That's point one. Point two is, they're nifty at blackmail.

You're a headstrong guy, they could have something on you. Point three, they have lots and lots of money."

"Fuck your points. I'm no *sapo*."

Top Dog looked at Toro. Christ, he was angry! All that violence inside and no way to vent it. What would he, Appley Thomas, do if the Agency offered him a caper? No action for a while and no prospect of any. If the Agency called, would he answer? He very well might.

"What about point four? You blabbed about it."

Righteous indignation: "I did not!"

Top Dog leaned forward. "You told everyone you'd been somewhere you couldn't mention, doing something you couldn't mention either. Are we supposed to be stupid?"

Toro glared back at Top Dog.

Top Dog showed his teeth and leaned forward at him: "Hunh?"

Toro nodded once slowly. "You're right."

"When we've done our thing over there, with you or without you, we can't have you assing around giving off hints. Any guy who wanted to know who did the caper could put your nuts in a vise and get the whole story. We could be fucked because you tried to impress someone. Am I going to have to worry about shit like that? Convince me, or you better be a good swimmer."

"No sir, you won't."

Top Dog gauged Toro. About whom his gut had always felt fine. Bluster? Sure, because timid. Touchy and quarrelsome? Yes, because insecure. But also bold because fearful, loyal because . . .

Top Dog's manner had made him a host of enemies. It had cost him general's stars and, more important, years of wearing his country's uniform. But it brought one great bounty: no one was lukewarm about him. Most civilians he knew dreaded and loathed him.

Most enlisted soldiers thought him insane. Most officers considered him a throwback, fit to rampage with Tamburlaine or Attila but out of place in a modern army. Most commanders wanted nothing to do with him. He told them the truth, not what they wanted to hear. On the other hand, a few in all categories prized him, and the men who went raiding with him . . . The men who raided with him, who put their lives in his hands and took his in theirs—they were loyal.

Only two motives for loyalty, love and fear. Toro loved Top Dog, he wanted to be like him. No, it was stronger than that, he wanted to be him. And who knew? He might even make it. There'd been a time, forty years back, when Top Dog was almost as full of shit as Toro. And, loving him, Toro feared losing his approval.

Love and fear were plenty. Besides, Top Dog's gut hadn't fooled him yet.

"Still want this job?"

"Yes, sir."

"If you have hard feelings, tough titty, I don't give a shit. Will they get in the way, affect your performance?"

"No hard feelings, Colonel."

"Okay, you're still in. The matter's over."

"It was Carlos, wasn't it?"

"It was Carlos what?"

"Who said things against me."

"You think this is a girls' school? Think I'd fuck up the esprit de corps of a unit by letting guys tell tales on one another? Carlos minds his own business. So does everybody in my outfit. The matter's over. Go tell Senior I'm ready to hear his confession."

By then Chivo, Hector, and Lilo were in Atacalpa. Rusty stayed long enough to police the island clean of Retriever traces. His plane touched down at Macagüita a few hours after *Princess Nan* picked up a mooring in Puerto Calbo. A car for hire took him to a safe house in El Maestro. Chivo, Senior, and Shooter were already in residence, Toro, Gato, and Doc at a safe house in San Lucas. Top Dog was with One-One in El Carmen, along with Hector and Lilo. Dude was on *Princess Nan*. Mac and helicopter were in Texas, on their way south. I was at Target's.

Rusty's job in the preattack phase was making charges, one for me and fifty for diversion. Explosives, detonators, and timing devices had come in by diplomatic pouch in care of the mil group, along with small arms and ammo, mortar tubes and rounds. One-One took delivery in a warehouse he had leased on the city's outskirts, a place big enough for vehicles to drive into, with a steel-doored concrete storeroom. Rusty and Shooter made the charges there under florescent lamps and a dinged skylight.

Hector, Gato, and Toro would arrange distribution, becoming garbagemen for the occasion. Some years back the municipality of Chilpanzango had put litter cans into the better parts of town. Fifty or so of these would be replaced with false-bottomed new ones containing Rusty's charges. This was sub-op Rhino One. My camouflage metaphor had caught on with Top Dog and One-One. Actually, Rhino One crossed the flea and the rhino, garbageman being the lowest job in society, zero prestige and so zero suspicion.

The point of the flash-and-bang was a fake insurrection. Target's defense force wasn't Top Dog's main worry. Mac would be in the air a long time getting over the cordillera to the Caribbean. Then *Princess Nan* had to clear Atacalpan waters. Top Dog didn't want anyone scrambling planes or patrol boats. He wanted the whole defense establishment handcuffed, and one did that by scaring the shit out of *El Comandante*.

Charges were going to go off in downtown Chilpanzango—the business district, the National Palace environs—and on Linda Vista near the commandant's compound. Next was a fake break-in at Target's gate to cover the actual penetration and prompt his defenders to call for reinforcements. Next a fake assault at *El Comandante*'s, a blast big enough to take out part of his wall plus a mortar barrage from Rusty and Chivo. The duty officer would think this the main show, the thing at Target's only a feint. He couldn't get in trouble protecting his boss, and his boss's self-importance would do the rest. Whatever plan the Atacalpans had for safeguarding the institutions of state would be put into effect, concentrating forces where they wouldn't bother Retriever.

Rigging the blast at the commandant's was called Rhino Three and involved a manhole in Linda Vista where power lines to several estates branched off the main. Rhino Two employed Mac and the helicopter to string a one-inch cable across the Barranca. Both depended on an electric power outage to take place Sunday night, December twenty-third, arranged from inside by a member of One-One's network. Rhino ops vehicles were at the warehouse and included an old Chevy truck for which Nico would steal a garbage department license plate, a heavier truck with a winch on the front bumper, a panel truck with power company markings, and an authentic-looking police car Lilo would drive dressed as one of Chilpanzango's finest.

Doc's job was keeping track of where everyone was, ditto for every piece of equipment, so that One-One could concentrate on final details. Taking over from One-One was like changing shifts in an air traffic control center. Doc had to pick up the blips on One-One's monitor.

Mauricio, for example, a fisherman One-One had found to serve as Dude's pilot and keep him aware of the north coast's shoals and currents, and Chepi, my onetime guide. They were scouting up a bay or cove or inlet where Mac could rendezvous with *Princess Nan*. They had to find three sites by D minus seven, safe anchorages unreachable by road with beach enough to land a chopper. Dude had to check all three out by D minus four and pick a number one and an alternate.

Two hundred yards of cable was a blip too. It was in the warehouse on a wooden spool mounted on a forklift pallet. It would go onto the chopper on D minus one.

Senior tested radio equipment—three base stations in a safe house in San Lucas, two on *Princess Nan*, fourteen hand-held transceivers. Toro and Hector checked weapons and ammunition, then set up caches where they might come in handy, off Road One between Maestro and Linda Vista, off Road Two outside San Lucas, near the field where the helicopter would be based.

Lilo got a tutorial from a retired cop, a man One-One knew from his mil group stint in Atacalpa. Top Dog roamed Chilpanzango with Nico, all day for days. When Mac came in Top Dog roamed by helicopter. His knowledge of the terrain got as good as One-One's. No one hung out in cafes or cantinas, but all were driven around the city and past the spots where they would be in action.

Drive-bys and run-throughs. I was there for the run-through on D minus nine, Sunday, December 16, 1984. Circle of chairs beneath the warehouse skylight, One-One on his feet in the center, turning and pointing.

"Monday," he says, "Christmas Eve," pointing at Rusty. "Seventeen hundred hours, D minus one."

"Chivo and I take the panel to Linda Vista, following Lilo in his police car. We set up at the manhole and put out a railing. Lilo puts out smudge-pot lanterns. Chivo tells the guards we're checking the power lines because of the outage your guys did the night before. Then I set my charge with a radio-controlled detonator. Then we drive off."

One-One nods and turns and points to Mac. "What about you? It's thirteen hundred on Monday."

"I'm stringing cable. Toro and Gato are on the north bank of the Barranca. Hector and Doc are on the south bank. Shooter and Senior are with me. We'll string north to south, high ground to low ground, what we worked out in the island."

"Okay," says One-One. He turns. "What about it, Gato?"

"Toro and I go out with Chivo in the panel, no later than eleven hundred hours. We go one street east of T Street in Linda Vista, park at the dead end, put out *'Hombres Trabajando'* signs. Then we go east along the lip of the Barranca, plenty of noise, no attempt at concealing our presence, to where the Barranca is narrowest, about eighty meters from Target's. Then we rig an anchor for the cable. Chivo leaves. When Mac comes by, Toro and I anchor the cable. Then we go through the Barranca to the San Lucas side and report to you at the safe house."

"Okay," says One-One. He turns and points.

Princess Nan had come in from scouting the day before. Everyone but Mac was present. First was a workout, Senior leading. Then One-One briefed the group on my infiltration, beginning with my trip to La Cañada. He had reached the part where I was in Target's household, when I arrived.

Claudio had collected me in Linda Vista. Nico had collected me from Claudio. He honked and got down and opened the door for me. I'd never been to the warehouse before. One-One hadn't told me the others would be in the country. As I stepped inside, Top Dog roared, "On your feet!" He and the rest stood up applauding. I was so firmly lodged in Juan Reyes's persona that I halted at once and pulled off my straw sombrero and held it by the brim before my chest. Then the penny dropped, and I grinned sheepishly. By that time the others were hooting.

"Cut me a slice of that ham," said Shooter.

One-One gave me my regular weekly debriefing, letting the others listen and ask questions. Then I sat with the extractors— Gato, Doc, and Toro—and went over the floor plan of Target's house. Later One-One led us all on a random run-through. After that the beer was broken out. Comradeship foamed about me like a warm sea. Other Retrievers dolphined in it. I waded pleasantly without plunging, making one beer last until Nico came for me.

One by one the others came up to me, each in his style, to congratulate me on how I was handling this assignment. Each time I joked through it, though with Toro, drunk and mawkish, it wasn't easy. One-One caught my eye, and I went over. He wasn't drinking much either.

"Find this childish? I do sometimes."

"No, not at all. I'd like to join in. The problem is, most of me is over at Target's."

Later, in the Wanderer on my way to meet Claudio, I considered this response and revised it. In part it was true, my mind was on being Juan Reyes, but my urge to join the party wasn't strong either. Months back I had longed for my comrades' acceptance. Now, though pleasant, it meant little to me. I remembered a thing my father had said a short while after becoming president: All you got by accomplishing something was the chance to start from scratch at a tougher level.

The next Sunday, D minus two, was a dress rehearsal. Dude came down by plane from Puerto Calbo. One-One had his model of Linda Vista set up in the warehouse and watched each man point his way through Golden Retriever holding a script that looked like a conductor's score: names on the left, a page for each half hour, beginning at daybreak on D minus one, Monday, 24 December, and ending when the last man left Atacalpa. It took most of the day and included costumes where pertinent. Toro, for instance, had three: power company T-shirt, garbageman's coveralls, Atacalpan army battle dress. When One-One was done, Top Dog spoke for a moment. I recalled the occasion, years before it seemed, when he first spoke to us after our workout.

"This isn't a pep talk, we don't need shit like that. This is just a reminder, don't underestimate these guys. We're well-trained and well-rehearsed and I hope well-commanded. We should be gone before they know what hit them. But remember, we're in their country, and they're going to be very pissed off when they find out what's happened. Let's do it and go home."

There was beer after that. No one clowned or got high, though. When it was time for me to go, Top Dog and One-One went outside with me.

"You've done well," Top Dog told me. "I liked the way you handled the test we gave you. I especially liked how you handled being set up, that you weren't caught off-guard or resentful. Life plays shitty tricks, we'd best expect some. Resentment and self-pity sap your strength. And you've done well inside Target's. That's how it looks at least. I hope it's true."

"I do too, Colonel."

"I was worried about you a little. I'm not sure what you're after. These guys I've collected . . ." He waved an arm toward the warehouse. "One-One and me too. We need this shit to feel alive. Sure, the money's okay, but we'd do it for nothing. Excitement and comradeship is what we're after. It's too bad there has to be killing, but that's where it's at. Other men trying to kill you, your life at risk. You trust your comrades with it, they trust you with theirs. The highly evolved can get kicks from sports or business. We need warfare."

He shrugged and looked down, then went on. "Anyway, you don't need it. You need something else. I hope you get it."

"Thanks, Colonel."

"Thirty-two hours more." This from One-One. "You want to be alert for signs they're suspicious. I'll send Claudio by tomorrow after work so you'll have a chance to report anything that's late-breaking.

"Take a couple of these." He handed me two Syrettes, collapsible tubes with hypo needles attached. "Doc and Gato have them, but if they're down you'll have to work with Toro, and I'd rather you do the injecting than him. And you've got a new radio. Nico has it. It's got an alarm. If you don't take the batteries out, it'll send a distress signal at H minus two hours."

"In case the other side takes me out of the game."

"You've got it."

"We've seen no sign of trouble," said Top Dog. "It's just that you're my pathfinder platoon."

I smiled. "And you don't want the guys going into a hot LZ. Leaders are to prevent that."

Top Dog grinned, showing teeth. "See you in Linda Vista, wiseass."

*"I*t puts me in an awkward position."

"But this isn't about you. It's about a woman who's lost her children."

"And their father, what about him? And you, you seem to be in it. Well, you're my wife, he's my friend . . ."

"How can you call him your friend?"

"Well, he isn't my enemy, at least not yet."

"He's a shit, Edgar. He had them kidnapped."

"After she stole them."

"That's not true, and you know it. Ellen's husband abused her, she'd had enough. She took her children and went home."

"What's she doing here anyway?"

"It's Christmas, Edgar. She wants to see them."

"Does she need you for that?"

"He won't let her. He won't even let her speak to them by phone. She's trying to get a *boleta* . . . A paper from a court requiring him to let her visit. She also wants to get the embassy to bring up the kidnapping with the government."

"That's it! Just mention my name at the American embassy!"

"Edgar, this isn't about you. Can't you imagine what she's going through? She hasn't seen her children for months and months. She hasn't heard their voices, doesn't know how they are. And you're worried about that shit."

"He's a big man in this little country. He's also my partner in some important ventures. It puts me in an awkward position if my wife takes his wife's part against him."

"She's alone here, Edgar. Her Spanish isn't that good. I said I'd keep her company."

"Company plus translation and transport."

"We'll hire a taxi then."

"You can't go unguarded. No, Diana, tell her you can't go. I know what's best for me in this business."

Diana Haft's peal of laughter was so rich I almost looked up at her. I was thirty feet away scooping bougainvillea blossoms from the pool and trying to stay in Juan Reyes's persona. The conversation had almost rattled me out.

"Edgar, you're wonderful! You know what's best for you! God, do you ever! Why didn't I know you when I was at Smith? I had a report to give on the narcissistic character type, and I killed myself writing it. All I'd have had to do was bring you to class."

I hadn't seen her the day before. Not down when I left in the morning or when I returned. A remnant of the tennis/pro-football bunch, Antonio Oliveira not included, was drinking in the *sala*, picking at a cold supper Marco Tulio had set out. Drank straight through the power failure, thanks to the auxiliary generator. At some point her friend Ellen had called her, and they'd made plans. Waited till now to tell Target, at a table by the pool on this pleasant morning—bright sunlight but cool enough for pullovers—after he had his decaf and his two-minute egg.

"I'd have gotten A-plus without . . ."

Her voice trailed off. I sneaked a peek. Something in Target's face had snuffed her sarcasm.

"I'm sorry, Edgar." She looked down at her hands like someone observing a moment of silence.

"Are you sure?"

She nodded without looking up.

"Good. It shows intelligence. I don't let people laugh at me, it's too expensive."

"I'm sorry."

"Have you promised the woman something, given your word?"

"Yes," she said, looking him in the face. "That I'd keep her company today and that we'd have tea here."

"All right, do it. But don't promise her anything else without checking with me."

"Thank you, Edgar."

No sign they had wind of Retriever. Not a wisp of uneasiness in either of them—not, that is, till Target made his face. I, on the other hand, had begun the day with a touch of premission tensies and now worried I might hear phantom children wailing.

I went back to the bougainvillea. Tingle of envy, pang of regret and longing. I love the way you make me nervous, Carlos. The tingle and pang were better than children sobbing.

"Juan." She called from where she was sitting.

"Mand' Usted, señora."

"This afternoon, please cut some nice flowers for the *sala* and terrace. I have company for tea."

"Como no, señora."

"Gracias, Juan."

"A la orden, señora."

Later, when she went off with Raimundo and Justo, I went up to the edge of the orchard and dug a hole. With a trowel, slow work, but Juan Reyes was no ball of fire—a plodding dull fellow who thought in months not minutes. I was safely back in Reyes's persona, having herded all thought of a woman named Ellen into a corner of my mind. The corner was back of my right eye just inside my temple. I herded my Ellen thoughts there and kept them pent.

The hole was circular, two feet across at the top. Bottom would be the steel skin of the Culvert. Exactly how far down that was I couldn't be sure, so I kept the sides as straight as I could manage. The explosive charge was almost a foot in diameter.

Blowing the Culvert there, just inside the orchard, left a lengthy stretch to cross aboveground but cut the stretch Target would have to be dragged and made for the shortest overall in-and-out time. It also gave me tree cover while I was digging. I chopped at the ground with the trowel, then scooped dirt aside. Later on I lifted dirt in trowelfuls. By the end I was in the pose of a Muslim at prayer, but no one paid any attention to Juan Reyes.

Toro, too, had a hole to dig that morning, on the lip of the Barranca east of S (for slide) Street, less than a block west of T (for Target) Street, eighty meters from where the Culvert opened. Gato could spell him, but Toro loved to show off his muscles and needed the physical stress to keep his nerves calm. I imagined him jabbing a spade into the clay, stepping on the blade, swinging his weight up, levering out a clod and tossing it forward. Gato watched. They wore hard hats and jeans and midnight blue T-shirts.

When my trowel hit steel, I widened out the bottom, then stood and stretched and went up to the garden and dug at the base of an oleander shrub. After a bit I uncovered a white plastic bag. I took this back to the hole at the edge of the orchard, lay down on my stomach, and took the charge out. It was Frisbee-ish, wrapped in black tape. A pair of wires dangled from it. Rusty had shaped it to breach the tubing but kick most of its blast up to open a passage. Claudio had got it into the compound under the roots of a potted plant. Holding the ends of the wires in my left hand, I placed it on the Culvert. Then, still holding the wires, I scooped some dirt onto it.

While Toro dug, Chivo mixed cement—a couple of pailfuls, up where the panel was parked, where S Street dead-ended. Lightning bolts were painted on both sides, along with *"Compañia Altacapeña de Fuerza y Luz."* I imagined the watchman from over there watching him mix: chunky, flat-faced, copper-skinned, three-quarters Indian; wide-brimmed hat, leather windbreaker, corduroy pants; pump-action shotgun, patent-leather holster, rusting long-barreled Colt .38.

"*¿Y este cemento pa' que?*" the watchman asked Chivo.

"*Ya verás,*" Chivo responded. "*Ya verás.*"

When the charge was covered with dirt, I dropped the wires, reached into the plastic bag, and took out the radio. When it received a signal on the right frequency, it put out a current to detonate the explosive. I reached into the hole and connected the wires. I opened the antenna and set the radio on the bottom of the hole with the wires bunched beside it. The bud of the antenna was above ground level. I spilled some dirt in the hole and patted it down, firming the radio in an upright position. I pushed a button on it. A red light came on.

At this point I began to feel eyes staring at my shoulders. I had a strong urge to get up and look around. Instead I rolled onto my left side and shoved some dirt into the hole from the pile beside it. As I did, I began to think of radio signals. The spectrum was full of them. What if some station happened to send a signal . . . ? Had I ever seen a man blown in half? I couldn't remember. Had I . . . ?

I breathed deeply, forced a smile and then a grin. I cupped my palm and pushed dirt into the hole. When the hole was full, I pushed down on the antenna till the bud at the end was flush with the ground.

Gato and Toro carried a six-foot length of railway track to the hole Toro had dug. Gato bent, putting his end in the hole. Toro walked the track up and forward till it stood upright, half in half out. A circular hole was bored in it near the top. Gato went on one knee and grasped the track with both hands, holding it upright. Toro turned and picked up a sledge. Sweat stood out on his face and darkened his T-shirt. He swung the sledge straight up above his head, grunted and brought it down on the end of the track: *thunk!* He swung the sledge up again and brought it down.

"Easy," said Gato in Spanish, "you're making me tired."

I got to my feet holding the bag and the trowel and kicked excess dirt to one side and the other. I stepped to my right and kicked some leaves onto the hole. The thought of pissing on it came to mind, a vestigial marking instinct, this turf is mine. I smiled and walked off toward the garden.

Chivo trundled a wheelbarrow full of wet cement toward the Barranca. The watchman followed. Two-plus feet of railway track protruded from the hole Toro had dug. With the front of the barrow almost touching the track, Chivo lifted the handles to dump the cement.

"Hang on!" said Gato in Spanish. "Let's do this right." He nodded to Toro. "Hey, hold that thing, will you?"

Toro got down on one knee and held the track. Gato stepped past Toro to the side of the barrow. He sifted spadefuls of loose cement into the hole.

I stood in the garden. Not a leaf stirred. Clouds had come over the sun. The air squeaked with tension. No, the tension was in me.

Thunderheads over the peak. Someone had forgot to tell them it was December, too late in the year for serious rain. No fun at all for Mac to be up in a thunderstorm, let alone a few feet over Road Two at the end of a length of anchored cable. The question for Top Dog and One-One was whether to send him up and risk the weather, or wait till the storm blew over and risk having to put the op back a week. Option Two won hands down. Wait till the storm passed, and if that left no time to string the cable today, go on New Year's instead of Christmas. I could imagine Top Dog fussing and One-One soothing him.

"They'll have a week to notice no power's attached."

"We'll wait until a week from today to string it."

"And this emergency? Busting their asses to get a line strung, and then they just forget it for a week!"

"Top, this is Central America, where the hammock was invented. No one wonders when a job is left half done."

Another week as Juan Reyes. I suddenly longed to be clean of him but had no choice. The charge I had just planted would have to come out, would have to go back to Rusty, be done over, brought back here, and then replanted. What else? I'd need a reason to hang around New Year's Eve. *La Señora* had said take Christmas Eve or New Year's. I'd said New Year's, so how could I stay? I'd get sick, that's how. Too bad everything wasn't that simple. What else? Make a list of what postponement entailed. No, forget that, I could do that later. The thing now was to cut *La Señora*'s flowers, then see what my favorite DJ was playing.

3 "We used to hate coming in here, even the pilots. Storms with no warning."

"Yes, but it can clear up just as quickly. See how nice it's been, letting us sit outside? And we're getting my favorite sunset, magenta between black clouds and purple hills."

They were on the upper terrace off the *sala*. Wrought-iron chairs, wrought-iron glass-topped table on which Marco Tulio had laid a locally sewn cloth, rich green embroidered with yellow quetzals.

"It's lovely here, Diana, and you've been wonderful. I'm glad I called. I almost didn't."

"Why, for heaven's sake! Did you think I'd hang up on you? I'd have been hurt if I learned you were here and hadn't called me."

I was to their left, a little behind them.

"No, it wasn't that. It was pride partly. I hate dragging my woe into other people's lives."

"That's silly."

"Maybe it is, but you'd feel the same way, I bet you."

"You're probably right."

After the storm hit, the DJ played "Besame Mucho," followed by "Un Viejo Amor." The op was on hold but might get back on schedule. I lay in my room and listened to boleros, getting more and more antsy but not over Golden Retriever. Later, when the storm lifted, I heard "Piel Canela" and "Tú, Sólo Tú." The op was on tentative Go; I should stay tuned. I should also lie low. Didn't need a special message for that. Going down to have a look at *La Señora*'s guest was a huge and needless risk to my cover. Still, at teatime I put the earphone on and the radio in my pocket and went down to trim the hedge beside the terrace.

"The other part was your husband. He and Antonio are partners in something, aren't they?"

"Yes. But I don't think we should let that bother us. They wouldn't let it bother them if the shoe were on the other foot. Look, there it is again!"

"It's heading across. What's that trailing behind it?"

"A power line, I think."

Mac was over the Barranca, thudding toward San Lucas and Road Two. The cable trailed behind like a giant's jump rope. I nerved myself for a glance at Diana and Ellen and looked down at once, trembling. I sidled to my right, farther behind them. Didn't want them looking over. (A) Ellen might recognize C. J. Wagram. (B) The left side of their faces might be missing.

"Justo said they're stringing a new one. The power went off for twenty minutes last night."

"Is he the bodyguard?"

"Yes."

"How can you stand him?"

"The one before was worse, if you can believe it."

Familiar agitation, mixed shame and joy. Couldn't grasp where I'd felt it before till I looked up again. She turned her head toward Diana, and I had a clear view of her profile, all features present. The strain she'd been under didn't show in her face. I saw grace, health, style, energy, spirit. And straight away began to shudder. I turned away and closed my eyes and saw Ellen walking beside me through Miami Airport. She smiled softly, at something I said or just from being with me, as at a wonderful secret that modesty forbade her to disclose.

"Edgar insists I be guarded whenever I go out. He says someone might try to get at me to get at him. He's probably right, but I can't take it seriously."

"You will if they do."

"Yes, I suppose . . . Oh, Ellen, I'm sorry!"

"Don't be, it's not you. It's that everything . . ."

My eyes were wet. Tears of shame and sorrow, for her, for myself. Stealing children was a form of self-punishment. Stealing hers was surrogate suicide.

"Oh, Diana, what's wrong with me? What happened to feisty Ellen?"

"You've been horribly hurt, that's what. Taken advantage of, tricked and humiliated, tormented with worry. Don't you dare be ashamed! You've kept fighting. If you just crawled off and died no one could blame you."

"I was that way for a while. At first I was okay, or I thought I was anyway. I filed a complaint, I wrote my congressman. Through him I got the State Department involved. Then our embassy here reported that as far as Atacalpa was concerned, Antonio was a model citizen. He'd sued for divorce and custody on the grounds that I had abandoned our happy home. He won, of course. I never heard of the proceedings. All they had to do was publish a fine-print notice in two newspapers here for three business days. Bringing Tonio and Elena here was perfectly legal. My custody order had no validity here. As for my rights, if I had any, the only thing the embassy could do was recommend a lawyer. The lawyer said there was no way to overturn the custody decree. He'd see what he could do about visitation privileges. That's when it got harder and harder to go to work in the morning, easier and easier to spend the day curled up on the couch, not even watching TV, not even crying. I snapped out of it, thank God, but I'd go right back if it weren't for Tonio and Elena. I just want them safe, out of this terrible country, away from that bastard!"

"You'll have that, Ellen. I'm going to turn Edgar around, I know how to do it. It will take a few days, but then you'll win. The wonderful thing about this place is that money buys anything."

"I can't let you involve Edgar."

"We'll be doing him a favor. You know I adore him, but it will be the first time in his life he does something for someone besides himself."

"You've been wonderful, Diana. And you're right, I've been ashamed. That man of Antonio's tricked me, yet somehow I feel it's my fault."

"That's how they beat us. Don't let them."

"You're right about everything. Even the tea; it's true, it helps."

"My Argentine mother, more Brit than the Brits. At least I gave you cake, not cucumber sandwiches."

"Lovely tea, lovely cake, and lovely flowers."

"Yes, I have a new gardener. *Juan, ¿estás allí?*"

4 *La Señora's* new gardener was in full retreat, but shame drove me off not fear of being exposed and wrecking the mission. At the same time I didn't want to leave. It was all I could do not to look up at Ellen. Somehow I kept the clippers working, kept from mutilating the hedge, and had enough shame to slink off when *La Señora* was going to call me over.

I hid out in my room. Dazed, twitching with remorse. It became a life-and-death matter to get my mind elsewhere, so I thought of what was going on with Retriever. I knew the plan well enough for that.

Mac, for instance. He had a perfect view of Diana's sunset but not the leisure to enjoy it. He was over the Barranca in the swirling gusts the storm had left there, trying to stay lined up on Doc and Hector.

They were forty feet below him—one-fifty, one-forty, one-thirty feet to his front. Hard hats and midnight blue T-shirts, plastic IDs dangling at their chests. In front of them was a metal post set in cement, behind them a truck pointed toward Linda Vista— winch on the front bumper, chocks under the wheels, power company lightning bolts on the cab doors. A police car was on the shoulder of Road Two. The driver's door was open, the roof light flashed. Lilo, by the rear fender, windmilled his arm like a third base coach sending a runner home. Sundown on Christmas Eve, plenty of cars. The motorists dawdled, gawking at the chopper.

Artistic success was hitting the post with the cable. Box office was doing the job in one pass. First of all, it was tricky to go backward. The slack had to come up, yard for yard, or the cable might snag. No possible outcome of that was very pleasant. If that wasn't enough, the light was fading. No way to be sure there'd be time for more than one pass.

If the wind would quit or blow steadily from one direction, if the turbulence would only call it a day, Mac wouldn't have to make any passes. He could go in high and sit over the roadway and pay out cable until Hector grabbed it. That was what they'd come up with on the island as the safest, solidest procedure. Altitude confers margin for error. So when One-One asked Mac's opinion, Mac said, do it early: oh six hundred or so, no wind, stable air. Top Dog kiboshed that. If they left the thing up all day, someone would catch on to it. Early afternoon was what they agreed on. Then came the thunderstorm, and there he was: wind and turbulence and time for one pass.

On the way in, bucking the swirls, Mac didn't think of the friend who ground-looped a Huey on an LZ in the central highlands, toasting himself and his crew, beheading his prospective passenger, a soldier headed for home on emergency leave who was waiting to board and got clipped by the rotor. He didn't think of friends lost attempting maneuvers with insufficient margin for error, or of drops and pickups he'd made under hostile fire. He had those thoughts later, along with the rush of surviving another near thing. On the way in he thought of hitting the post with the cable. Then he was thudding away in the gathering twilight to rest and refuel for the main show of Golden Retriever.

One-One was in the safe house in San Lucas with two radio base stations and three phones, with a street plan of Chilpanzango taped to the wall, six 18-by-24-inch sections, with the dining table piled with stuff from El Carmen—photographs, maps, guidebooks, schedules. Heavy drapes covered the windows. Beyond them lovely tall trees rose from back patios, fragrant creepers clung along the fences, homes and lawns showed Christmas lights and crèches.

Enjoying himself, just a step from gleeful. An out-of-season storm had scrambled his schedule, but he'd fiddled a little here, tweaked a bit there, and kept Retriever running without hitch or hobble, while Top Dog sat beside him fretting, watching him pull rabbits out of his hat.

Rusty was down a manhole in Linda Vista where the lines from several estates hooked to the main. Chivo's panel truck was parked beside it. A railing and lit smudge pots were set around. A drop light connected to the panel truck's battery filled the hole with buttery incandescence while Rusty unwrapped bricks of C-4 with a clasp knife.

Shooter was at the warehouse. He sat at a card table under a florescent lamp setting timers on litter-can bombs. The bombs were on circular pallets that fit under the litter can's false bottoms. Lilo attached the pallets to the cans. Hector took the cans to the garbage truck parked in the shadows near the big double doors.

The ride with Mac had jangled Shooter harshly—giddy sways, abrupt plummeting drops, sideways slings against his safety harness. Mac and Senior were used to that shit, Shooter was infantry. He'd been smart and lunched on soda crackers, but even so he was hard put to keep from puking. His fire point for later was lousy too. He needed a clear view of the guard tower, and of T Street from Target's gate back toward Road One, but all the trees and bushes were inside the compounds, the shoulders of the street were bare dirt two feet wide—no cover, no concealment, no alternate point to jump to after firing a few rounds. All Shooter would have was a net with leaves and twigs. Lousy!

Dude was on board *Princess Nan* on the Caribbean. When the rain stopped he went topside. There were no stars or moon. The beach was invisible sixty yards away. Even Mauricio's skiff, moored at the stern, was hard to distinguish. He sat down facing aft and sipped slowly. One beer. One more than the other Retrievers would get that night.

After a time he made out two shades of darkness, jungle below, cloud cover above. The last of the flood tide rippled past the hull. The radar arm purred as it circled above him. He imagined the scope, bottom half lighting up in the inlet's contour, whole thing going dark as the arm swept the sea. He got up and went forward. He pulled the plastic cover off the radar scope, a duplicate of the one below in the cabin except this one had a funnel-shaped rain-and-spray guard. He switched it on and checked it: the sea was still empty. He switched it off and switched the radio on: One-One might try to raise him.

He and Mauricio had reached the inlet at sundown, anchored, got the drums and pump ashore. Rolled the drums up the beach to the edge of the jungle. Almost twenty yards, plenty of room for the chopper, and the tide would be lower when Mac landed. Mauricio would pump fuel, Dude would take people. In the *Nan's* yellow inflatable with outboard—Target, Doc, and Senior in the first load,

Gato, Toro, and me in the second. Senior would have the anchor up by the time the second load came aboard. He'd steer for the rising sun, Mac would steer for the border, Mauricio would steer for whatever village he fished from.

The rain came in squalls. They *put-putted* back to the *Nan* under it, darkness coming down like a theater curtain. The scope and radio dial glowed in the cabin. Rain splatted on the windshield, on the deck above. He sent Mauricio down to sack out a few hours. He went below himself and got into dry clothes. He ate a sandwich, drank a pint of juice. He killed the lights and went back up to the cabin. He checked the scope, made a scheduled call to One-One, listened while the rain became a torrent. When it stopped he took a beer up to the flying bridge.

The breeze had gone round to the west, he could smell the jungle, rotten-sweet against the salt-tart sea. Soon the tide would turn and the *Nan* would swing on her anchor to end up with her stern aimed seaward. Which meant backing out of the inlet and then turning, a clumsy exit compared to bow first, but either way they'd be fucked if the bad guys sent aircraft. No aircraft no problem. He didn't worry about patrol boats. *Nan* could outrun anything the bad guys had floating.

He went back to his seat and felt on the deck beside it for the beer can. If the op was on schedule, the garbagemen were out planting litter-can charges. He took a sip and listened to the flood tide. "Here's to you guys," he said.

The garbage truck coughed through the old part of Chilpanzango, cobblestone alleys it had trouble negotiating and more than once had to reverse out of. Flat-roofed one-story dwellings pressed right to the roadway. Open-shuttered glassless windows. Families displayed in front of TV sets. People were still about, came and went on errands, stood at windows talking to people inside, sat on folding chairs underneath street lamps playing dominoes and *damas*. For a while a woman in native dress walked in front of them. Lilo, out front in his cop car, honked her to one side and pulled around, but the alley was too narrow for the truck to get by her. She had a cylindrical cushion over her cranium and on it a purple plastic basin. With tamales. Wrapped in bright green palm leaf, tied with black thread, stacked under a spread napkin. She moved at a stately saunter framed in the truck's headlights, beaded skirt brushing the cobblestones, arms at her sides. Every few steps she cried languidly, *"Tamal,"* halting now and then to make a sale. At which the truck halted also, full of explosives, and Toro in the cab beside the driver hunched forward so no one outside could see his transceiver and warned Lilo not to get too far ahead.

In time they came out in back of the Palacio. Gray-green stone, narrow windows massively barred, built by people who didn't mind being hated. Huge square in the front, broad facade with heavy columns, block-long row of steps, huge iron doors. Two sentries paced the length of the steps, met at the doors, presented arms to each other, shouldered arms, about-faced, paced toward the corners. Above them a huge flag drooped. Floodlights in the square lit up its colors.

The center of the square was raised six or so feet. Benches at the edges, fountain in the middle. Gato and Toro went up and got litter cans, brought them over, handed them up to Hector. He handed new cans down. The truck moved forward as they went for others. At the far end of the square was the cathedral. Mass was letting out, another would be starting. Lilo drove over there and parked and got out, stretched and stood leaning on the left front fender. The air was getting chilly. Clouds covered the stars. Toro handed a litter can up to Hector, who took it and handed down a new one.

In Linda Vista the script called for banging the cans, being a proper rhino. By then they were on the last lap. They left eleven litter cans near the general's compound and eight others elsewhere around the colonia. Then they descended the switchbacks to the warehouse. Gato and Toro rode in back with Hector.

"I guess the foreplay's over," said the one.

"I guess it is," replied the other.

My radio played boleros and rancheras, mambos and cha-cha-cha, bossa nova and tangos. Below my awareness mainly, like crickets or birdsong, though when "Flores Negras" followed "Por Una Cabeza" I knew the cable was up and that Golden Retriever was on unless canceled later.

My window went dark and I didn't notice, realized only when the intercom buzzed. *La Señora* wanted flowers, said Marco Tulio, I should cut some for her friend to take to her hotel. I said I couldn't do it, I was ill. No lie either. I was sick at heart when I thought of Ellen, sick to my stomach when I thought what I'd done. A woman I would have loved, who might have loved me, and I jobbed her children to a son of a bitch.

I went through the action phase minute by minute, my own part and everyone else's over and over. When I'd done, I played through it again. Time passed, my radio played. When it was time I took the batteries out so the thing wouldn't send an abort signal. When it was time I went downstairs.

*S*ilent night, holy night.

No wind, only a breath of eucalyptus. No moon, a great scatter of stars, very hard, very bright. 0344, H minus 16 minutes.

"Feliz navidad, mi sargento."

"Igualmente."

He had a tabloid, *El Independiente,* spread out on the guardroom table, phone and radio base station pushed to the right. Avelino Grimaldo, age, say, thirty-seven. He looked back down at his paper as soon as he answered.

"¿Todo tranquilo?"

"¿Porque no? Son las tres de la madrugada en Nochebuena." Annoyed at the interruption, at being questioned. *"¿Que haces tú aquí, porque no duermas?"*

"I woke up, then I couldn't get back to sleep."

"You've got a bad conscience."

I stepped back outside. Barely room for two in there, and I could hear Jaime crossing the gravel. He'd been making coffee on the barrack hotplate when I came down.

"Merry Christmas, gardener." Smiling toothily at me—stripeless private, always in good humor.

"Merry Christmas, colonel." That got a big grin. I was glad it wasn't his turn in the tower. That way he had a shot at surviving Retriever. He handed Grimaldo one cup and set one on the table; then he took the third cup up the ladder.

I hung around in the pool of light by the gate. I wanted to be on hand when Top Dog showed. He was ninety meters away on T Street, behind the wheel of the cop car Lilo had been driving—black shirt, black jeans, black nylon photographer's vest, pistol on the empty seat to his right, mammoth C-4 charge in the trunk behind him. Rusty had shaped it to blow to the left and backward. He was higher up on the ridge with Chivo at the estate whose owners were skiing in Vail. Shooter was maybe three minutes out of the cop car, slithering down the street to his fire point.

0349. The house was dark. Pools of light along the wall to my left where it stretched away toward the Barranca. Gato and Toro had spent the afternoon down there, chopping a path through the tangle on its flanks—betel palm, wild teakwood, bracken, vines. Gato tied a rope to the rail where they'd anchored the cable, and he and Toro went down it chopping, hanging by one hand. At the bottom they stepped across the muddy trickle that would be a torrent when the rains came, and chopped their way up to Road Two along a rope Doc had tossed down when he anchored the cable on that side. Then at H minus 90 minutes the three crossed to Linda Vista, carrying a body bag for Target and five sets of harness for the slide.

In Atacalpan army battle dress, U.S. issue from combat boots to olive green kepis, except they had pips instead of bars on their collars—one each for Gato and Toro, two pips for Doc—and Uzi machine pistols slung on their chests. They cached their gear below S Street where the cable was anchored. Then they crept around to their start line under the lip of the Barranca a few yards southeast of where the Culvert emptied.

0355. Shooter was making himself at home. He was forty meters from me against the wall of the property opposite Target's, just this side of the bend in T Street. Getting his left arm through the sling of his Springfield. Rolling onto his belly. Tugging the camouflage netting over his shoulders. Laying crosshairs on the guard in the tower, then on the sentry between him and the gate. Two AK-47s lay in front of him to his left, one for him, one for Top Dog. When he'd done his sniping and Top Dog had blown the car bomb, the two of them would put fire on the gate area to build the sense of threat there and make the defenders forget the garden.

Rusty and Chivo had set up the mortar. When the car bomb blew they'd put fire on Target's compound, air bursts with plastic warheads. Then they'd hit the commandant with real stuff.

0355. Toro was on his way up to do the sentry. The sentry sat over the pipe the Culvert emptied through, shoulders against the wall, feet dangling. I'd seen one sitting that way in an aerial photo, so that's how I imagined him. His weapon lay beside the wall to his right, his right hand lay near the butt plate, his left in his lap. Toro was ten yards below him out of sight, midsection and thighs pressed to the flank of the Barranca. Where he was the slope was almost vertical. Above him it flattened and was clean of cover, brightly lit by overhead arc lamps. Toro would work around to the sentry's right, then go up to the base of the wall beyond where it curved, where the sentry couldn't see him.

Where did Toro get the rage to murder? No doubt he thought of his mother, evicted from their home in Havana with nothing but the clothes she had on her back. Or no doubt he thought of his father, a doctor of law trained at Salamanca, selling ladies' shoes in Coral Gables. I knew exactly how he did it. Toro might have been my younger brother.

0357. Top Dog was into his deployment check. The transceiver was hung on his vest, earphone in his ear, loose cord in a shirt pocket, talk button under his right thumb.

"A-2, this is A-1, over."

"This is A-2, over."

"Are you deployed and ready, over?"

"That's a roger, A-1, locked and loaded."

I walked slowly from the gate to the barrack. I was halfway back when the radio in the guardroom started squawking. Grimaldo came out and hollered up at the man in the tower, "What's going on?"

"Nothing," came the call back, "just a police car."

I strolled away toward the garden, worried that I might have cut it too fine, wanting to hurry up but of course knowing better. Top Dog would roll down to the end of the street. Then he'd make a U and roll back to the gate, lay the car alongside it a yard out.

I stepped around the corner of the house. I stopped there half a second, everything still. Then I ducked back. My first job was to observe the car bomb's effect. Grimaldo went up the ladder, Jaime watching.

Toro strode along the wall to where it curved. He peeked around, the sentry hadn't budged. Toro walked toward him. If he went for his weapon, Toro would shoot him, though shooting was way too good for the useless donkey. Toro stopped a pace from him. The sentry looked up. Toro tasted his terror, then roared him to attention: *"¡Cuadrate, huevón!"*

The sentry jumped all different ways at once. He scrambled up. Toro smiled gravely at him. He put his left arm across the sentry's shoulders in what might have been taken for a fraternal gesture and drew his knife out of the sheath on his thigh. Holding the sentry firmly, he drove his knife, blade horizontal, into the sentry's throat just under the jaw, leaned on it, then raked it outward. A fan of blood sprayed out behind it.

Top Dog got out of the car and shot the gate sentry. I didn't hear him do it, his pistol was silenced. I heard the tower guard's shout, the bang of his handgun, the crack of Shooter's .306. It cracked again—Top Dog was sprinting up T Street—Grimaldo opened up with the M-60. Jackhammer bursts and no answer from the Spring-field. A litter can popped, then light flared and the gate flew back-ward.

Bulged, turned red and blew back like tissue paper. Part of the wall and the base of the tower dissolved. The platform rose straight up, Grimaldo still firing. Then it lay on one side and crashed down on Jaime. Unearthly noise and shock wave, Merry Christmas!

I turned and ran off to find the roving patrol, make sure they weren't around when I blew the Culvert. They were squatting on their heels a few yards off, staring wide-eyed, not sure they were still alive. I squatted down facing the three of them.

"Grimaldo sent me to get you, the radio's down. He wants you at the gate on the double."

They stared at me. A mortar round exploded across T Street. Lit-ter cans popped, I could feel time passing. I was about to grab the nearest one's weapon when another round banged hugely right above us.

I ducked my head though I knew there'd be no shrapnel. The patrol leader bolted past me, taking the other two with him toward the gate. Somebody, Shooter or Top Dog, was spotting for Rusty, but why didn't I hear any AK fire?

Sprint to the orchard. Found where I'd buried the charge, put a thick tree between us, reached around with the radio thing and blew it. Considerable crunch, dirt flew by on both sides, clods falling like hail through the tree branches. Where I'd dug was now a funnel-shaped crater six feet across. At the bottom the Culvert pipe was open.

A rifle cracked off to my left, then cracked again. I turned as it cracked a third time and saw a lamp at the top of the wall go out. Two more shots, and the wall along T Street was dark, five lamps with five shots. A mortar burst over the house, still dark behind me. Another burst ten seconds later. Then I heard automatic rifle fire. Then I saw Gato's hand at the crater bottom.

"E-3, this is A-1, what the fuck's keeping you, over?"

"This is E-3, I ran into the other sentry. I'm on my way again, where are you, over?"

The earphone plug was out of Gato's transceiver. I could hear Top Dog and Toro. Gato got to his feet and unbuckled the strap on his ankle. He pulled the body bag out of the pipe and handed it up. Then he took my hand and pulled himself out.

"The police car's upside-down in front of the gate. I'm behind it, shake ass. If you make it you win a Kalashnikov, over."

"Wilco, A-1, over."

"Okay, E-3, out."

"Shooter's hit," said Gato. "Top Dog's called Toro around to the T Street side."

Doc crawled out of the pipe and stood up in the crater. A mortar shell went off. Assault rifles rattled over by the gate.

"A-1, this is E-1, over."

Doc was calling Top Dog. I could hear him live and over Gato's transceiver. Then silence. Assault rifle fire from over by the gate.

"A-1, this is E-1, do you read me, over?"

"This is A-1, over."

"E-2 and I are inside Target's perimeter and have rendezvous'd with P for Penetrator, over."

"Okay, E-1. Let me talk to P, over?"

Bursts of AK fire behind Top Dog's voice. Gato handed me his transceiver. I pushed the talk button. "This is P, over."

"Status of Target's defense force, over."

"Three casualties in the blast, over."

"What about the guys patrolling inside the wall, over?"

"Bugged to the gate, I think. They're not in the garden, over."

"Put E-1 back on, over."

I nodded at Doc and handed the transceiver back to Gato.

"This is E-1, over."

"Grab Target and get the fuck out of there! Out."

Running between rows of shrubs, Doc and Gato behind me. Light from the lamps above the wall to our left scattered our faint shadows on the flowers. Small arms burped to our front. A mortar shell boomed and split the sky above us.

The house showed light at an upper-story window. I ran along the hedge then onto the terrace. A light gleamed beyond the glass door at the back of the living room.

"Should be unlocked," I said in Spanish.

"Vamos a ver," said Doc. He slid the door back. I led him and Gato in and to the stairway. Somewhere above *La Señora* said, *"¡Nos ata-*

can!" Then a mortar shell thundered. After it, Target moaned, "Oh, God! Oh, God!" Then, "What's the matter, Diana? Can't you make them see someone's trying to kill me?"

I led the way upward. On the landing Doc drew beside me. We went up the second flight together, Gato right behind. *La Señora* and Target were huddled on the top step. She was listening on a cordless phone.

"Señora," I said, *"estos oficiales han venido para llevar el señor a un lugar seguro."*

"What's he saying, Diana? Who are these men?"

Doc stepped ahead of me, clicked his heels, and saluted. "Señor Haft. An attempt against you is in progress. My orders are to convey you to the commandant's residence at once for your safety." He spoke slowly with lengthened vowel sounds: "ráy-zee-dance."

"Thank God!" said Target. He got up and stepped over Diana's legs down the stairs. I turned and went past Gato down to the landing.

"Are you sure you should go, Edgar?"

"What are you talking about, Diana?"

"He must, señora," said Doc. "I have my orders."

"What about me and the servants?"

"I can take only one person and my orders are to take Señor Haft. Your guards are holding the gate and have been reinforced. Another patrol is on the way."

"We're wasting time!" said Target. He went down past Doc, past me and Gato. "Come on!"

La Señora called, "Juan!"

I half turned and looked back at her. Her face was gray with anxiety. Mine, I guess, was gray with guilt. Gato took my arm and drew me downstairs.

"Wait a minute!"

We were in the garden, headed back to the hole in the Culvert, Gato in front, Uzi at the ready. Target was right behind him, then me, then Doc. Moving at a fast walk, which seemed about top speed for Target, but now he had stopped and was looking back at Doc.

"Where are we going?"

"As I said, señor, to the commandant's residence."

"But . . ." A big blast rumbled higher up on the ridge. Rusty had blown the charge he'd put under the manhole. Target turned some more and looked back at the house. Gato and I had turned and were looking at him.

"There's a fight at the gate, señor," Doc said. "We are going to take you out another way."

"What's he doing here?" Target pointed at me.

"He suspects something," Gato said in Spanish. "Sharp instincts, or he couldn't have swiped all that money."

Target spun toward Gato, then spun back. "What's he saying about me?"

"We can't stand here, señor."

"Wait a minute! Show me something that says you're from the commandant!"

"Very well, señor. I have my orders."

Gato was slinging his weapon when Doc nodded. Gato stepped in and spun Target, pinning his arms. Doc got a Syrette from his breast pocket. He pulled the needle guard off and hit Target's bicep through his shirt.

Target squealed. Doc clapped a hand over his mouth. Target thrashed and tried to bite him. Then he slumped. In a few seconds we were on our way again, Gato still leading. Doc and I hauling

Target by his belt and arms. Mortar shells were exploding higher up the ridge.

"Make better time like this anyway," said Gato.

Dank in the Culvert pipe and dusty also. From the explosion. I got into it feet first to help Doc get Target in, zipped in the body bag. Then I had to crawl backward. Gato had gone first. When I started crawling I felt him pulling the line. It ran below me between my knees and hands. Took an hour for me to crawl through, I don't like confined places. Began to get panicky and claustrophobic, queasy I'd get left behind. The others would go; I'd be stuck in Atacalpa.

Total bullshit, Top Dog never left anyone, never headed for home till all were present. No one just accounted for, everyone there! The dead went home along with the fit and the wounded, and there was a story about when a guy lost a foot, Top Dog sent a patrol for it and didn't take off till the lost foot was on the chopper. I was scared I'd be left because I wanted to stay. Just about when that came to me, Gato grabbed my ankle. I scrambled out and helped him pull Target.

The three of us lugged the body bag with Target. Gato and Doc had hold of the loops at his shoulders, I had his feet. Along the lip of the Barranca. At the corner of the wall we ran into Top Dog with Shooter on his back in the fireman's carry, Shooter's Springfield in his free hand. I heard small-arms fire up the street behind him.

"You guys lead," he said, "you know where the slide's anchored. Shooter took an M-sixty round and he's got to go on it, but we're short a rig."

"I'll stay," I said as Top Dog fell in behind me. The words were out before I knew I'd said them.

"Fuck that," said Gato, "you've been here for months already."

"Exactly right, I know my way around."

"His wife saw you with us, Carlos, you're probably compromised."

"So what? I'll get other ID, I have One-One's network."

"Carlos is right!" growled Top Dog. "Shut up and shake ass!"

We moved along the lip of the Barranca, between it and the next compound's wall. Ahead, at the top of the ridge, mortar rounds were air-bursting.

At the cable we set Target down. Gato went to get the harnesses for the slide, rigs that went on like parachutes—straps at the crotch and over the shoulders—with a pulley-wheel dingus that clamped over the cable. Doc and I eased Shooter down from Top Dog's shoulders. He was breathing deeply and quickly through his nose. His eyes were open, but he didn't look at us. He was in lots of pain and had withdrawn into himself to fight it there. Doc bent over him.

"The entrance wound's in the back of his right shoulder," Top Dog said. "The exit wound's at the point of his right hip."

"Things will start getting better quickly," Doc told Shooter. "You're no more than ten minutes from morphine. There's plasma on the chopper and whole blood on the yacht. I can operate there if surgery's needed."

Gato came back with the rigs. "Where's the line?" Top Dog asked him. "Carlos and I will bug out through the Barranca."

"Right here below the cable." Gato showed us.

"Give me the burp gun," Top Dog told Gato. "You take Shooter's Springfield. If you drop it in the gorge, better jump right in after it." He looked down at Doc. "Hook up and get out of here. I'm going back to cover Toro's withdrawal." He turned to me. "Grab Doc's gun and Shooter's transceiver and come along."

Top Dog wheeled and ran off back toward T Street. I caught up
with him at the corner of Target's wall. He shot out the light above
it with the Uzi. "Got the other five with five shots." He grinned,
baring his teeth. "If we were back on the island you'd owe me a
quarter. Stay here. Let me know when our guys are off this ridge.
And watch out Target's guards don't crawl through the Culvert and
get on our rear."

He trotted up T Street. After a bit I heard him on the transceiver
telling Toro to fall back while he gave covering fire. Then I heard
his Uzi, *burp, burp, burp*. Then Toro ran by and sprinted for S Street.

Silence. I couldn't see the spot where the cable was anchored, but
after a bit I heard Doc.

"S-3, this is E-1, over."

"This is S-3, over."

I looked out over the Barranca. Senior's down-east baa came
from out there.

"We're about set to come across. Are you ready, over?"

"Affirmative E-1. Let me give you some light, over."

Headlights came on to the left of where I'd been looking.

*"E-2 will lead. We've a casualty in the two slot. Then Target, then me,
then E-3, over."*

"Roger, E-1, come ahead, over."

"Okay, S-3, out."

I imagined Gato hooking onto the cable, clamping the pulley so
he wouldn't leave prematurely. I imagined Toro and Doc getting
Shooter hooked on. Then I imagined them hooking the body bag.
Then I waited. Not enough light to see the cable itself. It was very
quiet. Then I heard an engine growling behind me.

"P, this is A-1, over."

"This is P, over."

"Those guys off yet, over?"

"Not yet, over."

"Ever seen a Saladin armored car, over?"

I was wondering whether Top Dog wanted an answer when I saw a form sail left to right toward the headlights. Then another, then another, sailing through air.

"They're off!" I called, forgetting to say "over."

"Good deal! On my way back, out!"

I turned and ran up the street a few steps to cover him. He came down along the wall on the opposite side and took off toward S Street. As I sprinted after him I saw a flash up T Street and heard a cannon, saw flashes and heard a machine gun spurt.

Top Dog hit the dirt where the cable was anchored and went down the knotted line Gato had tied. I followed. In thirty feet or so we were in complete darkness. Top Dog stopped a few feet below that.

"S-1, this is A-1, over. S-1, this is A-1, over."

"This is S-1, over."

"We're done on Linda Vista. I'm in the Barranca. I've got P with me, he missed the slide. How should we withdraw, over?"

"Wait one," said One-One. Somewhere above men were shouting.

"A-1, come up to Road Two and I'll collect you. In twenty minutes. But I don't want P with you. He's liable to be hot, and I have no clothes for him. Have him . . . Have him follow the stream at the bottom to the southeast—that's his left, upstream. Almost eight hundred meters, about a klick walking. He'll come out on Road Two a hundred meters or so south of where it meets Road One. Someone he knows will meet him there in an hour with good ID. Have him wait in the brush on his side of the road. Over."

"Roger, S-1, over."

"See you in awhile, over."

"Roger, S-1, out."

"Get that?" asked Top Dog.

"Got it."

From then on we went carefully and slowly, putting no weight on the line in case someone on top found it and cut it. We were on the bottom soon enough. Down there one could see nothing. We felt our way along the line to where it was tied to the line running up to Road Two. We waded the stream. The upward slope began a step beyond it. Top Dog kept his hand on the line and turned around. I couldn't see him but could feel him a yard or so off.

"Carlos?"

"Yes, Colonel."

Silence. Then, "Thanks for giving Shooter your place on the slide."

"You don't get to thank me. I didn't do it for you."

"Fuck you, Fuertes." His bared-teeth grin was in his voice.

"Fuck you, Ape."

The stream was never more than ankle deep but full of slippery rocks in assorted sizes. I went slowly, slower than I had to, stopping, staying a bit, moving on, stopping.

Think of a man waking up after long sleep the first day in many when he can take things easy. He's been on a tough job or on a hard journey. The job or the journey ends, he has a long sleep, then he begins the next part of his life, taking his time getting up on that first morning. Stares at the ceiling, pulls himself up out of bed, sits on the edge, stands, pulls on his trousers. Recollections and snatches of dreams come to him. He sighs, scratches his head, lets them sort out.

In a bit I found myself smiling in the dark. I looked up, but there were no stars—clouds, or maybe the overhang of the Barranca. I thought of my father. What I got for doing Retriever was a chance to start over at a tougher level. Nealy, too, would have liked it. What did I tell you, Tommy? That I wouldn't do a snatch in Atacalpa, too much downside.

I walked on, following the stream, smiling in the dark.

GLASS MOUNTAIN

*"H*e's a businessman, new style."

"What does that mean, professor?"

"In the seventies cocaine caught on with affluent gringos. Wall Street wizards, sports stars, fashion models. But the United States is a democratic society. What the beautiful people prefer finds its way to the masses. Crack is the Model T of chemical happiness."

Cruz spread his arms and paused to let note-takers scribble, though the balcony was tiny and we were alone—drenched in brilliant sunlight, perked by cool air, 0720 the morning after Retriever.

"Supplying the U.S. mass market is a big challenge. One response has been airlift via a chain of strips in Central America. Coming this way avoids a long leg across the Caribbean and permits larger payloads. It also circumvents the South Florida bottleneck, opens the whole Gulf Coast from Brownsville to Tampa. And of course there's a local market here—limited, it's true, but money is money. So a vibrant industry comes to Atacalpa."

"He's in it?"

Cruz held up his hand like a traffic warden: "Wait." Seven stories down the swimming pool shimmered between ranks of white wooden chaise longues.

"Another springs up to employ the first industry's profits, cocaine dollars looking for honest employment. Our economy isn't large but we do our bit. The money-washing business has arrived also."

He reached down and picked his cup from the plastic-topped table, sipped, sipped again, and looked at me calmly till it was clear I wouldn't interrupt. Then he went on.

"Meanwhile, civil wars are in progress. Vigorously in Salvador and Nicaragua, on and off in Guatemala and here. They support a thriving weapons traffic that makes use of clandestine airstrips and employs cocaine dollars. He's in cocaine, money-washing, and weapons."

"How?"

"As managing partner for a group of investors. He's connected to the cartels. He's connected to funny banks in Panama. He's connected to Israeli weapons dealers."

I was staying at the Crillon as Richard Engel, one of two identities Nico had for me when he picked me up on Road Two on Christmas morning an hour into the withdrawal phase of Golden Retriever. I crouched in the brush while the Wanderer rolled by, while it made a U and rolled back toward me. Then I stepped out on the shoulder and hopped inside. Engel, a travel agent from Kansas City, had arrived in Atacalpa three days before and had a flight out to Houston later that morning. Also available was Gabriel Anaya, local hewer of wood and drawer of water, in case Nico and I got stopped on the way to El Carmen. Shooter's transceiver and pistol went out the window. Reyes's ID card went up in smoke. Engel's passport went under the floor mat, along with his ticket and money and my two Syrettes. It was just getting light. No one was on the spur where the cable was anchored, but where the road bent northwest toward the center of town soldiers were stopping traffic in both directions, scanning people's papers under flashlights. Gabriel Anaya's caused no stir.

In El Carmen I showered and shaved my moustache, put on a suit, left a note where One-One would find it. I had Nico drop me beside the Camino Real where months before he'd first collected me. I walked through the bar and lobby and out the front door and took a taxi to the Crillon, letting the driver drag me all over town padding the meter. The sun was up, the city awash in soldiers, but no one was looking for Richard Engel. I checked in, had breakfast, went to sleep.

One-One came by at dusk. Ill-humored. Wouldn't take a beer. Wouldn't even sit down until I pressed him. His victory high was over. He hadn't slept. He'd driven to Tiltenango, driven back, seen to leaving the warehouse and safe houses traceless. Didn't like me missing my flight. Liked it even less that I'd missed it on purpose. West Point, after all: for them orders are orders, and besides he was sweating the withdrawal, aware we could get nabbed if the bad guys got lucky, while I (the fuck knew why!) was prolonging it need-lessly.

"I have to talk to you. I didn't know how I'd reach you if I left Atacalpa."

"Talk."

"I need your network here, part of it anyway."

"What for? You're flying out tomorrow morning."

"I'm coming back, next week at the latest."

"What's this about?"

"Some months back I stole a woman's children."

"I heard you were in that business. So what?"

"They're here. I'm going to steal them back."

Before I got much farther he decided I'd jeopardized the mission, put private goals before it and my teammates. Which stung. I was bonded pretty tightly to those bastards.

"What was I supposed to do? Quit when I learned the op was in this country just because I knew a guy from here?"

"You should have told us."

"Tantamount to quitting. You and Top Dog would have thought I had cold feet. As for stealing the kids back, I decided that at five o'clock this morning. I'd forgotten the thing, put it from my mind. Then their mother showed up here. She had tea at Target's yesterday afternoon."

"Did she see you?"

"No."

"What about Oliveira?"

"Once. He looked right through me. I could have said something at the briefing when I learned he was an associate of Target's, but I didn't want to lose my slot in the mission. Which, by the way, if you haven't noticed, worked. And I was straighter with you than you were with me. I never got you locked up in Robledo."

For a second I thought he'd come back at me. Then, all at once, he was his old self again, sheepish grin and twinkle. "Won't you even offer a guy a beer?"

I had bottles in the sink under cracked ice. I got two out and uncapped them and brought them back.

"What do you need?" he asked me. "I can't let you keep the passport, it's just to get out of here. I got it from DOD, and it's got to go back."

"I don't need it. I do need a passport for the woman and kids— the name and number of someone who can supply it and you as a reference. Any English-speaking country. U.S. or Commonwealth would be best."

One-One took out his notebook and wrote in it, tore out the page and handed it to me. "What else?"

"I need to keep tabs on the mother while I'm away. I need to begin finding out about Oliveira. That's short term. When I'm back here I'll work out the rest. What I need most is someone like you, a guy who knows this place and can arrange anything."

"Thanks for the compliment, but I'm not staying. How will you do it?"

"No idea."

We sipped beer. Then One-One asked, "Why?"

"Yesterday, when I saw her . . . Look, I shouldn't have taken them in the first place. This morning, walking out to meet Nico, it came to me I'm going to get them back. That's as far as I've gotten. But planning is planning. You look at the thing from all sides and something suggests itself. Sooner or later. You have to have faith."

"And time, which you may not have. If someone fingers you as Target's gardener . . ."

"Worrying about that won't help me get those kids back."

One-One said nothing.

"What scares me most right now is facing the mother."

"Fell for her, didn't you?"

"It shows?"

"Oh, yes. That's why I'm not trying to talk you out of it. You could tell the wrong people a lot about Golden Retriever."

"The only name I can give them is Top Dog's. Anyway . . ."

"I know. A man's got to do what a man's got to do."

"Did you get Claudio clear?"

"He left this morning."

"Good. Then I won't worry. So, what do you say, will you help?"

"Sure." He put the empty bottle on the table and got up. He looked very weary. "Nico will take you to the airport tomorrow. He'll bring someone by here first, around oh seven hundred. Then someone else will ride out to the airport with you. The man you meet here can tell you about Oliveira. Don't offer him money. The other man can help as a business arrangement. He can do all kinds of things. Both dislike the people who run this country." He smiled wanly and shook his head. "The beer may have been a mistake, I still have things to do."

"Thanks for the help, Colonel."

"I'll throw in a couple of maps. They may come in handy." He grinned and laid a finger alongside his nose. "Take care."

Cruz came by on schedule the next morning. The front desk called to announce him, but the penny didn't drop till I saw his face.

"Professor!"

He stood blinking, then smiled in recognition, but was discreet enough to come in and let me shut the door before speaking.

"Carlos Fuertes. How is your brother, Camilo?"

I was impressed. I was ten or eleven when a group of men brought him to meet my father—not an uncommon thing with prominent visitors in the days when my father was president of the assembly and the coming man in the country. The next time I saw him my father had been dead a year. Cruz was in town for a conference and came to pay his respects to my mother. Four years later, in Chilpanzango, he watched me play tennis. Mind more like a pol's than a professor's.

I called him professor on my father's advice, not that I ever heard my father address him. "Professor is a loftier title than doctor," my father said once, apropos of someone else to whom both applied. "When Einstein and Freud corresponded that's what they used. 'Dear Professor Freud,' 'Dear Professor Einstein.'" Cruz looked the professor too: rumpled seersucker, silver goatee. I didn't pick up on the reference to my brother. How to explain no contact with him in years? I'd had coffee sent up. I took the tray out on the balcony— plastic chairs and a plastic-topped table, just room for us two.

"Is Richard Engel joining us, or is that you?"

"For the moment, Professor."

He looked at me and nodded. Then he told me about Antonio Oliveira.

"Nothing new-style to dealing in weapons, Professor."

"Don't be too sure. His group buys for use here as well as sale elsewhere. Guess what's being airdropped near our Indian villages: booby-trapped toys the Soviets make for their war in Afghanistan."

"*¡Hijo de puta!*"

"Exactly. But novelty of product line isn't the main point. The main point is that his partners run this country. Command the army, direct the police, control the means of communication. Manage the economy, administer the justice system. That gives them a novel edge, wouldn't you say? It's not a question of corrupt officials, or of criminals with influence on high. The men who run the country are principals in a diversified criminal enterprise doing hundreds of millions of dollars each year. That's the new style: government of, by, and for criminal entrepreneurs. In your country too, Carlos."

"Professor, I haven't been there for years and years."

Cruz looked away toward the mountains beyond Chilpanzango. Instantly I felt stupid. To Cruz, I was sure, as to my father,
a person with no sense of duty toward his country—of continu-
ing obligation, continually discharged, to nurture and improve as
well as defend it—was an idiot. My father, in fact, had instructed
Camilo and me on the word's etymology: idiot, a mental defec-
tive, from the Greek *idios*, a private person who doesn't participate in his community. How stupid! Years and years an idiot,
concerned with no one but myself, no country and no family
either.

"How come you know this, Professor?"

"No choice, I'm afraid. This is a small country, and I have the
habit of inquiry. It's an open secret that Colonel Tovar and others
in power are professional criminals. Open secrets are safe in a police
state. Most people avert their eyes, but I have bad habits. As for
Oliveira, we're of the same class. My wife and his mother were
school friends. One of his uncles married one of my cousins. We
belong to the same club, see the same urologist."

"Which club is that, Professor?"

"The country club. Where they held the open you played in. But
tell me, will he be kidnapped like Mr. Haft?"

Yes, I said to myself, that might just happen. "What's the take on
Mr. Haft, Professor?"

"It's an open secret that the Americans did it, but the government blames it on a dissident group. I assume you took part, along
with the gentleman who arranged this meeting. Are you in the
American service, Carlos?"

"No, Professor. I was for a time but not now. And my business with Oliveira isn't political, though it's possible I may cause him some inconvenience."

"The more the better as far as I'm concerned. But the gentleman said you were flying out this morning."

"I am, but I'll be back."

"As Engel?"

"No, Professor, as a man called Austerlitz, or Borodino."

Cruz nodded. "I hope someday you'll be in your own country with your own name."

"So do I, Professor, so do I."

 2   *"I*'ll do him myself."

Tuñón sat twisted around looking back at me. Traffic oozed along the Paseo de los Invictos carrying us with it. He, Nico, and I were in a station wagon, one of three cars I had just rented as Engel. The other two were a commonplace sedan and a luxury model, flea- and rhinomobiles.

"The beginnings of a pattern is plenty," I told him. "If you get his usual day and evening, terrific. But not at the expense of making him nervous."

"Since yesterday morning everybody's nervous."

"You don't want this one to catch you on his tail. His business partner is your Colonel Tovar."

Tuñon nodded. *"Ya veo."*

"Documentos," said Nico.

Tuñón twisted around and faced front. I looked between him and Nico. White-gloved policemen stood between the lanes, stopping cars, saluting, checking papers. Beyond, in the plaza, soldiers in combat rig lounged about, thumbs in the slings of their rifles.

"I'm the gringoest gringo on earth," I said. "Can't speak or understand a word of Spanish. Here." I tapped Tuñón's left shoulder with Engel's passport. "You be my keeper. I couldn't fart without you to interpret."

White-gloved hand held out at waist level, deferential salute. *"Sus documentos, por favor, caballeros."* Great show of respect here on the boulevard, worlds away from the *retén* at Cedral. No one was looking for Engel today either. In a minute we were on our way. Past the plaza we picked up the airport highway.

"What about the woman?" Tuñón twisted around and handed the passport back. He'd been in the car when I came out of the Crillon. Early forties, hook nose, olive complexion. His business card said "Research & Translations." His physical assurance and seen-it-all air said he'd been a plainclothes cop at some juncture.

I reached into my jacket and took out an envelope with the Crillon logo. Wrote on it, handed it over, he read aloud. *"Ellen Gonders, norteaméricana, ojos verdes, pelo casteño."*

"Oliveira's ex-wife. As of yesterday she was at the Fenix. Don't lose track of her, but be careful. There's little if any risk of her spotting a tail, and nothing she could do if she did spot it, but Oliveira might be having her watched. It wouldn't do if his watchers spotted yours."

"Why? I mean, why would he tail her? If you don't mind my asking."

"It's a reasonable question." I thought for a moment. "He took things from her. She'd like them back. He may want to know what she's up to, who her allies are if she has any. He may want to dissuade her, make her go away. All I need is for you not to lose track of her. Exactly what she does isn't important. So if he's having her watched, your people should be behind his. You want somebody invisible on her base, and somebody invisible tailing her loosely. Women might work."

"I know some smart kids. Street kids."

"Excellent! No one pays any attention to them. Are they trained?"

"Enough. And I'll have a woman too, you're right about that."

"Over forty, ill-tempered, ugly."

"Worse." He returned my grin with a seen-it-all one of his own.

"Get what you can of his pattern, keep track of her. And look into penetrating the country club. See if you know someone who works there, or if someone you know knows someone. My main area of interest is tennis. And, can I become a temporary member?"

"I think the Camino Real has a plan where guests can have use of the facilities."

"Check that, please. Also, we'll probably need a discreet place to entertain someone. Find something appropriate and when I call give me the name of the agents. I'll wire them three months' rent and have them leave the keys with a hotel concierge. That way no one can trace it back to you. And find me a pilot, one who will take four passengers over the border. Same way, find the man and let me make contact. Here." I handed him another Crillon envelope, got out a plastic pen and handed it to him. "Put down all the numbers where I can reach you."

Tuñón wrote and handed the pen and envelope back. I went into my shirt pocket, took out hundreds, counted some off. "That do for now?"

He nodded and took the money.

"How do I get you, Nico? Do you have a number?" We were in the circle at Macagüita, coming up on the international terminal.

"Negativo, señor. Call El Presidente and ask for the taxi line. Everyone knows me."

"A few days, then. Remember, when you see me, I can't speak Spanish."

Two document checks between curb and ticket counter, three more between ticket counter and gate. Uniformed cops backed up by thugs in civvies, all flights delayed due to security measures.

Tiny departure lounge, tiny green plastic chairs. People kept coming through the door on the left. No one came to open the door on the right. A baby squalled. A quintet of teenaged androgynes for Jesus clutched their Bibles and brayed a mantraish chant. A gentleman wedged in beside me opened a tabloid, but I mustn't peek, no truck with the tongue of Cervantes. A six-year-old wandered by brushing my knee, twanging my nerves in tune with Ellen's anguish. Were they frightened? Were they sick? Was someone harming them? Instead of pinching it off I tasted it carefully. Wormwood. That was how her life had tasted for months. Should share it instead of sweating my own safety.

Airborne I did. When the final thug handed Engel's passport back to me, when I went up the ramp, when the plane began moving, when it shrugged free of the runway, I felt wonderfully eased but refused to enjoy it. Instead I worked myself into Ellen's skin.

Fist in the face, they were gone! Piercing pang, the school bus wouldn't be stopping! Evenings not drawing their bath, not fixing their dinner. Nights twisting in worry and self-reproach. Are they frightened? Are they sick? Is someone harming them? Why wasn't I careful? Why didn't I suspect? And the weariness of telling the story over, the loneliness of knowing no one cared. That's how I spent the flight to Houston.

There it turned out that Denver was having a blizzard. Airport closed until tomorrow at least. I found a good hotel and took a suite and had a manicure along with a haircut, reflecting that Texas was used to fellows like me, coming in from the wilds and getting cleaned up, cowboys and miners as well as for-rent *pistoleros*—though my manicure and haircut, and my suite too, were because I was going back to Atacalpa. I didn't want to look or feel like Juan Reyes.

After the barber's I called the number One-One had given me. A woman with an interesting voice said she could do British. Kendall, who kept good files and kept them forever, arranged for the photos Oliveira had provided of Ellen Gonders and her children to go to the woman with the interesting voice. I called an investigative service Carl Marengo subscribed to and asked them to find out what property Antonio Oliveira had in the United States. Then I pushed the sitting room chairs against the wall and put the coffee table up on the sofa and had a workout. After that I did my breathing and meditation. After that I showered and went downstairs and had dinner. When I came back up I called my brother.

I didn't plan it. My plan when I came back upstairs was to watch some TV and get caught up on current events. The last event I'd heard of was Reagan's reelection, and I might need fresher information. But when I reached for the remote on the sofa end table, my hand picked up the telephone receiver instead, my finger dialed "O," my voice asked the hotel operator for information in what had been my country. Just like that. I assume I had pondered the action unconsciously.

My brother came on the line at the third or fourth ring. I knew his voice at once, though I hadn't heard it in, God! maybe twelve years. At which I panicked. I almost hung up, but he said, *"Digame"* again, and I said, "Camilo?" In a questioning tone, although I knew it was him.

"Carlos," he said. No question in his voice. Then he sensed my fear and said, *"No me cierras."*

"I won't," I said. Both of us waited. I heard my breathing, or maybe it was his.

Then he said, "You're alive."

I didn't have to be. My brother Camilo's belief system is elastic. It could accommodate a call from the dead. After a beat I said, "Yes. Yes I am. I don't really know why I called. Maybe something to do with a man I met this morning. He was in our house years ago, he knew our parents."

"Are you coming home, Carlos?"

"Yes," I said. "Yes, I am." I hadn't thought about it till he asked me. When I made the call I had no home to go to.

"I've a job to do," I said. "When it's done I'll come home."

"Good," said Camilo.

"Is Clara . . ."

"Clara is married, has kids. I'm married, have kids. Including a boy called Carlos."

We both waited. I heard his breathing, or maybe it was mine. "I was dead, Camilo."

"I know," Camilo said. "I felt it."

I made it to Denver on Thursday but not until evening. The next morning I got Austerlitz and Borodino out of the bank vault and mailed Richard Engel back to the Pentagon. Then I took an airplane to Miami and another to an island in the British West Indies with the bank that had my Golden Retriever money. I had a whole weekend to wait until it opened, so I took a suite in a place that had tennis courts.

Three pros there, and at dawn I was on with the youngest, a local boy with a compact underspin game like the Frenchmen I sometimes played with in Southeast Asia. There was also a girl from somewhere in the States. I hit with her when the local boy was tired, then I hit with him again after lunch. Nothing wrong with my wind, thanks to Top Dog and Senior. I stayed on all day Saturday, except for an hour signing for stuff in the pro shop, tennis stuff and some golf clubs. Golf bag too, the biggest they had, and a two-wheeled cart to trundle it around in.

The head tennis pro was a Brit who'd been ranked at one time and who preened as if he'd won Wimbledon, though maybe he was all right and it was me. Sometimes I put men off by my presence, convey the equivalent of a threat or an insult to receptors the cortex doesn't process. I was thinking a lot about Ellen, the pain she was feeling, and laying it off on Oliveira, generating lots of anger. Maybe the Brit sensed hostility and was put off. Anyway, after lunch on Sunday, having spent the morning wearing the boy and girl out, I asked if he would play a set with me—as a paid lesson, of course, but keeping score.

"Sorry, old fruit. Don't play sets with hackers. Hit the ball with you all day, though, if you like."

I'd have made him play by betting I could beat him, but I hadn't much cash. I just smiled and said fine. He made the mistake of taking the first court, putting us on display to his junior colleagues and the folks coming in to play or finishing up. Within ten minutes I had him in a match. De facto, we weren't scoring, but that made no difference. I began putting sting on the ball, running for everything, lacing shots down the line, lacing shots crosscourt. He was over forty and not in good shape, and though his play was levels above mine, he couldn't keep the rallies going without taking me seriously, and had to hit winners to get a chance to rest. It was better than playing a set. He'd have beat me 6-1 or 6-2, and that would have been that. This way, I just smiled and enjoyed the workout till he ran out of gas and "remembered" a meeting. Meanwhile my strokes picked up a lot of polish.

Monday was New Year's Eve, but the banks were open. I got a chunk of my bounty in cash and took an airplane to Kingston and another to Panama. My suite there had stateside cable TV. From it I learned over coffee the next morning that fugitive financier C. Edgar Haft had been apprehended by treasury agents in a motel in San Juan, Puerto Rico, where he was sleeping off a heroin binge. After breakfast Charles Borodino flew to Chilpanzango, where Carleton Austerlitz had a room at the Camino Real. It was Tuesday, January 1, 1985.

I'd called Tuñón every evening. He and Nico were outside customs when I came through. Nico's Mayan face tipped nothing, but I could tell from Tuñón's that we had trouble. He was going to tell me, but I shook him off. I sat in the back while Nico loaded my tennis and golf stuff, while he started up and headed off toward town.

"Okay, tell me," I said, but I still wasn't ready. Ellen Gonders was missing.

3 "Seven to nine weekday mornings, that's when he's scheduled. In practice he's on the court around seven ten, dressed and on his way by eight forty, eight fifty."

"What does he have on when he gets to the club? Where does he put on his tennis stuff, at home or there?"

"He keeps tennis clothes at the club, they have a laundry. He changes before his game and changes back after. When he leaves the club, he goes straight to his office."

"How?"

"Three Japanese four-bys, the biggest they make: this year's model, forest green, opaque windows. He varies which one he rides in, what place in the convoy."

"When I saw him he was driving a sports car."

"Since I've been on him he goes everywhere in convoy. Each vehicle has a bodyguard and a driver, so normally his escort is six. Today his children went with him. They have their own guard, so today the escort was seven."

"Armed how?"

"The bodyguards have handguns in shoulder holsters. I assume the drivers carry the same. And other stuff in the vehicles, that's the style here, Uzis and shotguns."

I put the thing on pause and thought for a minute. The number of guards didn't matter, I decided. Or how they were armed. They'd obey Oliveira's orders or they wouldn't. I was betting he ran a tight operation.

"Do the children go in convoy also?"

"When they leave Los Delfines, but they haven't left often. Three times in six days, always to the country club. On Saturday and Sunday they went at ten thirty. Oliveira went out early to play tennis and sent the four-bys back for them. Today they all went together around eleven, I guess because last night was New Year's Eve. Other than that they've stayed in the *colonia*. There's a jungle gym and swings, the brochure has a picture. I haven't tried to get in, you advised discretion."

Mint iced tea for one on the country club terrace, microcassette recorder with earphone plugged in. I sat facing west, getting the premium vista. The golf course had been laid out (a bilingual card told me) to take advantage of Chilpanzango's surroundings, in this case a volcano, extinct yet impressive, high enough to have some snow on top. I looked past the first tee and out the fairway toward an oblong green backed by white sandtraps, blue-green pines at attention left and right. Above, the monster hulked hugely, a somber presence, while the show-off sun, who'd just done a header behind it, splashed the sky with purple, crimson, and gold.

I'd taped myself debriefing Tuñón and associates—in the wagon on the way in from the airport, on a back street near the cathedral, in my suite at the Camino Real—one cassette for the surveillance of Ellen, another for the ditto of Oliveira. Not enough neurons to memorize the whole business, and minor details could fix or nix my plan. Decanted the Q&A into cassettes and was sipping it now.

"What about getting in?"

"Not easy. There's a four-meter wall around the whole *colonia* patrolled inside and out, and only one gate, with guards on duty twenty-four hours. Residents and employees have *colonia* ID, visitors and deliveries are cleared by telephone. I'd tail a maid on her way home and then romance her. Or give her money. Or romance her and give her money both. To clear me in when I showed up delivering something. Oliveira has his own compound with its own wall. His partner, Arnaldo Ramirez, has a house inside it next to Oliveira's."

The tape ran on, hissing. Then my voice came again. "Okay, the club. Have you got someone there? From what you said before it sounds like you do."

"The son of a woman I know works there as a busboy. He gave me names. One turned out to be perfect, a locker room attendant, an Indian named Amador, that's his first name. In the right place and will do whatever we ask him."

"Why?"

"The village where he was born was wiped out entirely. All the houses torched, little thatch-roof *ranchos*. All the people killed and thrown down a ravine. He didn't tell me about it, I knew on my own. I collect things like that, for later on when these shits fall from power. I asked him where he was from and he wouldn't tell me. Funny how a thing like that makes you ashamed. Of having survived, of not doing something to stop it, as if he could have."

The tape ran on, hissing. Tuñón cleared his throat. "Anyway, when he finally said where and I knew the story, it established me in his eyes. Who I asked about sealed it. He knows Oliveira is in with the top shits. He gave me his pattern, his morning game with Roldan, the tennis pro. And while Oliveira is out there, Amador keeps him under loose surveillance. I'm giving him money, of course, but he'd help for nothing."

"Good. See if he can find out if Oliveira will be there tomorrow."

"He already has. I had him take a peek at Roldan's appointment sheet. The time is blocked every weekday through the eleventh. Seven till nine, Antonio Oliveira."

"I need to talk to Amador tonight."

"I know where he lives."

"I need to see the club too. When does Oliveira leave there?"

"I've no pattern for him when he's with the children, but I'll get word when the four-bys clear the gate."

"How will you know he's on board?"

"I'll call out there and ask for him."

Tuñón got word around four, and I came straight out. With racket case and sports tote, golf bag and cart, in lizard polo shirt and canary trousers and aviator shades to hide my worry. Flashed my hotel key and signed "Carleton T. Austerlitz" in a hardwood-paneled lobby I remembered. Got a bilingual card with the club's facilities and a caddy to show me to the locker room. There, with the caddy interpreting, I signed for a locker and arranged to leave my golf gear where members left theirs. The attendant was a Mayan about five feet tall, skin as dark, flesh as firm, as a hardwood panel. I didn't tell him we had a mutual friend. The place hadn't changed much—stand-up lockers, fixed wooden benches, a little workout room and off it a sauna. The last was the only thing I didn't remember. It was Oliveira's ground, though—more of an edge than I wanted to give up. I changed into tennis clothes. The courts were where I could start feeling at home.

Two kids were hitting where I played the final. Home from college in the States for Christmas, that was the look of them, surfing shorts and tank tops, designer sneakers, blasting every ball with maximum violence. The lower court had their fathers' generation, four men playing doubles while another watched. When the set was done the watcher and I played the winners, one of whom had been a regular at Target's, a plump Atacalpan with accentless English. Who recognized me on an infraconscious level—so, anyway, it was exciting to think—picked up my scent and matched it to data from memory but couldn't allow the finding to enter his consciousness. Haft's gardener on the country club court hitting twist serves? No no no no no, that was too zany. My brain, meanwhile, was abuzz with nontennis business—Ellen, Amador, my plan for the morning. Then my partner stayed back on his second serve, and our plump opponent cuffed a little drop shot that grazed the net and fell in the far alley. I sprang along the net for it, but with no anxiety. The ball would wait for me, and so it did, bounced and hung in the air and waited serenely until I arrived and flicked it into the backcourt out of both opponents' reach. In that instant all my other concerns fell away. My brain kept chewing on them, I'm certain of that, but discreetly, so as not to stain the present moment.

"You play a nice game," the plump man said when we finished.

"I was lucky, my first serve was going in."

"Looked like more than luck to me. Come out Sunday morning. There's a pair who think they're good. It will be fun to let some wind out of their sails."

Oliveira, perhaps, and some buddy—or so, anyway, it amused me to imagine. I said, "Fine," though I didn't think I'd be around.

I put on a dry shirt and strolled around to the terrace. The sun was about to plunge behind the mountain. A last foursome was putting the eighteenth. I sat down and got out my recorder and let Tuñón tell me about Oliveira and Ellen. She had moved out of the Fenix the day I flew to Houston, into a place called the Pensión Romero in the oldest part of the city behind the cathedral. Leaving word. That made things easy for Tuñón. He had people in place that afternoon.

A woman and two kids, Alva, Pili, and Jaime. Alva had a folding chair and a tray of lottery tickets. She set up on the sidewalk in front of the *pensión*, between the door and the pay phone on the corner, a woman in her fifties, the kind that wizens with age not the kind that spreads out, in a faded dress and a man's leather jacket. Pili was twelve but looked younger. The streets of Chilpanzango hadn't helped his physique. They'd taught him, though, to trade on his waifish aspect—thin shirt, short pants, grime-specked neck and forehead. He had One-One's flair for seeming innocuous. He had a shoeshine box and stayed by the barbershop across the street. Jaime, meanwhile, worked on his motor scooter. Tuñón had supplied it, and it didn't need work. Jaime had the engine cover on the sidewalk beside him and poked around inside with a long screwdriver, but he could be mounted and gone in fifteen seconds—an unkempt sixteen-year-old crouched on the corner opposite the pay phone.

Ellen showed around six, stalked down the bystreet from the bus stop near the cathedral ("Like a cat twitching its tail," was Alva's description) with Oliveira's snoops three yards behind her in a four-by-four that took up the whole narrow pavement. No, not accurate, more goons than snoops. Their aim was intimidation more than surveillance. Ellen crossed to the *pensión*. They parked with two wheels up on the opposite sidewalk. She turned and glared, they leered back. She stalked inside, they settled back waiting. Alva went to the pay phone to call Tuñón. Jaime, no more than a yard from the four-by-four's tailpipe, put the engine cover back on the scooter and walked it across the street past the pay phone and Alva to a spot around the corner from her chair.

Goons sat on Ellen all week long in relays. When she walked, the four-by-four crawled three yards behind her, blocking traffic where the streets were narrow so that a cry of car horns bayed in her wake. When she got on a bus, a goon got on with her, hung buzzarded over her if she sat down, stood brushing against her if she didn't. When she entered a building, a goon followed, got on the elevator right behind her, rode to her floor, trailed her to the office she meant to visit, was slouched beside the door when she came out. And when she went for a bite to eat or some coffee, both came in and took a table near her and leered at her until she left. Meanwhile Pili and Jaime tailed the tailers.

What was Ellen about? Finding a lawyer for one thing. She visited four firms the day after she moved, getting the runaround, so Tuñón put it.

"I'll bet every one of those bastards claimed conflict of interest, told her Oliveira retained them for something, or that a partner was married to his aunt But the real reason why none of them will represent her is that Señor Oliveira is influential, and more than just a little prone to hard feelings. They'd lose their corporate clients and retaining fees."

Next she decided she didn't need a lawyer. She'd get an order from a neighborhood magistrate for Oliveira to bring the children to his chambers for her to see and speak with in his presence. That, anyway, was Tuñón's explanation for her spending all day Friday at the *corregiduría* for the part of town Colonia Los Delfines was in. Anyone proving parenthood could get such an order, any Atacalpan or resident foreigner, but Ellen's residence permit had to have expired, and there was no way she could renew it. Her right to residence proceeded from her marriage and ended with it.

On Saturday she lunched with Diana Haft, whose cortege made even goons keep distance. A jeep with a major aboard preceded the town car. A six-by-six with a squad of soldiers followed. Then reporters, paparazzi, TV crews—just what neither woman needed. Retriever had to have hit Ellen hard. Diana had put her hopes up, Retriever smashed them. I asked Tuñón about Diana and was glad to learn that news of Target's capture in Puerto Rico had been in the Chilpanzango papers, and that she had left for the United States a few hours before I returned to Atacalpa.

On Monday Ellen was back with lawyers, criminal lawyers now with offices closer by near the National Palace. Someone had pointed her in the right direction. A lawyer with no retaining fees couldn't be blackmailed, and most criminal lawyers love a good scrap. One appointment that day, however, was different. She had lunch with a law professor, a woman who had pled a high-profile human rights case some years before while Ellen was still living in Atacalpa. Tuñón told me about it.

"Two university students disappeared, boyfriend and girlfriend. They were weekending at the lake near Tiltenango. It's pretty clear they ran into some soldiers—at night, in or near a cantina, the soldiers were drunk. Evidently the girl was raped and both were murdered. Their families were middle class, so the case got some notice, but in the end they might as well have been Indians."

"Why would Oliveira's ex meet with her?"

"Maybe to hire her, she is one tough woman, taking on the army in a country like this. But hiring her would be an error. It would make her custody case political, and the judges here know what's what, you can bet on it. And I don't think Señor Oliveira wants that lady lawyer in his private life."

"You think that's why they grabbed her?"

"I do."

A bit before noon New Year's Day Ellen had come out of Pensión Romero. The four-by-four was parked right in front. One of the goons got out and took her elbow and put her in the back.

"He got in back with her," Tuñón said, "and they drove off, got on the highway south to Albamorada. Jaime couldn't keep up. He went back and reported to Alva and she called my house. I got the word just before you landed."

I shut the thing off. Night had come down. Faintest wisp of orange to the right of the mountain inked away even as I watched.

I sipped some tea. Not that cold anymore but still tasty. Came in a thermos pitcher so it wouldn't get watery, mint sprigs mulled and brewed in it, just right. Everything right since the fellow hit that drop shot. Body singing, worry fallen away. Harming her would be foolish, hence out of character. Tomorrow it would be my serve.

4   *A* pink arrow made wangish thrusts in a heart-shaped pink sign.

The place, Villa Amor, was a shagging spa not a whorehouse, find them from Rio Grande to Patagonia, one of Latin America's great institutions. You and your true love drive in and see rows of carports. Pull into an empty one and push a button. A door comes down behind your license plate. Put money through a slot and push another. A door opens before you onto a bedroom—soft lighting, mood music, room service, pornovision, mirrored ceilings in the deluxe units.

Slow tonight after last night's excesses, after this morning's hangovers and resolutions. No lovers in all the time we'd been there. No lights beyond the arrow or on our side, no cars in either direction for almost an hour, though once a big jet whooshed in a few feet above us, undercarriage groping for a runway no more than fifty yards to our left rear. The airport and the city lay behind us. Ahead a heart-shaped sign and a thrusting arrow and a scatter of stars above invisible mountains.

The Parador Caracol was to our right front, a two-story, cement-block building back from the road with seven vehicles parked head-in along it, including a big Japanese four-by-four. *Parador:* inn, hostelry, roadhouse. This one catered to low-budget travelers from the provinces with early flights out of Macagüita. Sixteen rooms upstairs at one per window, fewer below assuming a lobby and dining room, fire exit at the near end but no back door. I'd had a quiet look around it. The sign on top had gone off a bit after we got there, but light showed beside the entrance at the far end and in two windows on the second floor. Nico was parked well shy of the inn, on the opposite shoulder.

Crunch of my shoes on the gravel beside the asphalt. I went around to Tuñón's side of the wagon. "Time?"

"Four forty."

"*Bién.* I'm on my way."

"Still going solo?"

"*Correcto.*" He and Nico lived in Atacalpa. I didn't want anyone seeing their faces. I bent and looked past him at Nico. "When I'm inside, pull up to the exit door. No lights."

"*Está bién.*"

I crossed to the Caracol's side and walked toward it. Dank chill, I was glad to have Tuñón's leather jacket. Besides warmth, it gave me the look of a local. He had also provided a Spanish revolver. It made a tumorous bulge over my appendix. And a *cachiporra*—a blackjack, a cosh: tumorous bulge over my right buttock. Very much loaded for bear and I liked the feeling.

Tuñón and I had been to see Amador Quilche in a *barriada* on the city's north side that spread like a fungus up the slopes of a ridge. We left Nico at the bottom and went on foot. No streets up there, a tangle of dirt pathways full of mongrel dogs and naked children. "In your country too, Carlos," Cruz's voice whispered. We got lost a few times, Tuñón hadn't been there at night. Then it took time to get to the point of the visit, which was scripting Amador into my thing for the morning. *Chicha* had to be sipped—ritual foreplay before one could touch business. Which was fine with me. The purpose of the moment was to make my thing work. I was fully focused on it. Extraneous matters couldn't seep in to disturb me, even the whereabouts of Ellen Gonders. Tuñón, on the other hand, started to fidget. He'd been out of touch with his watchers too long. He had hunches and had learned to trust them. Something was telling him Alva wanted to reach him.

He stood up. "Unless you need me . . ."

I sipped *chicha*, then nodded. "Go ahead." He'd got me there and made the introduction. I didn't know what he was up to, but he'd earned my trust.

"Can you find your way down?" he asked me.

"Of course."

"Then I'll see you at the car."

A lie as it turned out. By the time I got down to where Nico was parked, Tuñón had called his house, got a message from Alva, and had taken a cab to Pensión Romero. He was waiting for us one block up toward the cathedral with a big, seen-it-all grin on his cop face. Oliveira's man had come by for Ellen's luggage.

This just before ten. He parked out front, went in, stayed less than five minutes, came out with a carry-on and a tote bag. Maybe Señora Romero had packed them for him. He didn't bother to open the four-by-four's tailgate but slung the bags up on the rear seat and drove away with Jaime and Pili behind him. To the airport and past it. Then he pulled in at the Parador Caracol. Jaime continued on, then came back and watched. When the four-by-four had been parked for fifteen minutes, he crossed to the Villa Amor, found a phone, and called Alva.

It was closing on midnight when we got there. We stopped at Tuñón's for the jacket, revolver, etc., at an all-night pharmacy for adhesive tape, at Macagüita for flight information. The next plane north was Atacalpeña 100, departing for Miami at 0810. That had to be the one they were putting her on. No fuss from a national carrier when the CIM came up with a last-minute passenger, bump people to make room if the flight was full. The men who had Ellen were probably cleared with security to drive her right to the ramp and walk her up it without even stopping by the airline counter. Goon escort handcuffed to her, seats in the last row, gauntlet of gapes and whispers to traverse.

—Who do you think she is?

—A whore or a druggie.

Passport stamped *"NON GRATA."* Deportation papers for the Miami authorities. Why front for Colonel Tovar in a criminal combine if you can't get your ex shunted out with maximum anguish when she threatens to smell up your life with human rights lawyers?

The impulse was to free her at once. Nothing in the books my mother read me beat rescuing a maiden in distress, and there was nothing I craved more than credit with Ellen. I didn't think they'd harm her, but I couldn't be sure. I didn't think they'd move her, but if they did the next spot was liable to be harder to handle. On the other side there was my thing for the morning. Oliveira might want to check with his goons before sleeping, might wake in the night and want to check with them then. The longer we waited the more likely it was that Oliveira would get up and go to his tennis game confident that he was in charge. Everything would work out if he went to play tennis.

"Perdón, señor!"

"No hay de que." Mid twenties, white shirt and tie, regaining composure. Asleep in his chair and didn't hear me come in, jumped like a scalded cat when I rapped the counter. I gave him a big jolly smile, think nothing of it.

"A room, señor?"

"Ten steps to financial success." His book had gone onto the floor. I peered at it over the plywood counter. "When you're done with it, lend it to me."

He managed a thin smile. "A room?"

"No, gracias." Shook my head, smiling, and took out a thick fold of pesos. "My friends are checking out, how much do they owe? Two men and a woman, driving a *cuatro por cuatro*."

Jumpy again. "You friend . . . Lieutenant Acuña . . . He said I had to give him two rooms gratis. They had no luggage, the lady's came later. In such cases the policy is payment in advance. He said it was a military matter, that there'd be no charge."

Chiseling on his expense sheet. "Did he show you military ID?"

"No, señor, he showed me his pistol."

"Really? Where did he carry it, here?" I raised my left arm and patted under it.

"Sí, señor."

"He likes to joke, pay no attention to him. Did you call anyone?"

"No, señor, I made a note. My instructions are to cooperate with the authorities."

I nodded. "Good idea. How much are the rooms?"

"Forty pesos, señor, twenty each."

"Any other charges?"

"No, señor."

"What about phone calls?"

He touched the phone on the counter. "He made one local call, no charge."

I looked behind him. Box of numbered pigeonholes, but no switchboard. "No phones in the rooms?"

"No, señor."

"What about pay phones?"

"None, señor. Only the phone here."

I gave him fifty pesos. "The last ten are for you."

"Gracias, señor."

"What rooms are they in?"

"Two zero seven, señor, and two zero nine."

"Are there stairs down there?" I pointed down the corridor.

"Sí, señor."

"Then we'll use the door at that end. I have my car there."

"Como guste, señor."

"Bueno." I stepped toward the stairs to the right of the counter, then turned back. "If anyone calls, don't mention I was here, just say they checked out."

"A la orden, señor."

Dim in the corridor. Cement floor, no carpet, excellent traction. On my right was 209, light showed under the door. I knocked twice softly. *"Mi teniente."*

I was going to knock again when the door jerked open. *"¿Tú, quien eres?"*

Walther PPK pointed at my chest, nine-millimeter short cartridge, brass-jacketed round. The hammer wasn't cocked, but that was no help. Shoots the first round double action like a revolver.

"I'm the desk clerk, señor." Tremor in my voice, no acting required. "You have a call." Was going to add, From a Señor Oliveira, but thought better in time. Not like Oliveira to give his name, connect himself to this business unnecessarily.

"What happened to the *chico* who was on last night? He said he didn't get off till six in the morning." Shirtsleeves and shoulder holster, flat glassy stare. Shorter than I but wider, face and eyes a blank wall.

"He got sick, señor, I came in early."

Still staring, he put the pistol back under his arm, held a forefinger up for me to wait, drew back into the room and closed the door. In a moment he came out wearing a suit jacket. I stepped back, shoulders slumped, a dawdling dolt. He turned his head, flat stare, upper lip curled. Then he went by me along the corridor. I stepped in and coshed him behind his right ear. Up on my toes for a downward, sweeping motion, turned my wrist on impact, followed through. Then I lugged him back past 209 to the far stairs.

Forearms through his armpits, hands on his chest, lugging and dragging. To the stairs and down, one step then another, ten steps down to a landing, then ten more. Backward through the door, my back against the bar that unlocked it, Nico there to keep it from closing behind us. I laid him on the ground in front of the wagon.

Tuñón came over holding a pair of handcuffs.

"Give me the key to those things, they may have her cuffed. See if he's got the keys to the four-by-four. I'll be back with the other one in a minute."

A lie as it turned out, took a bit longer. Back upstairs I got a Syrette from my shirt pocket and took off the needle guard. Then I knocked. Knocked again. At length a man asked, "Who's there?"

"Desk clerk, señor. *Mi teniente* Acuña has a message for you."

"Where is he?"

"Downstairs, señor, talking on the phone."

"All right, tell me the message."

"*Por favor, señor,* the message is, uh, confidential, about the foreign lady you have with you. Open the door, please, I don't want to say it too loudly."

The door opened two feet. A man my size wearing a suit stood in the opening. Not flashy with his pistol, which was pleasant. His right hand was on the doorknob, his left hand was empty. Unlike Acuña, whose face betrayed nothing but malice, his showed annoyance, boredom, and fatigue.

"All right, tell me."

I charged him, hitting the door with my left shoulder. That turned him to his right, brought his left side toward me. I grabbed his chest with my left arm and drove the needle through his clothes into the muscle on top of his right shoulder, squeezing the Syrette. After that we tussled. He tried to get at the pistol under his left arm. I hung on to his chest and tried to get behind him. Then, abruptly, he slumped.

I went to one knee, easing him down. The door was wide open onto the corridor. I reached out to swing it shut and heard something behind me. A terrible swat hit the back of my head.

"Bastard!"

I got up. Instinct says, On your feet, confront the danger. A second swat hit the back of my neck. I turned, raising my hands, covering up. The next swat went through my left hand and caught the hairline over my left temple. My hand took some of its zip, though, and turned it a little. It didn't hit straight on but skidded.

"Bastard!"

Blood poured down my forehead, scalp wounds are like that. Ellen Gonders had one of those big, square glass ashtrays and was swinging it at me.

"Bastard!"

The ashtray came roundhouse at my left cheek. The odd thing was part of me said, Welcome. Things had to be even between us. I owed her her children back and was going to get them, but I also owed her for a lot of pain. Her hitting me was bringing that debt down. Instinct, on the other hand, said, Put your guard up. Also, she was getting arm-weary. And the spectacular display of blood had to be triggering compassion in her, which in turn reduced the force of the blow. Healthy humans will feel it unless it's trained out of them. Anyway, swat 4 hit my left forearm, stung like hell and numbed it but did no damage.

"Bastard!"

"Wait! I'm trying to help you!"

Took another swat, which I blocked the same way.

"Wait!"

"Why should I believe you?"

"I took out two of your husband's goons, for one thing."

"They were going to take me to see my children."

"They were going to ship you out."

"Yes, but first they were going to let me see them."

"I don't believe it, and neither do you."

"Bastard!" She raised the ashtray.

I dropped my arms and stuck my chin forward. "Okay. You hit me with that thing till you feel better. When you're done, I'll get your children back."

We stood like that. Then she said, "How?"

"The first step is leaving this place, but we have to clean up."

I turned and went into the bathroom and looked at myself. I had blood all over me, but the wound was clotting. I folded the hand towel and used it as a compress. Ellen's face came into the mirror and stared at me.

"Take the bath towel and get the blood off the floor."

I put toilet paper over the wound on my forehead. Then I wet the end of the towel and sponged my face. I'd buy Tuñón a new jacket. I had clothes for myself, my bags were in the wagon. When I came out Ellen Gonders had finished mopping and was standing beside the man on the floor. "Is he hurt badly?"

"Not hurt at all. Sedated." I took the towel from her. "Get your stuff. If he or the other one left anything, bring it with you."

I draped the towels over the man and tucked a fold of each into his belt. I found the Syrette on the floor a few feet from him and got the needle guard out of my shirt and affixed it, put the Syrette in my pocket. Ellen came through the door to 207 with her bags.

"Go ahead, and close the door after me."

I got down in a squat behind the man on the floor. I put my hands under his shoulders and got up with him. Weighed tons. The adrenaline was washing from my bloodstream. My head throbbed back and front. The effort of lifting popped the wound on my forehead. Blood came down my cheek in a warm trickle.

Backward into the corridor, backward along it. Lugging and dragging. Ellen followed, a bag in each hand, her eyes on mine. Hatred or maybe just fury, a need to do damage. In my dreams of her those eyes had other looks in them, but I owed it to her not to look away, and bearing her look helped me keep concentration. My head throbbed, I was woozy. Good odds I had a concussion, maybe two. Beyond her eyes the corridor stretched away dimly, its end obscured by the curvature of the earth. I sensed the same immensity behind me.

In the stairwell, back to the wall, goon collapsed at my feet. I'd lugged him the first five steps one step at a time, then my foot slipped and we did the next five in full stumble, slammed against the wall knocking my breath out, rapped the back of my head on the concrete. Ellen on the steps above looked down at me. Concern in her eyes, involuntary compassion. Tuñón and Nico came up the lower flight, Tuñón with a pistol held up beside his right ear, right hand on the grip, left hand cupped beneath it. Winced when he saw my face, put the pistol away. He and Nico took the prisoner.

Outside in the night. I stood with both hands against the side of the four-by-four. It was next to the wagon, tailgate open. Acuña lay on his face in the back, hands cuffed behind him, eyes and mouth taped. Tuñón and Nico were doing his partner. Tuñón, crouched at his waist, cuffed one hand then the other. Nico, crouched at his head, spread tape over his mouth. They worked quickly, we were vulnerable out there. I felt I should help but couldn't think what to do. The ground turned beneath me.

"¿Estás bién, Carlos?" Tuñón looked up at me. "Are you badly hurt? What happened up there?"

"Bastard! Why don't you tell him I hit you? Why don't you say why?" Ellen beside me, glaring.

Turned my head to ask her the time. Had to be at the country club at seven. No words came out. Then I was on the ground beside her feet.

5 Weights, of course, a barbell and one-hand dumb-bells, and an adjustable bench for doing sit-ups. A bicycle, a ski machine, a treadmill, a step-climbing thing with poles you pull and push to work your arms and upper body. The treadmill had poles and also handrails, a brisk walk being enough for your older geezers. Opposite was a Universal gym with chinning and dipping stations and high and low pulleys and a leg-and-thigh exerciser and a press. I lay under the last with my hands on the bar, as if I had just finished a set of bench presses.

Originally I was going to be on the step-climber. That's how I saw the thing the evening before when I explained it to Amador Quilche. The climber was near the door, I could get off it quickly. That's where I'd be when Oliveira showed. In the morning, though, I opted for the treadmill. I'd have handholds to grab if I got woozy. Then I thought, Why risk wooziness in the first place? I adjusted the sit-up bench to horizontal and put it under the press and lay down. My head still hurt a lot, but that didn't matter. The throbbing had stopped. My pulse was steady. Not 100 percent, but I could function.

The door he'd be coming through was on my left. Amador would bring him. He had insisted.

"He'll come after you later. I don't plan to kill him."

"No me importa!"

Stolid stare, nothing tougher than Indians. Reminded me of my make-believe guitarist, two-by-four on the nose and he wouldn't blink.

"It might matter to them." His wife—who looked fifteen, sixteen at the most—sat on the shanty's dirt floor nursing a baby. Another, two years or so old, sat beside her. Opposite them Bugs Bunny cavorted mutely on a TV screen the size of my spread hand. The TV cord rose above our heads to a socket that also held a naked bulb. The socket cord rose to a nail in the ceiling, then slanted away and out the window—an opening in the wall, there was no glass. Someone had put a tap on a power line somewhere, and the whole ridge would have juice till the company found it.

"We'll go over the border, I have family there. We were here before there were borders, they don't matter to us."

"Let me give you money for the trip."

"It's an easy walk through the forest, three or four days, and no one asks your name on either side. We'll leave from just this side of Tiltenango. The bus to there is ten pesos, five pesos each. They don't charge for babies."

"I have plenty of money, more than I need."

"Give me what you like, then. But I'll give you Señor Oliveira for nothing."

The door to the sauna was on my right with a handwritten sign taped over the little window:

CERRADO

MANTENAMIENTO

LO SENTIMOS

("Closed. Maintenance. We're Sorry.")

My golf bag and cart were inside, minus the clubs. They were in my locker where Amador had put them. He'd put the bag in the sauna and made the sign and was going to deliver Oliveira. Then he'd walk across the border with his wife and babies. He hated the shits who ran Atacalpa. I wanted to snatch one, that made me a good guy.

Ellen Gonders hadn't made her mind up. "I want to believe you," she'd said two hours before. I wasn't sure she did and kept my mouth shut.

"Believing you hasn't worked out for me."

Safer not to believe, not get her hopes up. More fun too, being angry, lashing out. Couldn't vent her rage on Acuña, a very scary guy with that flat stare.

She looked at me closely. "You're going to, aren't you? You're going to try."

I nodded—hint of a nod in any case. One, my head hurt; two, the ice pack might slip.

"No. I won't put them at risk. I'd rather not have them."

Partly she meant it, partly she liked saying no. Made her feel in control, a new experience lately. "No risk," I said. "Not to them, they won't be there."

Tuñón was off ditching the four-by-four, with Nico behind to give him a lift afterward. Ellen and I should have been with Nico. That, anyway, was how he and I had seen it beforehand. One, get rid of the four-by-four and take the goons where they can be held for a couple of days; two, drop Tuñón and Ellen at the safe house; three, be at the country club by seven. I hadn't anticipated she'd try to brain me, though in retrospect it was entirely predictable. Now I was regrouping. No way to postpone my thing with Oliveira, so get some ice and rest and try to be up for it.

"I don't know what you mean, 'They won't be there.' And why are you doing it? I don't have any money. No, I don't believe you, it's a trick."

She turned and went to the door where my bags were. Bolero

violins swirled faintly between us. She'd put the volume down as far as it went. I kept quiet. Eyes half shut in the half light from the alcove, towels packed with ice on my temple and under my head. Box in the alcove wall they serve you drinks through, or a grocery bag full of ice cubes if that's what you've ordered, using the telephone beside the bed. Must have thought they were for some kinky delight, cubes on your pubes for a postorgasmic chill-down.

She came back and looked down at me. "If you're going to get them, tell me why?"

"Last year, when I took them, I was on the wrong side."

"Didn't you know that then?"

"I had ways of fooling myself, but yes, I knew."

"Bastard."

Hint of a nod.

She turned away. "Now you want to make up for it."

"Yes."

Turned back and dropped her eyes to where her hands were, clasped together lightly below her waist. The pose was achingly familiar. No wonderful secret, though, she wasn't smiling. "You can't," she said. "You'll never be able to."

Cold rage. Had she been here before, indulging passions more appropriate to the place and its appointments? I found myself replaying dream views of her. Gave herself like leaping from a bridge. Later on a rueful, "You! You do something that unhooks my spine." Spell of the place working on me, quanta of sexual energy discharged in a small confine. No mirror on the ceiling, but a length-of-the-bed one on the wall to my right. Looked at her in it. She stood by the door like a cat flicking its tail. Sat down in the alcove, crossed her legs, uncrossed them, caught me looking at her, glared, looked away, and I, ashamed, looked away quickly also.

I'd given her the option of staying with Nico. She was up front, I was laid out in the back. Rear seat folded down, bags pushed to one side, a lily on my chest was all I needed. Nico and Tuñón had hefted me in there. I offered no help but hadn't lost consciousness.

"*¿Y ahora?*" Tuñón peered in through the open tail door.

"*¿Que hora es?*" Got the words out this time.

He looked. "A quarter to five."

"It's okay, we're on schedule."

"Yes, but you don't look good. Think you can make it?"

Growled back, "I'll be all right," but then thought better. "Wait. Okay, take me to the Villa Amor. I'll get some rest. When Nico drops you, he can come back and get me."

"What's this for?" Ellen asked when we pulled in. Archly, as if she thought I might have designs on her virtue.

"Going to get some rest," I croaked from my bier behind her. "I don't go on again for another two hours. Tuñón's going to put the goons on ice and ditch their vehicle. Nico will follow, take him to a safe house we have. Go with him if you want. When he drops you and Tuñón, he'll come back for me."

"No." No hesitation. "I'll stay with you."

Which pleased me. As if it meant that she enjoyed being with me, instead of that she preferred the devil she knew to riding around in the night with a total stranger. Nico got out, put money in the slot, pushed the doorbell, came to help me out. Tuñón had kept the four-by-four out on the highway.

It turned out I could walk. I told Nico to bring my bags and followed Ellen. She went right in when the door opened, straight to the bedroom and snapped off the TV, which was putting out male grunts and female moaning. Then she turned down the music. I went to the telephone and ordered ice cubes, made the packs and used one as a pillow, held the other balanced on my temple.

She came back and looked down at me. "Will you be all right?"

"Sure. I'm all right now. Enough to do what's needed to get your children."

"I didn't mean that. I meant, I hope I haven't hurt you badly."

Hint of a head shake, half smile. "Blows to the head? Can't do me much damage that way."

Small smile back, then she looked away smiling to herself, the smile I liked, the one I'd dreamed of seeing. Just had time to catch it, then it faded.

"If I'd had a gun I would have killed you."

Said nothing. Eyes locked on hers. I think she would have.

"I'm glad I didn't have one, but how could you? We'd done you no harm. You were in our home, you ate at our table. Lying and lying. Bastard, how much did you get? How much did Antonio pay you for breaking our lives?"

Eyes locked on hers. My head was throbbing. Forehead or back or both, I couldn't distinguish. Met her stare, I had to. Said, "I was wrong." Said, "I'm going to get them, you'll have them back."

She turned away, walked two steps, and then turned back. "How will you do it? I meant what I said, I won't have them at risk."

"They won't be. I'm going to kidnap your husband, Oliveira. He will have the children delivered to you."

"Are you sure? Don't underestimate him."

"I won't. But if he were to die, you would get custody. When he understands that you'll have them one way or the other, he'll give them up."

"He's their father. I won't let you kill him."

"Fine. I won't. But he doesn't know that, does he?"

Throwing men from helicopters was the preferred method when it came to establishing seriousness of purpose. Don't believe we mean it? How about this? A-one, a-two, a-three, and out goes his buddy. Or blindfold him and take him up alone, then lose altitude slowly, hover at two or three feet. Over grass if he mustn't have bumps or bruises. A-one, a-two, a-three, and out he goes. In flight less than a second, fifth of a second in free fall, but it's enough. He's going to smell pretty bad, but he'll be tractable, won't ever say or think you're bluffing again. Other things work when there are no choppers handy.

"Have it all thought out, haven't you, you bastard? Has it occurred to you that if you hadn't taken them in the first place . . . ?"

Kept quiet. And since I hadn't said it, she did. "I know, someone else would have. Lucky, lucky me that it was you!"

Flush of self-pity as she turned away. Who else would get her children? Ought to appreciate. But I was too healthy to stay in that mode long, not that my head hurt less or had stopped throbbing. Urge to laugh out loud that I managed to stifle. The place, the two of us, the conversation, the mission that by then had been running a week.

"Glass Mountain."

"What's that?" She was over in the alcove.

"Mission name, only one I can give it."

"I don't understand."

"Missions have names. Two words is the style now. I think of it as a mission, getting your children."

"Yes, but why Glass Mountain?"

"Oh, that's a long story, goes way back. When this is over, I'll tell it to you. Assuming you're interested. Probably only be interested in getting home."

"You sound cheerful."

"Do I? Maybe I do. I was thinking how funny all this is. I don't mean your situation, what you've been suffering. But, you and I in this place. Me trying to unkidnap the children I kidnapped last year."

No answer. Faint tango guitars. In a bit she said, "If it works, if you capture Antonio, and he lets me have Tonio and Elena, what happens then?"

"I have a plane chartered. We'll fly out of this country, and you'll go home."

"I wasn't lying, I don't have any money."

"It's not a big plane. I can afford it."

Guitars. Then, after a little, "Can I do something for your head?"

"Before we leave you can put a bandage on it. I have a first-aid kit in my bag. I don't want to be all bloody and scare your husband."

"Not my husband anymore." And a bit later, "He brought me to this place when we were dating. There's something funny."

Tension draining from me, drifting toward sleep. "Yes, it is, I was wondering if that had happened."

"The other man called you Carlos. Is that your name?"

"Yes. My real one. Carlos Fuertes. Time we were introduced. We've been in this place how long, half an hour?"

"More." Then, "Carlos, I think someday I may forgive you."

"That would be nice. Then I can forgive myself."

Rap on the door. Oliveira was on the premises. I checked the Syrette in my sweatpants pocket. When he was in tennis clothes, Amador would bring him.

I'd made it to the club in plenty of time. Dozed a while, put on gym stuff, had my head seen to. Swelling down front and back, no dizziness standing, professional job of bandaging by Ms. Gonders, who'd aced the first-aid course in stewardess school. Coffee for two while we waited, no conversation, worn out as though from a normal Villa Amor visit.

"You're sure trying to kidnap him is the way?"

Tuñón had picked up the sedan, and come out behind Nico. That way I could go directly to the club. Ellen had let him in, then turned back to me.

"I am. You don't want me to go directly for the children, and I don't think I could swing it even if you did. I think this will work. If it doesn't, there's no risk to them, and I can't see anything very bad happening to you, an American woman, after what he's done."

"Don't forget yourself. He's a very vindictive person. You could be killed. Do you know that?"

"I know about him. But thanks for asking. Whatever happens, I really want to do this."

"Good luck, then," she said, and went out after Tuñón.

Two quick raps, and the door opened. In strode Antonio Oliveira—diamond pinky ring and Rolex Oyster. Amador Quilche was a step behind him.

I got to my feet slowly, no wooziness thank you. Big smile, right hand out, left hand on the Syrette in my sweatpants pocket. I had practiced removing the needle guard with one hand.

"Hey, Mr. Oliveira, how's it going? Carl Marengo. Remember me?"

Amador helped me put him into the golf bag, a bit like putting a limp dick into a condom. Then we put the bag into the golf cart.

Amador did most of the hefting. Big green four-by-fours were parked between the clubhouse and where Nico had put the station wagon. Goons, goons, goons. I resisted the urge to wave as I trundled their boss by.

6 *"T*ell me."

"They've left Delfines. Walked out through the gate and took the taxi."

"No one followed?"

"No."

"They could have had a car outside the gate."

"Pili, the kid who just called, was on the next corner. He watched the taxi reach him, turn right, and drive on—as it was supposed to. No car on either block pulled out behind it."

"I'm afraid to believe this will work. If I do and it doesn't . . . Oh, God!"

"One step at a time, so far it's working. At Invictos we'll check again, in case they put cars farther out on several streets."

We were on the side of a ridge south of town. The road climbed the north face to Colonia Something, and a flat-topped spur left a bulge of ground alongside it that somebody had made into a mirador. Railed because the brink dropped away steeply, and at the tip a large map of Chilpanzango and a coin-operated telescope. The cafe was on the right back by the road, a counter with umbrella'd tables in front. Ellen and I were at the one farthest out.

"Invictos is the arch, isn't it? What happens there?"

She wore a denim jacket and a man's white shirt. I wore a panama hat over my bandage. Nine-thirty of a limpid dry season morning.

"Cars go around it, avenues spoke off. The taxi's going to circle it three times, then start around again and take the third spoke. If someone's following, Alva will spot it."

Meanwhile Tuñón would spot a homing device. According to Pili's report, they'd followed directions. Only the kids and the woman went to the taxi, and all they did was get inside. Nothing was clamped to the chassis with a magnet. No one carried anything either, but if a device was taped to the woman's leg or sewn inside one of the little boy's pockets, Tuñón's scanner would pick up the signal. He would be getting behind the taxi right now.

"Who's Alva?"

"You'd know her if you saw her. She sat outside your *pensión* selling lottery tickets from the day you checked in until Acuña grabbed you. She'll call and say if there is a tail or there isn't."

"If the phone doesn't work?" Her smile toggled between anxious child and parody of one.

I smiled back. "I only bought it yesterday. I've got the receipt. If it doesn't work I'll get my money back."

Cordless, pastel blue, top of the line. Charged from seven last night till seven this morning. My deal with the cafe proprietor was that he got to keep it, along with a hundred dollars. I got exclusive use of the line that morning. If someone called for him I'd say call later.

"It's going to work, isn't it? I don't mean the phone, getting my babies. Tell me it will work."

"They've let them leave Los Delfines, that was the first threshold. So far no one's following, that's the second." To my right the sky above the city was empty. A hawk or two, no light planes, no helicopters. "I've told them that this morning is a dry run, an obedience test. The children and their nanny will drive around town. We'll see if they're followed. Tonight will do it for real, children and money. One hundred thousand dollars, my supposed fee. It was partly to make my pitch credible to Oliveira. He knows you don't have what a thing like this costs. And to make them relax. With luck we'll be airborne before they realize we only want the children. Even if they see through the demand for money, it comes down to whether they'll obey Oliveira. I think they will, you've seconded that opinion. He's told them to do what I say. It'll work."

She didn't know how I'd got Oliveira to do it. Not the details. She and I had talked the previous morning, as soon as I got him to the safe house.

It was on the fringe of the city but must have been well outside when it was built. Rutted drive and pine trees, it felt rural. I'd leased it unfurnished and Tuñón had put in essentials. All Ellen's room had was a cot and two folding chairs. I didn't know why I found it familiar, then it came to me. Her suitcases, the room's fugitive air, reminded me of the hotel in Miami. She, too, of course. She had bathed and washed her hair but had put on no makeup. The change in her fortunes showed in her smile. In the sunlight that flooded through uncurtained windows, her freshness was breathtaking—that and all the love I'd dreamed us sharing and her having accepted me as her champion.

"Your ex is downstairs sleeping."

"What will you do?" Her eyes shone.

"Let's talk about that. You have to know what we're into. Otherwise I'll have trouble being effective."

"Go ahead."

"What he did was theft. I sneaked in and stole the children for him. What we're doing is warfare, imposing our will by violence or the threat of it."

"No, Carlos. It may have been theft to you. To Antonio it wasn't even that, just taking his property from someone who didn't matter. But to me it was worse than being killed. It's been war all along as far as I'm concerned."

"Good. That makes things simple. But lighten up, we're winning."

"It's you who looks tense. Does your head hurt?"

"No, it's that I need sleep but have things to do first, work this out with you, get our guest tucked in, give Tuñón and Nico their assignments."

"Work what out with me?"

"What you're going to know. I'm glad you understand the situation. I should have known you would. Now, how much do you want me to tell you?"

"I don't know what you mean."

"Well, maybe all you want me to say is that I'll persuade him to have the children delivered. If that's it, we're done."

"You'd prefer that, wouldn't you?"

"Probably. Probably that would be easiest for me. But you're the principal. My convenience isn't important except as it may coincide with success. For instance, it will be easier for me if I don't have to check each step with you before I take it, but the main point is that checking with you would delay things, and time's important. By this afternoon Colonel Tovar will be beating the bushes. If we don't get this done quickly we'll get caught."

"You say we're going to impose our will by violence."

"Or the threat of it, pain and fear. Pain and fear are like energy and matter, they convert. Pain is frightening and fear is painful. Dread of annihilation is almost unbearable. Most people will do anything to relieve it."

"You're going to torture Antonio."

I grinned, almost told her I loved her. "That's it precisely, though I wouldn't have had the guts to be that precise. How'd you get so honest?"

"Don't you think I've thought about this moment? Night after night. I told myself to face facts, it would never come, but I dreamed it might, that I could make him give back my babies. Tell me, Carlos, will you have to hurt him more than he's hurt me?"

I thought for a moment. "No. Not at all."

"Then go ahead. Do what will be most effective."

Phone ringing, I listened to Alva. Anxiety on Ellen's face; I smiled to relieve it. Listened to Tuñón, then put the phone down. "No tails," I told Ellen. Tuñón had said there were no devices either.

"Are they coming here?"

"Not yet. They have to change taxis." A yellow bus pulled off the road and rolled by us.

"At the department store?"

"That's it."

I'd had Oliveira insist Tovar's people stay clear, but I couldn't guarantee they actually would. Say they had someone near the gate, got the taxi's number, put out an all-points bulletin on it. They'd have a good chance of locating it after we had checked it for tails. So I set up a switch. Tuñón would pick Alva up at Invictos and take her a few blocks along to a public phone where Jaime was waiting with his motor scooter. Jaime would go after the taxi, tell the driver to take his passengers to the Alameda entrance of Galerias Primavera, and hand him a note I'd had Ellen write the kids' nanny. Meanwhile, Tuñón and Alva would call me. Then he'd take her to the Galerias, where she'd wait just inside. When the children and the nanny came in, Alva would lead them through the store to the next street, where I would have another taxi waiting.

Ellen smiled wanly. "How much longer?" Kids poured off the bus and ran squealing toward the telescope.

"Depends on traffic. Ten minutes to the store, a half hour to here."

"Tell me it will work."

Tuñón had put a cot in the cellar storeroom set up on cinder blocks almost waist high. He, Nico, and I carried Oliveira down there, stripped him, and laid him out on the spring. We cuffed his ankles and right wrist to corners, taped his left wrist to the rail by his hip, put tape through the springs and around his chest, but not so as to interfere with his breathing. His breathing was slow and deep, the sleep of the just. We blindfolded him and put a strip of tape loosely over his mouth to mute the shouts he might make when he came to. Then we covered him with a blanket and left him in the dark. That was right after my talk with Ellen.

Oliveira's men had seen the station wagon at the country club, so Nico drove it to a supermarket and wiped it down and left it. Tuñón followed him and brought him back after they had bought provisions. Then Nico went down to sit by the storeroom door and Tuñón called Oliveira's office and told the receptionist where to find Acuña and his partner, then went to scout locations for the next day's action. I was fast asleep by that time.

I woke around one, bathed and shaved, put on a business suit. From now on I was Charles Borodino, who dressed more formally than Carleton Austerlitz, last seen trundling a golf cart through the country club parking lot. I went to see Ellen, who had also been napping, and while I made myself a meal and ate it, she told me all she could about Oliveira's household and guards and lieutenants and confederates. We were more or less done when Tuñón came back. He drove me downtown, where I acquired a panama hat, pruning shears, and two cordless telephones. We discussed the next day's action en route. Police stopped us to check our papers at two points on the way down and at four on the way back. From the attention mine got, it appeared gringo businessmen were coming in season.

Oliveira was making noises when we got back. I had Nico go in and remove the blanket without turning the light on or saying anything. I sent Tuñón off to brief Alva, Jaime, and Pili. Then I put on the sweat suit and sneakers I'd worn that morning and went downstairs.

The cellar was cool. I wasn't at all uncomfortable in my sweat suit, but Oliveira had to be getting chilly. The light was just over his head, a strong bulb in a concave reflector. He tensed when it came on. Certainly he felt eyes on his body.

His body was fit, well-proportioned, and very smooth—wispy hair on his forearms but none on his torso. As I looked, goose bumps came out on his chest and flanks. He began to speak through the tape over his mouth, tried to anyway. What came out was blurred Spanish in a gruff tone—transforming some of his fear into anger, I figured. Some of his shame too. He was naked for one thing. The floor beneath him was puddled for another.

"Hang on," I said in English. "I'll take the tape off."

I put the shears and my first-aid kit on a folding chair near the cot. I stepped to his left side and pulled the tape off. Then I undid the blindfold.

Oliveira glared up at me. "I'm going to kill you."

I looked back and said nothing.

"Slowly. You'll beg for death."

As a strategy it had merit. If I bought any part of the view that I was in trouble, his position improved. Still, I think it was custom not calculation. He was accustomed to killing those who crossed him, to being feared. His current predicament hadn't curtailed his assurance. I, on the other hand, felt lousy. A person was naked before me, and I was doing nothing to ease his helplessness. Worse, I'd contrived it. Worst, I was going to exploit it. I was going to torment him from a position of safety.

I had ways to feel better but mustn't use them. I could turn my shame into contempt, pretend his being my prisoner made him less human, then turn contempt into cruelty and start having fun. Turning my shame into anger would be even easier. How dare he go on about killing me when I'd taken the trouble to have him at my mercy? Why not ball my fist at brow level and bring it down on his hairless belly, *thump!* like a speaker banging the table for emphasis? But I mustn't indulge myself. Do what I had to do and bear the dishonor. Getting drunk on anger or cruelty would only compound it. I reached down and took his penis between my right thumb and forefinger, putting up with the disgust occasioned. I raised it out of the way and put my left hand between his thighs. I bowed my middle finger against my thumb and flicked him crisply on the scrotum.

He had started squirming when I touched him. When I flicked he convulsed, tried to curl into a ball, which of course he couldn't, which must have hurt his wrists and ankles. He didn't make much noise, though, for which I admired him. Since he couldn't curl up, he straightened as far as he could, arching his back, and began breathing deeply. I kept my gaze on him as he dealt with the pain, making sure my face was empty of smugness or sympathy. His scrotum stayed drawn up toward his abdomen, but bit by bit the color returned to his face. Then his eyes returned to mine, glowing dully in hatred.

"This is like the dentist's," I said. "It's unpleasant. Unpleasantness is built in. Don't make it more unpleasant than it has to be. Try to relax. Cooperate. It will all be over pretty soon."

He met my gaze and said nothing.

"I'm acting for your wife. She wants the children and one hundred thousand dollars."

"Former wife."

"The decree you got here isn't valid in her jurisdiction. Nowhere in the U.S., so I've been told. Anyway, that's what she wants. The hundred thousand, actually, is my fee."

He met my gaze.

"Her view is you paid to take the children from her, you should pay for their return. In any case, I won't do this for nothing. She has no money, so she's asking you."

"*¡Puta inmunda!*" He said it softly but with great disgust.

"I've a recorder. I need you to make a tape for your partner Ramirez. I'll say what to say. If everyone plays ball, you'll be back home this time tomorrow."

He rolled his hips a little. The ache had to be radiating through his lower body. He was having trouble keeping still. But he met my gaze with hatred and said nothing.

"Plan B is I kill you."

"Kill me, then. You'll get nothing."

"Well, she'll get the children. She's their mother, after all. If you die, she'll get custody. It might take a little time, that's all."

"She'll never get them. My friends run this country."

"How many friends will you have after you're dead? I think there'll be a lot of sympathy for her. Already is. She was on the front page of the Miami *Herald* this morning, all bandaged up in Hialeah Hospital. Acuña broke her cheekbone and two of her ribs."

"What day is it?"

"Thursday. You were unconscious almost thirty-six hours." He couldn't check his beard like the man in Poe's story.

"I don't know how smart it was having Acuña rape her. Or maybe that was his idea. Either way she blames you. Maybe you're right, maybe she won't get custody, but right now she doesn't mind a bit if I kill you."

Worry crept into his face, but he chased it out. "If you kill me, who pays you?"

"She does. As your wife she'll inherit the Key Biscayne condo. It should bring about a million. And we just began looking. I'll bet you have more property in the States."

Silence. He'd gone back to staring at me, saying nothing.

"You have till tomorrow. If your people don't deliver as per instructions, you'll die. But no more unpleasantly than necessary. I got a suit back from the cleaner's yesterday morning and kept the plastic thing it came in. It goes over your head...Two or three minutes, maybe less."

"You don't want to kill me. You'll have to wait months, maybe years, to get your money. You're fucking her, aren't you?"

"No, actually. I'm not."

He eyed me closely. "Maybe not. And if you aren't, you certainly don't trust her. Why should she pay you? You have no way to make her. No, you don't want to kill me. If you don't collect the money yourself, you won't get it."

We eyed each other. I was more ashamed than when I started. I admired Oliveira more as well. Splayed out naked in a dank cellar, yet he showed no hint of weakness. Anyone raised in a Spanish-speaking country admires courage above all other qualities, even though it can exist in reptiles.

"You don't believe me, do you?" I said at last.

Oliveira said nothing.

I was sad it had come to this, though I knew it would. I was happy too, having foreseen the moment and prepared for it. Happiness, sadness, admiration, shame. All those emotions played healthily in me, but the look I wanted and felt pretty sure I was getting was the look on a cop's face when he writes a summons. I went to the wall where we'd dumped Oliveira's clothes and got one of his socks—good, thick white wool. I put it on the folding chair. I picked up the tape roll and tore off a strip a foot or so long and stuck it to the rail of the cot. I took the sock in my left hand and pinched Oliveira's nose with my right thumb and forefinger. When his mouth opened, I stuffed the sock in. I put my left palm over it and let go of his nose. He was twisting his head, but that was no bother. I peeled the strip from the rail and taped the sock in. His cheeks were sweaty, but the tape held fine.

I stepped back and looked at Oliveira. He had come close to panic, as I had in Robledo. Now he was recovering control. It occurred to me he had asked for nothing. Water for instance. I was thirsty, he had to be much more so, but he hadn't given me a chance to say no. Well, I'd give him something to drink when this was over, but I had to press on. I took the shears from the chair with my left hand. With my right I gripped Oliveira's little finger. Guiding along the rail of the cot, pulling on the finger, pushing on the shears, I sheared back through his hand between the bones. Blood splurted. Oliveira convulsed and gave muted bellows. I sheared back toward his wrist. When the shears were within an inch and a half of it, I swung my left forearm over the cot and sheared outward, through the bone. The finger and chunk of hand came off.

I held it up, diamond ring turned toward him. He lifted himself toward me as far as the tape around his chest allowed and stared at me, eyes bulging.

"The good news is you can still play tennis. The bad news is what I'm going to cut off next."

"Do they know they're going to see me, Elenita and Tonio?"

The day campers were lined up at the telescope getting their five-centavo looks at the city. Ellen had been gazing at them but now looked at me.

"They can't know, they may guess. I figure your note has just been delivered. If the nanny says, 'This note's from Mommy,' maybe they guess, but I didn't mention you to Ramirez."

All I said in the first call was cancel the spot checks. "If I'm stopped tomorrow I'll send you his ears." That was the night before, after he got Oliveira's finger and tape. The tape said please do what I wanted and keep Tovar out. In the morning the streets were clear, or it might have been risky to take Ellen out of the safe house. Was she a personal or a business problem to Oliveira? In the latter case, Ramirez would know about her being in Chilpanzango and the busted plan to ship her to Miami. He'd get a photo of her to the police.

A kid Pili found dropped the package at Delfines gate. Oliveira gave me a way to know whom I was talking to.

"How long have you known your partner Ramirez?"

"Since we were sixteen."

"Tell me a girl who dumped him, who he was hung up on."

"Nadia Montiel."

By then we were virtual buddies. When I waved his finger at him, his moxie vanished. Then I bandaged him up and replaced the blanket and held a big can of V-8 juice while he sipped it, winning what looked a lot like his eternal gratitude. I'd seen the reaction in torture victims before—though not all, by any means—where after a session of torment the mere decency a healthy man shows a dog is welcomed like the purest loving kindness. Shame choked me. He'd stay trussed up where he was, however, till Ellen and I and her children were safe. The buddies phase wouldn't last forever.

Ramirez insisted on talking to him. We did that in the morning. First I arranged the taxis. Nico recommended reliable drivers, but I made the arrangements to keep Nico clear. Next I went to the mirador Tuñón had found, where I could direct while checking for air surveillance, and made my deal with the cafe proprietor. Then I called Ramirez from a public phone.

"Señor Oliveira will call you in awhile. He'll speak very briefly, just enough for you to know he's alive and well. If someone else answers or if there's the slightest delay, I'll send you some more of him. In awhile I'll tell you how to get him back."

That was in another call from another pay phone—the dry run, the hundred thousand, the real thing that night. "Have the kids and the nanny ready to go by nine." Then I went back to the safe house and held the cordless phone for Oliveira.

"Arnaldo, por favor, haga lo que él diga. Sí, estoy bién, pero haga lo que él diga o me va matar."

The last call was from the cafe with Ellen beside me, nine-twenty of a limpid dry season morning, after Pili called to say that the taxi was at the gate. "As soon as I put the phone down, have the children and the woman walk to the gate, alone, carrying nothing, and take the taxi that's there waiting for them. They'll drive around and be back in about an hour. If they're followed or if these instructions are disobeyed, Señor Oliveira will lose something important."

"Did you mention me to Antonio?"

"Oh, yes. I said I was acting for you. But I let him think you're in Miami."

"Why there?"

"That's where they were shipping you out to, the men who grabbed you and held you at the Caracol."

"Miami." She dropped her eyes, and the soft inward smile that moved me crossed her face, but even as I recognized it she looked up at me. "Do you go there often, Carlos?"

"I've been in Miami Airport a hundred times, but I rarely stay. Once or twice for a night." Except for dreams, I thought.

"How did you know I was here," she said suddenly. "In Atacalpa."

"I saw you."

"Where?"

I looked back at her smiling. Her tone wasn't hostile, and I was happy she was interested in me, but I couldn't answer truthfully and was not going to lie.

"How come you were here? It wasn't to get my children, was it?"

"No. That came into my mind after I saw you."

"Were you part of what happened to Edgar Haft?"

No hostility, interest. I looked back at her calmly. Kids were filling up the tables behind us. Sodas were likely the next item on their agenda.

"You were, weren't you?"

She was going to say something else, but the phone was ringing. I picked it up, listened to Alva, held it toward Ellen. "They're in the store. The nanny wants to speak to you."

Worried look at me, she took the phone. *"Bueno?"* Listened. Nodded. *"Sí, Amalia, soy yo, la señora Elena."* Smiled and began to weep, *"Sí, Amalia, ¡sí!"* She put the phone down and looked at me, smiling and weeping. "They're coming," she said. "They want to see me."

Alva called again in a few minutes. Children and nanny had taken the second taxi. I didn't tell Ellen. She wanted to be alone, was in the sedan. I could imagine the feelings swirling inside her. Jaime called a bit later from the phone near Invictos. The taxi had made three circuits and was tailless. Twenty minutes, it would be here. Then it and Amalia the nanny would go back down, Ellen, her children and I would go on up, a quarter mile to where Nico was parked with the flagship of my fleet. Amalia would see the sedan and was probably under orders from Ramirez to call him at once if she became separated from the children.

I went to the counter and got myself a soda. I watched a hawk wheel and soar off to my right, over the ravine between Linda Vista and San Lucas where a cable had stretched on Christmas morning only ten days before. I watched the day campers get back on their bus and chug away. I watched a taxi climb toward the mirador, a big gringo gas guzzler ten years old, immaculately kept, from the line at the Hotel Presidente.

Ellen must have been watching also. She got out of the sedan and waved as the taxi pulled across the westbound lane onto the mirador. I got up but watched from beside the table as two kids jumped from the taxi and ran toward her, as she bent to clutch them. Then I walked toward them.

I'd taken eight or ten steps when I heard the phone ringing. It was Tuñón. His assignment, after dropping Alva at the Galerias, was to go to the small airport where my charter was based and let me know if anything was amiss. Since I hadn't heard from him, I assumed nothing was. In fact he had merely been prudent in not wishing to call from the place itself. Then he ran into trouble finding a phone.

"They're doing their best to be surreptitious, Carlos, but you can't miss them. The place is crawling with CIM agents."

7   After we crossed the stream, the trail began climbing. Hardly a trail at all, palm fronds all around, ropy vines overhead, ten yards visibility. Rhythmic machete swipes, wrist flicks left and right, Elenita behind me so no backswing. Easy pace but steady was what we wanted, put some ground between us and the highway.

"Mami, tengo sed."

"What is it, darling?"

"She's thirsty, Mommy."

I stopped. Two canteens on my belt, but to my right a vine hung at chest level, light green with white patches, three inches thick. I chopped a three-foot section. Water began to drip from the lower end. I turned and mimed attention from the kids and Ellen, held the vine canted above my lips, let the water fall on the back of my tongue the way you do drinking from a wine sack—one swallow, a little barky but cool and refreshing. I offered the section of vine to Elenita.

Who wouldn't take it. Ellen did instead, drank as I had, held the vine to her daughter. "Try it, it's good."

Still leary. Tonio took the vine and drank. By the time Elenita was ready the thing was empty, but there was no shortage of that sort of vine in the forest.

Farther up we got onto a long low ridge. A partridge flushed to my front with an explosive flutter, but otherwise I saw no game, though now and then an iguana rustled nearby us. Smooth gray-white *cuipo* trees poked up through the forest, narrow at ground level, swollen as though pregnant six or eight feet up, then pillar-like till their crowns spread far above us, eighty, a hundred feet up, shutting out the sky.

Here there was less growth, but I still machete'd. Constant generation, constant decay, forest floor soft with impacted vegetation. In one spot it was strewn with yellow, pink, and purple *membrillo* petals, but mostly one saw only grays and greens. I stopped and plucked an unappetizing green pod somewhere in size between a pigeon's egg and a golf ball. I turned and sliced off the top and mimed sucking at it and handed it past Elenita to Tonio. His eyebrows went up. I nodded and patted my stomach. He raised it and poked his tongue gingerly inside. Then his face lit up and he sucked out the sweet-tart jelly whose flavor I remembered as lemony quince. I gathered and sliced three more, one each for the rest of us, miming to Ellen and Elenita.

"Why don't you talk, Carlos?"

"Me Indian. No speak white man tongue."

We came off the ridge along a rocky brook on whose banks tree roots lay like sleeping serpents. The way was steep, my rucksack thrust me forward. I sheathed the machete, went carefully, dead slow, holding onto trees beside the bank.

"Just a little more," I called behind me. "I think there's a place to stop before the bottom."

"I thought you were an Indian," said Tonio.

"I'll be an Indian later or tomorrow."

Below and to the right the greens were lighter. When I reached that level I left the brook. In a few steps we emerged into a clearing, someone's last-year's slash-and-burn yam and maize field squatting on a hump of ragged hillside. One minute forest gloom, the next bright sunlight, though the sun was close to the horizon.

"Will we stay here?" asked Ellen. Her face was flushed by the afternoon's exertions. And by Tonio and Elenita—they were a big part of the health that glowed in her face. And by our adventures. Much action during the last thirty-some hours. How good she looked scared me.

"We've got the brook and level ground to sleep on. We're at least two, maybe more miles in, five or six from the highway. No one's going to ask for our *documentos*. Is the place to your liking?"

She nodded, smiling.

"Then we'll stay."

I shrugged out of the straps and set my rucksack down. As I did

a blue butterfly larger than my spread hand flapped by me indolently as a vision.

Had they found my pilot, or were they just watching airfields?

That's the question I asked myself in the sedan while Ellen's
children jabbered to her in Spanglish. Either way we weren't flying, but the answer had bearing. If they found my pilot by checking all charter takers, knowing we had to have a way out of the
country, maybe they were also checking real estate agents, knowing we had to have a safe house. If so, bingo! They'd find Oliveira.
Patrols would be out again checking ID, equipped with a police
artist's likeness of me. I was that far along when we got to where
Nico was parked.

"The airfield?" I was beside him, Ellen in back with a child on
either side.

"No."

"Where, then?"

"Out of town, take the first road." It had to be right to get clear
of Chilpanzango. Breathing exercise, get my nerves under command. Reading the signs, give my mind calming distraction. Speed
limit 65 klicks. Jalapa 40. No U-Turn. Tiltenango 79. El Caballero
Verde came up on our left, and I turned my head and body to watch
it go by. Smiling grimly, it was safer being Juan Reyes.

"You look happy," said Ellen. First words she'd addressed to me
since greeting her children. "Is the plane far?"

"We've had a change of plan, we won't be flying."

She looked at me steadily. "You got my babies back. You'll get us
out."

She turned her attention back to her children. I turned to the front and leaned back and replayed what she had said. Several times. Each time sounded better. "You'll get us out."

She was right. I knew how we'd get clear of Atacalpa. We'd walk out through the forest like Amador Quilche, starting just this side of Tiltenango.

We camped just inside the clearing. I brought flat rocks, firewood, a pot of brook water. Tonio tagged along, carried some of the wood. Elenita was fast asleep on a rubberized ground cloth. Ellen sat beside her watching. I got a fire going. I hung the pot over it on a bamboo crossbar between two forked stakes. Then I cut palm saplings for shelters.

I made two, one for Ellen, one for the kids. It wasn't going to rain, but they'd feel better. Lashed the crossbars with thin vines. Thatched the sapling frames with palm fronds. The things will keep you dry even in a downpour. Building one takes no more time than changing a tire.

"How'd you learn to do all this?" asked Ellen.

I was on one knee facing Tonio. I frowned and grunted.

"He's an Indian, Mommy."

We woke Elenita for dinner, which was consommé with noodles, corned beef, and fruit cocktail. The beef came from Argentina in a red and yellow can with a bull's head on it. I sliced it and fried the slices. By the time I fetched the fruit cocktail from the brook, night had fallen. I took the mess kits to the brook while Ellen put the kids to bed. In the morning I'd show them how to scrub a mess kit out with brook sand, but for now I'd do the housekeeping, like a hired guide. I concentrated on giving Ellen time. If I concentrated, I'd be able to do it.

When I got back, the kids were asleep. Ellen was in her shelter.

A light breeze had come up. We were exposed a little in that clearing. The breeze was nice. Ellen raised up on one elbow. I'd cut the stakes that held the high end of her shelter to almost three feet. The fire was still burning. She looked as good in firelight as she had in sunlight. Maybe better.

"I want to talk to you, Carlos, but not tonight."

I smiled and nodded. "Sleep well."

"You'll be here, won't you?"

"Oh, yes. Right over there." I nodded toward the far side of the kids' shelter. "I'll be back in awhile."

I walked to the far end of the clearing, where the hump it was on fell away steeply in tangles of growth. Give her time. Give her time.

"¿Son gringos?"

"¡Por favor, mi sargento! Aquella es la bandera de Gran Bretaña."

The *retén* at Jalapa. A sergeant in green fatigues stands beside Nico, who points in bruised dignity at the flags on the front fenders. A CIM agent in shades and a flowing *guayabera* ambles across the road toward us from the guard booth.

"That's true," the sergeant admits, glancing at the flags. "The gringo flag has stars and this one doesn't."

"The lady," Nico continues, adopting the haughtiness of his imagined employer, "is the daughter of His Excellency the Britannic Ambassador. The tots are his grandchildren."

When I learned which country's passport Ellen would carry, a gleam of Brit arrogance crept into my mind's eye. The result, purchased during my weekend in the West Indies, was a pair of small metal Union Jacks, colors ablaze in rich enamel, that could be affixed to my Rhinomobile's front fenders. We stopped to put them up on the way to Jalapa. Ellen put on a linen dress. Nico put on a chauffeur's cap and jacket. I put on boots, wrinkled khakis, and a T-shirt. Then Ellen, her children, and I played Movie. I was Gabriel and spoke only Spanish. The children were John and Jane and spoke only English. Ellen starred as Mommy and directed.

"And that one?" the sergeant asked with a gesture toward me.

"The gardener," said Nico, handing him Gabriel Anaya's ID card. "He's going to get orchid cuttings in Tiltenango."

The CIM man arrives, gets our documents and a rundown from the sergeant.

"Why no diplomatic passport?" he asks Nico.

"She's not a diplomat, your honor. She lives in England and is here just on a visit."

He steps to the rear door and makes little circles with his right forefinger. Nico fingers a button. The window descends.

"What you do here in Jalapa?" His English is passable.

"We are going to have lunch at the Posada del Rey. Then we will visit the ruins at Tiltenango."

"And you?" He pokes the same finger at Elenita. "Are you speak *inglés?*"

She turns from him and clasps her mother's neck, says (softly but clearly), "I don't want to talk to him, Mommy."

Which gets laughter and kisses from Ellen, applause from me, as soon as we are out of sight of the guard booth.

Jalapa province was the center of tourism in Atacalpa. In the low-lands near Tiltenango were the restored ruins of a Mayan metrop-olis. Jalapa the town and environs, in a high valley, had a five-star resort hotel and trails for hiking. Ellen and her children ate on the terrace of a colonial patio to the music of a marimba band. Nico and I went shopping: blankets, ground cloths, cooking gear, provisions, mess kits, matches, canteens, insect repellent, a machete, a compass, a Swiss Army knife, a rucksack.

The place Amador had mentioned was easy to spot. The highway ran for a bit by the rim of a lake on whose northern shore were indigenous settlements. A dirt road led out from the nearest of these. Where it met the highway was a bus stop. Half a dozen Indians were waiting there. We passed a couple more on the dirt road. It ended almost three miles from the highway. Ellen changed into jeans inside the car. Nico put an edge on the machete. I packed the rucksack. What didn't fit went into string bags hung from it.

At first we walked on a wide path from village to village—if you could call two or three houses a village, houses like my foster father's raised on stilts. At the last of these I asked for the trail to the border. The fellow I asked, a man my age or younger, came down from his house when he heard us. The way up and down was the same as with my foster father: an upright log with steps cut in it. He wore a pair of jeans cut off at the knees. I don't know what he thought about us.

"There," he said, pointing to a break in the forest. "Look to your left after you cross the stream."

Before we went in I set our line of march. I'd lead, then Elenita, then Tonio, then Ellen. "If anyone loses sight of the person in front, give a yell."

"I remember you," Tonio said suddenly. "You were with my dad when he took us on the plane. You look different, though."

Different movie, I thought. In this one I'm a good guy.

I stayed a long time at the far end of the clearing, standing for a while, then sitting. There weren't many stars, but the moon came up. While I sat I watched it. When I went back to the fire, Ellen was sleeping. I made no noise, but at my approach she sat up.

"Elenita? Tonio?" I don't know if she was awake or not.

"They're right beside you, Ellen, sleeping soundly." I think that was the first time I spoke her name.

"Oh," she said. "Okay." She lay down.

I put some more wood on the fire and spread my ground cloth. I lay down on it and rolled up in my blanket. How many nights, I wondered, had I slept on the ground? That thought of the past prompted a thought of the future. How many nights besides this would I have with Ellen? How many nights would I have to wait before she was ready? Then I laughed to myself. How foolish! Why care about nights past or future? What's wrong with this one? A breeze, a moon, three people in my life, and almost to the top of a glass mountain.

8 Our route ran toward and then parallel to a small river that emptied into the river that formed the border. The first leg was at a high elevation through pretty thick forest. The rest was lowland. The whole thing took us five days. Easy days, why tire the kids and Ellen?

My M.O. was to be on my feet at first light when tendrils of mist lay on the forest, and go off a ways to cut wood lest I wake someone early. I'd get a fire going, make coffee and cocoa, mix the pancake batter when the kids were up. After breakfast I'd douse the fire and bury our garbage and have a seat till the others were ready to travel, watching Ellen get to know her kids again. When that was done, she'd get to me. I felt no impatience. To be impatient you need a sense of time passing. At first she'd glance at me to see if she should hurry them. No rush, we're safe, is what my return glance said.

Once we were moving through it, the forest took me where I hadn't expected. Not to Vietnam, the last jungle I'd been in. Not to the war, though for years, wherever I was, I found myself interpreting my surroundings in terms of military terrain, scanning for cover and possible enemy positions. Instead I was restored to my own country, and to my first stay with my foster father's people. Their presence walked with me. A tree, a plant, a feature came into focus, and an Indian voice or mimed gesture gave me its story. Which often I passed on in their way or my own.

"That's a tree-killer tree."

"A what?"

"*Matapalo* in Spanish, Elenita. See, through that gap, you can see the tree it's killing. It starts as a shallow root that throws out vines, that twines around and climbs another tree. It encloses the other tree and climbs all the way up it, using it for support. The other tree dies in the process."

"How horrible!"

"If you think so, Ellen. Or maybe the other tree is fulfilling its destiny. Or there are no individuals, just one big thing that both the trees are parts of, along with us and everything else. Anyway, the root is good for love charms. The juice in it, the sap. If you dab some on your girlfriend, she'll never forget you."

I showed them balsa trees, and *chunga*, whose wood is too heavy to float, and black palm savagely spined with two-inch needles. We saw a kind of fig tree that dropped roots from its branches, so that it seemed to walk through the forest on crutches, and *ceibal* trees with roots like flying buttresses, three or four inches thick, hollowish when you knock them. The roots scarcely push beneath the ground's surface but may reach outward thirty or forty feet and be higher than one can reach where they join the trunk. We passed through stands of corozo palm, thick and branchless, more plants than trees except for their size. Their dark green fronds, toothed with thorns, spread above us like tongues, larger and broader, shutting out the sunlight, so that we moved in subaquatic gloom over ground as empty of growth as the sea floor.

The corozo has a soft core that gives moisture and nourishment but takes a lot of chopping to get at. Near noon on our first day, however, when we were resting, I saw one of the corozo's slender cousins near where Ellen was sitting and got up and felled it with two machete swats.

"*Maquenque,*" I said. That's what it was called in my country.

I swatted a length off and took it back to my rucksack and rummaged out a mess kit and our packet of salt. I swatted the palm lengthwise, splitting it. Then I sat down cross-legged and began peeling, keeping my eyes on my work, feeling eyes on me. In a bit I'd peeled the length of palm open, revealing a moistly shiny, yellow-white tube something less than an inch in diameter.

I opened the mess kit and put it outside my crossed ankles. I got my Swiss Army knife from my shirt and opened the main blade. I took the length of palm in my left hand and sliced the slick tube into sections, levering each from the palm into the mess kit. When the palm was empty, the mess kit was pretty full. I reached into the packet, pinched up some salt, and sprinkled. The saw blade of my knife had a forked tip. I speared a chunk from the mess kit, sampled, and nodded. Then I rose and handed the mess kit and knife to Ellen.

"Heart of palm, lady. Don't say it isn't fresh."

On the afternoon of our third full day in the forest I saw a bees' nest on the ground beside a tree root. I moved everyone back to a safe distance and set my rucksack down and went back to a brook we'd just crossed and got two big handfuls of mud. I got up to the nest very softly and quietly. Not a single bee caught on till the hole was plastered. Then I swiped the closed end open with my machete and came away with a cupful of wild honey. We had it for dessert that evening.

The river was on our right from then on, once or twice visible, often within hearing. The trail ran under triple canopy, wide and well-traveled, rarely in need of pruning from my machete. I made Tonio happy letting him lead for long stretches. Two or three times a day we saw dwellings, typically three or four houses set up on stilts with eighty or so yards of forest between them. Our next-to-last night was spent in one just built by a boy of sixteen but not yet moved into since his wedding was still a few days off. We'd bring it luck, his bride's father said, and many children. He assumed Elenita and Tonio were mine as well as Ellen's. We woke late the next day and had a big Indian breakfast, yucca and maize as well as broiled fish from the river. The sun was low when we reached our last camp.

The silent jungle wakes up for an hour at sundown: birdcalls, the buzz-saw whine of locustlike *cocorrones*, now and then a monkey's phlegmy bark. That night, too, we had the river, less than twenty yards wide, barely knee-deep at midstream but flowing swiftly, nois-

ily, over round rocks. A squadron of parrots flew in from the northeast, seven flights of two, and settled in a glade across the river,
adding their treble squawks to the brief serenade. We bathed before
dinner, Ellen and her kids by our campsite, I downstream. After dinner I took my ground cloth and blanket down to the river. The
moon was behind the trees on our side, but all the stars were out. I
sat and watched them, listening to the endless rush of water. When
her kids were sleeping, Ellen came and joined me, as I thought she
might. She sat down beside me and said nothing. When I thought
she'd never speak, she did.

"Did you dream of me, Carlos?"

I held my breath, listened to water rushing over round rocks.
"Yes. Night after night. How did you know?"

"Recently? Last week, last night?"

I breathed deeply. "Dreaming is one thing, remembering it is
another. Months ago, when the dreams started, I worked on
remembering. I woke early and lay still. That way I could gather a
whole dream. Then my life changed and I couldn't do that. I still
had dreams, but I lost them. I'd know for a second on waking I'd
been dreaming. I'd get a flash of a dream during the day. That's all.
Then my life got really busy, and even that faded. But I'm sure I still
dream of you. I bet I dreamed about you last week and last night.
How did you know?"

"In the dreams you remembered. Did you just dream of me, or
were we together?"

"As together as we could get, as together as possible." The moon
had risen above the trees behind us, and the corner of my eye
caught Ellen smiling, caught her give her teeth a feral lick.

"Did you know it was me?"

I could feel her warmth beside me, smell the soap she'd bathed with. "Interesting question. No, I didn't. I dreamed of a woman. She and I were crazy about each other. But when I woke I couldn't recall her name. I couldn't make out her face in my reconstructions. I didn't know it was you till I saw you two weeks ago, having tea with Diana Haft on her terrace."

"You were part of that thing with her husband. You were there."

"Behind you to your left, trimming the hedge. How did you know I dreamed about you?"

I felt a breeze on my face but couldn't hear it. I heard water rushing over rocks.

Ellen said, "Why was it, do you think, that you didn't know me?"

"Oh, that's simple. I was ashamed. I'd hurt you, the person I loved, and couldn't face it. So I blocked you out. That came to me when I saw you, when I knew you were the woman in my dreams."

"And you decided to get my babies."

"No, that was hours later, and I didn't decide. When the operation was over and I could act freely, it came to me I was going to get your children."

"Just like that? No thought?"

"No thought required. You love a person, you've hurt her, you make it up. How did you know I dreamed about you, Ellen?"

"I'm not ready for that yet. Can I go on?"

"Sure."

"When you dreamed of me, were we any place special?"

"Miami. Neither of us lived there, we just met there. I think I was coming from my country. I think that now, looking back. I was involved in a conflict of some sort and went to Miami to see my commanders. You and I took advantage of that to see each other.

There was a hotel we stayed at, a hotel where we had drinks. Restaurants. In one you . . ."

"Stop. Don't go on."

I turned to her. She sat with her knees drawn up to her chin and her arms clasped around them.

"This is getting interesting," I said.

"It's getting scary."

I looked at her. Then I turned back to the river. Strands of moonlight wove themselves in its ripples. When I thought she wasn't going to speak, she did.

"We were in a place late at night, hardly anyone there. We were sitting side by side, you on my left. We were talking and I put my leg over yours."

"Taking possession."

"Yes."

My heart turned over. I held my breath. "You dreamed it," I said finally.

"Yes."

I lay back. The moon was just over the trees. Beyond its halo spread a sea of stars.

"Carlos?"

"Yes?"

"What are you thinking?"

"In the operation I got to know an Atacalpan named Claudio. Older guy. He used to say, 'The world is my favorite place.'"

The river rushed on over the rocks.

"Ellen?"

"Yes?"

"When did you dream that?"

"Six weeks ago, two months, I don't know exactly. When those dreams began, I didn't try to remember them."

"Weren't they good?"

"They were wonderful!"

I turned to her and would have drawn her down to me, but she'd lowered her eyes and was smiling to herself with the soft look I loved. I just watched till she was done with her reflections and looked toward me.

"When I woke from them, though," she said, "I thought it was wrong. Having wonderful dreams when my babies . . . So I didn't study them the way you did, I just let them go. Now I've been having them again the last three nights. The restaurant dream came back just now when you told it. You didn't even tell it. You were about to tell it, and it came back. I was sitting beside you and put my leg over yours."

I waited, looking up at her.

"I've never done that, Carlos. Put my leg over someone's leg like that. But when I dreamed it, I felt it, just now I felt it. How did I dream it if I've never done it?"

"When you first dreamed it, did you know it was me?"

"Not at all. Not till I saw you at that place near the airport. I was with this marvelous man, that's all I knew. Just the thought of him made me nervous."

"Yes. You told me. But I'm not sure I get it."

"You don't know much about women, do you, Carlos?"

"I don't know much about anything, except maybe jungle craft and small-unit warfare. Women are what I know least about."

"Women find most men too easy. A man who makes you nerv-ous is something else. You want to be perfect for him. You were marvelous, Carlos. Everything you did, it was as if you were dancing. But I didn't know it was you. Shame, just like you. I was ashamed to love a man who'd harmed me. Finding out made me furious."

"Was that why you hit me?"

"No. I hit you because I wanted to kill you. You took my babies. Then I realized it was you I'd been dreaming about, and I was furious at us both. At you for taking my babies. At myself for loving a bastard. It's all right, I got over it."

"Got over what, loving me or being furious?"

"I don't know, you decide."

I looked up at her smiling.

"Was it real, Carlos? Even if we both dreamed the same dreams?"

"Will it be is the question. If the dreams were about anything it's a possible future."

"Only possible?"

"Possible's plenty. Nothing's sure."

"Carlos, were we together in that motel?"

"I don't know, you decide. You told me unforgettable things there. That you wanted to bathe me. That you liked the person you were when you were with me. That I did something that unhooked your spine."

"You!" A rueful grin, then her lips were on mine. When I could, I mumbled something stupid about the children, and she sat up and gave me a look and said impatiently, "Oh, Carlos, they won't wake up."

They didn't.

We didn't sleep much that night, Ellen and I, but we woke refreshed, I by the river, she higher up in her shelter, for she left me before dawn so her children wouldn't miss her when the light roused them. Elenita and Tonio were happy setting out. As much as they'd enjoyed camping in the jungle, they were ready to get back to clean clothes and hot water, and beds and playgrounds and other kids and TV. The ground was easy and the day fine. A quarter mile on we reached the confluence of the two rivers, after which we walked upstream along the larger, mostly on sand spits, to where we could ford, every step in bright sunshine and a fresh breeze. I tasted the wholeness of the moment and resisted projecting it into the future.

When we reached the ford I crossed first, confirming that the river was no more than waist deep. I left my pack and crossed back, then we all crossed together, Tonio on my shoulders, Elenita clinging to Ellen's neck like a monkey. Then we walked downstream along the left bank in the sovereignty of Atacalpa's neighbor, six or so miles to a town called Las Conchas. I had thought of cutting straight to the road, which was not only closer but more discreet, but our host of two nights before had counseled otherwise. The daily bus out of Las Conchas often left with passengers on the roof and no room to pick up others on the highway.

The ground was easy. On both banks the forest had been slashed and burned off and the sandy soil exhausted by cultivation. The people we saw lived in dirt-floor, palm-thatch huts several levels of squalor below Indians in the jungle. I noted scrawny children with pushed-out navels and tried to temper the happiness I felt, while Ellen talked back-to-school with her son and daughter.

The highway was the only paved street in Las Conchas. It began abruptly at the river. There was a one-story customs house called, rather grandly, the *Capitania del Puerto* and opposite it a cantina, *La Flor de Azalea*, then on each side half a dozen buildings ending in a barrack and a church. On the Atacalpan side was something similar, at least from what I could see across the river, which looked to be a little short of a hundred yards wide. No bridge, but there was a ferry—a barge with a diesel engine on it taking up and letting out cable strung between the two banks. It was hauling away toward Atacalpa with eight or ten people and their belongings on board. The bus had come in about twenty minutes before.

And was already full, every seat taken. I found the driver—not in the cantina, I was happy to learn, though I looked for him there since the bus was parked almost in front of it. He was lunching a few doors down and agreed, in exchange for our fares and a ten-dollar tip, to let me negotiate with seat-holders. Two soldiers had the front seat on the right side. I offered them forty dollars apiece, and they took it—hardly surprising, it was at least a month's pay. Ellen and the kids would have plenty of room, and I could sit in the aisle beside her.

I handed my rucksack up to the boy on the roof for him to tie down alongside other baggage. I got four cold Cokes from the cantina and handed three of them in through the bus window. I bought provisions: bread, deviled ham, raisins, a box of cookies. I also bought a plastic bucket. When I had delivered the foodstuffs, I turned to the cantina. The ferry was almost back from Atacalpa with four or five people on board. For their sakes I hoped none expected a seat on the bus.

Was I buckling under the unfamiliar stress of furnishing my sudden family civilized comforts, or was I merely addled by too much good luck? One, the other, or both are equally possible. While the *cantinero* chopped ice for my bucket to keep another half a dozen Cokes cold, I went AWOL from the present moment into a daydream of time future. There was a fair-sized town two hours off. We could leave the bus there and hire a car to the capital. The capital had to have at least one good hotel. The hotel had to have a two-bedroom suite. Elenita and Tonio would probably doze in the car, but that didn't mean they'd be wide awake on arrival. Not at all, they'd be sound asleep in five minutes. And then, and then, after a steaming hot shower, room-service cold cuts, a bottle of Bordeaux, I would spend the rest of the night trying to discover if it was more fun to make love with Ellen in a bed with clean sheets than on the ground beside a jungle river. It doesn't take long to chop a bucket of ice. I didn't hurry my daydream. Anticipated joy still absorbed me when I stepped through the cantina's swinging door and bumped smack into a short, thick, brown-skinned fellow in a corduroy cap.

He stepped back, recognizing and smiling. My daydream smirk must have stuck to my face.

"Hey! You look glad to see me. I'm glad to see you."

His jersey was green, but he still wore his sleeves rolled. He still carried a pistol in his trouser waistband, probably the same one I took from him in Robledo and later slung in a corner of the safe house. I had a plastic bucket in one hand and a paper bag full of Coke bottles in the other.

Cap kept smiling. "You know, I owe you. Thanks to you I have this wonderful job here on the border. I thought I'd never get to pay you back."

No one was near us, though two minutes before the space where we stood had been bustling. Behind him to the left Elenita waved to me from the bus window. Beyond him on the right two men in uniform came out of the customs house and started across toward us and the cantina. If I swung the bucket and threw the bag at the same time . . . Even as I thought this, Cap's pistol came out of his waistband and leveled at me.

"You've been on my mind for months. I know what you think before you do."

The bus started up. The driver must have come back while I was inside. The men in uniform stopped walking toward us and faced each other in the street, conversing.

"Now you're thinking you should have killed me. I think you're right."

I said, "You're on the wrong side of the river."

"You know, I don't care. This is like one town anyway. We come over here, they go over there. I'll put the gun in your hand and say it was suicide. I'm not worried, don't you worry either."

I kept my eyes on his smile but took in much more—the noon sky, the dusty street, the river. I wasn't leaving a minute before I had to. I was going to throw the bag and dive to my left, and probably take a bullet—in the shoulder if my luck held, in the chest if it didn't, then we'd see. No time for a muster, but two thoughts flashed through my mind. I was glad I'd joined Ape and gone to Atacalpa. Cap was wrong, I didn't wish I'd killed him.

Cap thumbed the hammer back. The bus pulled forward and swung left in a turn. Ellen put her head out and called, "Carlos!"

Cap turned to her, surprised.

One of the uniformed men looked up and called, "Hey, Carlos, what brings you over to this side?"

The other said, "Carlos! Let's have a drink, you're buying. All right, for God's love, put the gun away, I'll buy."

"Was he trying to sell you a gun?" Ellen asked when I sat down in the aisle beside her. "The man with the cap with the buckles. Do you know him?"

"Hardly know him at all, but it turns out we both are called Carlos."

April 1980–April 2000

ACKNOWLEDGMENTS

*P*eople helped me write *Glass Mountain*.

David Fechheimer, the legendary private investigator, gave me the plan for stealing Ellen's children and ironed out kinks in my plan for stealing them back. Colonel (retired) Bill Coy, U.S. Army, helped with all phases of Golden Retriever and played an extended cameo role. Chief Warrant Officer (retired) Don Mann, U.S. Navy, let me kibitz elite unit training in Panama and provided insights into the warrior psyche.

My son Rick believed in Carlos and wouldn't let me quit until I'd told his story. Adam Novak was generous with enthusiasm. Peter Matson was generous with wisdom. Jane Cornwell encouraged me when it mattered.

Otilita lo sufrió conmigo.